A DETECTIVE'S DEADLY SECRETS

Anna J. Stewart

HARLEQUIN

ROMANTIC
SUSPENSE

HARLEQUIN®
ROMANTIC
SUSPENSE™

Recycling programs
for this product may
not exist in your area.

ISBN-13: 978-1-335-59388-7

A Detective's Deadly Secrets

Copyright © 2023 by Anna J. Stewart

For questions and comments about the quality of this book,
please contact us at CustomerService@Harlequin.com.

Harlequin Enterprises ULC
22 Adelaide St. West, 41st Floor
Toronto, Ontario M5H 4E3, Canada
www.Harlequin.com

Printed in U.S.A.

"I made you a promise after we first worked together—what was it, three, four years ago? I said then if you needed me for anything, *anything*, all you had to do was ask."

It had been an easy promise to make to a woman he had no business caring for.

"I know. I kept telling myself that on the flight down." Her lips twitched as if he'd triggered a spark of humor. "If I don't get to the bottom of this, I'm really scared I'm going to lose my mind."

"That isn't going to happen." Especially if Eamon could do anything to stop it. "Whatever it is, you've got my help."

"You say that now," she hedged with a disbelieving shake of her head.

"There's nothing you can say that'll change my mind." He gripped harder on her hands to help her focus. "When I make a promise, I keep it. Let's have it, Lana."

She let out a long, controlled breath. "I need you to help me find out who murdered my husband."

Dear Reader,

This series started with *More Than a Lawman*. That very first scene in Eden and Cole's story was actually a writing exercise for my local writing group. When I finished that scene, however, I knew there was so much more to the story. One book became three, then eight. Now, with Eamon's story, this story, the series has come to a full circle close. I think I saved the best for last.

Eamon has always been a back burner character, popping up in the stories and lending a hand and earning himself a place in this "family" I created. He is dedicated, loyal and protective, most of which stems from losing his sister when she was nine. I knew whoever his heroine was needed to be equal to him in all ways. Enter Detective Lana Tate, a woman Eamon fell for years before, but for reasons you'll soon learn, she was off-limits. Well, she's off-limits no longer, only she brings some heavy secrets and mysteries with her when she returns. From the moment they reconnect, the sparks fly and the adventure begins.

I want to thank all of you for coming along for the Honor Bound ride. For now, this is the end of this series, but I never close the door completely. I hope Eamon and his cavalcade of friends and family have found a place in your heart. And hopefully, maybe your bookshelf, actual or virtual, as well.

Happy reading,

Anna J.

Bestselling author **Anna J. Stewart** honestly believes she was born with a book in her hand. After growing up devouring every story she could get her hands on, now she gets to make her living making up stories and fulfilling happily-ever-afters of her own. Her dreams have most definitely come true. Anna lives in Northern California (only a ninety-minute flight from Disneyland, her favorite place on earth) with two monstrous, devious, adorable cats named Sherlock and Rosie.

Books by Anna J. Stewart

Harlequin Romantic Suspense

Honor Bound

Reunited with the P.I.
More Than a Lawman
Gone in the Night
Guarding His Midnight Witness
The PI's Deadly Charade
Deadly Vegas Escapade
A Detective's Deadly Secrets

The Coltons of Roaring Springs

Colton on the Run

Visit the Author Profile page at
Harlequin.com for more titles.

To my own circle of ride-or-die friends: Mary, Cari, Melinda and Judy.

What a boring world this would be without all of you in my life.

Chapter 1

FBI special agent Eamon Quinn pulled in behind the Brass Eagle, the downtown Sacramento bar that had become his home away from home over the past few years. Bouncing between the state capital and the Bay Area had begun to take its toll, but working out of both branch offices gave him a wider range of focus. More potential cases. More people to connect with. More predators to stop.

He parked in the back corner, killed the engine and, with a sigh, dropped his head back and closed his eyes.

The adrenaline and energy that had been coursing through him for the better part of a week finally abated. Exhaustion crept into the void and made his eyes droop even as his stomach growled. Beneath the dim glow of the overhead streetlamp, the city, unaware of the nightmarish scene that had played out just a few hours prior, drifted silently into slumber, something Eamon planned to do just as soon as he dragged himself out of the car and up to the third floor.

The back door slammed open. Eamon blinked his eyes open, turned his head and spotted Vince Sutton, owner of the Brass Eagle, as he hefted three giant bags of garbage into the dumpster. He dropped the lid closed, brushed his hands on the back of his jeans and, after a quick glance around the parking lot, headed Eamon's way.

"Been wondering when you'd get here." Vince, all six-plus feet of him, rested a hand on the roof of Eamon's vehicle as Eamon grabbed his duffel out of the back. "Simone called." While Vince had become one of Sacramento's premier private investigators in recent years, it was his marriage to Assistant District Attorney Simone Armstrong that would have clued him in on Eamon's now closed case. Leave it to Simone, who was currently on extended maternity leave, to continue to have both ears perked for information. "Want to talk about it?"

Vince wasn't a coddler. He wasn't a hand-holder. What he was was a realist with a sharp eye for the tough world he and Eamon both inhabited. "Not much to say." Eamon locked his jaw. "Girl's back with her parents." Forever changed, but at least she was alive.

"You got him," Vince said simply, although the takedown had been anything but simple.

The standoff had lasted for almost twelve hours and ended in a hail of bullets.

"He had her for more than two weeks, Eamon. The odds of him surrendering peacefully—"

"You know I don't play the odds." After more than ten years with a dedicated task force in the Crimes Against Children division of the FBI, Eamon had learned a long time ago that expecting a positive outcome was the shortest route to burnout. He always hoped, but even that fire didn't burn as brightly as it once did. Cases like this one rarely ended with the victim being recovered alive. Even knowing that, it didn't stop Eamon from trying to save as many as he could. He really should be considering this one a win.

He hefted his bag over his shoulder and followed Vince into the bar through the back door. "She couldn't have been his only victim," Eamon said. "With this guy dead, we may never know how many there were. Forensics may come up with something, but—"

"But by the time they do, you'll already be on to your next case." Vince finished the frequently spoken thought. "You did good, Eamon. Whatever else happened, that girl is alive partially because of you."

Yeah. But how many had died before they'd discovered the pattern? It was a thought that would keep him awake—in the future. But for now?

"I'm glad to be here for our dinner tomorrow night." Always anxious to lighten the mood rather than darken it, Eamon ignored the way his heart twisted at what the annual get-together with his friends represented. His sister had been gone for more than twenty years now and yet… "Looks like the sleepless nights are treating you okay, Vince," he teased. "Come on. Let's see the latest, Dad."

Vince grimaced, but there was a twinkle in his eye. "I really don't want to be one of *those*—"

"As one of Caleb's honorary uncles, I refuse to let you finish that statement." Eamon held out his hand for Vince's phone, which was now displaying the most recent picture of his and Simone's month-old son. "He definitely got your hairline," Eamon teased.

"But his mother's eyes," Vince said. "Other than him being healthy, that's all I wanted. We're thinking he might have gotten Eden's attitude."

"For both your sakes, I hope that's not true," Eamon laughed. Their friend Eden St. Claire had a bit of a reputation of varying degrees, but despite her prickly flaws, her heart was probably bigger than everyone's combined.

The noise of the familiar Friday night crowd erupted through the swinging doors into the kitchen, which was buzzing with dinner activity. Eamon took a long, deep breath of stomach-tempting grilled onions, roasting meat and that always-there hint of bacon sizzling on the flattop.

"Thanks for the use of the apartment again," Eamon said as Vince stopped to let one of his servers pass. "I wasn't looking forward to the drive back into the city."

"No thanks necessary. Since Jason moved in with Kyla, the place is yours whenever you need it. Besides, you're family." Vince's lips twitched in an uncharacteristic grin. "After the last few years, I'd have thought you'd accepted that. Which reminds me—Jason slipped an invitation to his and Kyla's wedding under your door. And before you argue, attendance is mandatory."

"I thought they were keeping it small."

"They are," Vince said. "But there probably wouldn't

be a wedding if you hadn't gone out on a limb with the O'Callahan case. My brother and Kyla aren't ever going to forget you helped save their lives. Neither am I."

"Like you said. Family." Eamon shrugged, not able to voice how much being included in the tight-knit group of ever-growing friends meant to him. He'd spent a lot of years—too many years—alone. Now he had more people in his life than he actually knew what to do with. His contact list had gone from near-empty to blowing up his phone. He readjusted his bag and made his way through the crowd at the bar. "I think I have just enough energy to wait on a burger to take with me upstairs."

"You might want to make time for a drink," Vince suggested and nudged Eamon in the opposite direction of the stairs. "Back corner booth. Pretty brunette with sad eyes. She's been in the past few nights asking after you."

"You're kidding, right?" Eamon wondered if his friend had begun to speak in code. Women didn't come looking for him, but Vince's shrug told him otherwise.

"She stays long enough to finish a club soda and lime. Never orders any food. Normally she's left by now, but as soon as Simone called about your case, I let her know I was almost sure you'd be here tonight." He glanced at his watch. "She's been here a good few hours."

Despite being so tired he had to will his eyes to stay open, Eamon's gaze landed on target. Exhaustion evaporated, replaced by a long-dormant buzzing that accompanied anticipation and, more importantly, long-repressed attraction.

"Lana."

Pretty brunette didn't come close to describing Detective Lana Tate. Every cell in Eamon's body shot to attention. Just the sight of her was enough to supercharge his drained system. She always was—to his mind, at least—the personification of a strong, capable, kick-butt female with enough smooth edges to make the smooth bourbon she preferred seem sharp.

Eamon blew out a small, steadying breath. He hadn't often met women who ticked all his appeal boxes: independent, athletic, smart, wicked sense of humor, dedicated.

They'd laughed together, worked together, coasted case highs and lows together. Lana was one of the best cops he'd ever worked with, and the case they'd closed had earned both of them commendations and, in Lana's case, a promotion.

There had only been one thing wrong with her.

Lana Tate had been very, *very* married.

"I'm going to take that look on your face to mean *Lana* is a welcome surprise." Vince grabbed Eamon's bag and slung it over his shoulder. "I'll have the kitchen send out that burger and a double order of fries. In case you want to share. With Lana," he added with a grin that had Eamon suspecting Vince was going to be making a follow-up call to his wife to fill in the blanks.

"Thanks, Vince." Eamon scrubbed his suddenly damp palms down the front of his jeans. No one had ever made him feel quite as nervous as Lana Tate. Clearly the time since he'd last seen her hadn't done much to temper that sensation. One glimpse of her and he felt as if he'd been shot out of a cannon, straight back to his insecure teenage years crushing on the head cheerleader. Not that Lana...

She turned her head, dark eyes catching his in the blink of a heartbeat, and in that moment, he forgot to breathe. Her smile, when it curved those amazing, plump, unpainted lips of hers, carried an unfamiliar hint of uncertainty.

"I'm feeling the urge to quote Bogart," Eamon said by way of a greeting as he took the final few steps to her table and slid in across from her.

"I trust you to resist the urge." One hand clenched into a fist while the other tightened around the half-filled glass in front of her, and she let out a sigh of relief as her eyes softened. "Hope you don't mind me dropping in on you this way. I know it's been a while."

Eighteen months, twenty-two days, but who's counting? "Thanks, Travis," Eamon said to the bartender who set a beer in front of him. "You want another?" he asked Lana, who shook her head.

"I'm good."

"Burger will be out in a few, Eamon," Travis said before moving off.

Seeing her close-up now, Eamon couldn't help but think Lana appeared almost as an apparition of the woman he remembered. She'd lost weight, and not in a way that appeared healthy. She looked gaunt. Fragile, even. At the funeral he'd understood it. But now?

She sipped her drink, her hand trembling a bit when she set it down. Eamon focused on keeping his expression passive even as concern cycloned inside him. There was a familiar tension tightening her body, from her fingertips all the way down to her toes. She was pulled taut and appeared to be waiting for someone to snap her free. He'd seen this before, a number of times, in his fellow agents. In other cops. In dozens of people with high-stress, demanding jobs.

The wedding ring she used to wear on her finger now hung suspended on a thin gold chain, along with the familiar key pendant he'd never known her to be without.

He pulled the bowl of spicy pretzels and peanuts closer, tamping down on his growing worry. "So." He munched in an effort to keep his nerves at bay. "How long have you been?"

"Been what?" Lana blinked as if coming out of a fog.

"Sober." He inclined his chin toward her glass. "How long have you been sober?"

"Oh." She closed her eyes and let out a breath that, when she looked at him again, allowed the Lana he remembered to shine through ever so slightly. She opened her fisted palm to reveal the round plastic chip noting ninety days' sobriety. "I should have realized you'd... You never miss anything." She shoved the chip into her front pocket before flipping over her cell phone that had been facedown on the table. "Four months, seventeen days." Her smile was quick and cursory. "Six hours."

"Not counting the minutes, then?" He nodded with approval. "If me drinking will bother you, I can—" He signaled Travis, pushed his beer to the edge of the table, but Lana's hand whipped out and caught his. Her hold on him was so tight so instantly, every alarm bell in his head went off.

"It doesn't. You're fine." She hesitated. "I know it's

strange. Me just showing up like this, tracking you down. I'm sorry we fell out of touch. I was a mess after the funeral." There was an intensity in her voice that didn't quite seem like Lana. "I should have… I know I said it at the time, but I appreciated you being there. Marcus would have appreciated it as well."

His gaze dropped back to the wedding band she still wore. "He was a good man, Lana. And it was a big loss for you. You don't owe me an apology. The phone works both ways. I could have called and checked in." Looking at her now, he realized he should have.

How many times had he stared at his cell phone, looking at her contact information, finger hovered above the "call" button, knowing her voice was only a few seconds away? But that might have given up his deepest secret. That he'd been in love with her almost from the moment they'd first met.

That he'd have given anything, *anything*, if she hadn't been married. And then she hadn't been and the idea of being near her while she was still grieving… No. The best course of action—for the both of them—had been to put as much distance between them as possible. She'd needed to grieve and move on with her life—without him hovering, waiting, hoping that perhaps someday she'd see him as more than a shoulder to cry on and someone to turn to.

But as much as he wanted to be a part of her life, he did not want to be the rebound guy. The man who helped her move past her sorrow and on to someone else. Eamon was capable of a lot, but that he was not equipped to deal with.

When he'd first seen her in the bar tonight, fresh hope had sprung to life, but whatever that hope might have been was now tempered by the cloud of sadness that enveloped her.

"I've spent a couple of nights in here hoping to catch you," she said quietly, then looked down at their hands as Eamon resisted the overwhelming temptation to slip his fingers between hers. "I meant it. You drinking isn't going to derail or tempt me. Please, Eamon. Don't change anything for me."

"All right." Because he knew those in recovery needed to get used to being in a world of temptation, he nodded and pulled his drink back in front of him. He did take a long drink, but it was more to get rid of it than to prove any type of point.

"When I stopped by the FBI field office in San Francisco, they said you were working a case up here. Special Agent Sarah Nelson told me about the Brass Eagle." Lana glanced around the bar, lips curving at the sight of meticulously polished and maintained wood, shiny vinyl-padded seats and the large brass-cast emblem of the Marines hanging over the bar. "She said you crash here when you're in town. The owner sounds like he's a good friend."

"He is. Both Vince and his wife. They're two of many, as it turns out." Eamon tried to ignore the fact he was still holding Lana's hand. More to the point, that she was still holding his. Clinging to his, her fingers tensing as if he were some kind of life preserver. He could feel the slight chill from the glass on her skin, but also a tremor he was unaccustomed to.

"That's nice," she murmured. "I don't remember you having many friends."

"I've put many ghosts to rest. A lot's happened since we last spoke."

"Yes," she practically whispered to herself as she glanced out the window. "It certainly has." Before he could press for elaboration, she turned her attention back to him. "I take it since you're back here your case is over? Good result?"

"Mixed." He knew when someone was making small talk, even if that talk revolved around work. "Repeat sex offender broke probation and lured a teenager across state lines a few weeks back. We managed to track him down through his activity on the dark web. Girl's been returned to her parents, but he's—"

"Dead," Lana finished for him, as the "mixed" was understood. "One of the lessons you taught me," she said in a tone far too light for the topic. "Offenders like that should be taken alive if at all possible. It's the only way you find out about their previous victims. If there were any."

In this case there was no "if" about it. But Eamon's opportunity to bear witness and get confessions on the record was flat-out gone. "True as that might be, I'm not going to cry in my beer over him. On the bright side, the girl won't have to testify and her parents won't have to sit through a trial." And hear firsthand what had been done to their child. Therapy, on the other hand, was a different story. The family was going to need a lot of it.

"Answers have always been important to you," Lana murmured.

"They have." Eamon inclined his head. Was it his imagination or had this conversation suddenly turned into some kind of test?

"Because of Chloe." She was watching him now, with that pinpoint assessing stare she'd honed as a cop. It was the first time since he'd sat down that he saw a hint of the woman he'd worked with. "Because of your sister. You knew what it was like to have questions. To not have closure."

"Closure's a myth." He didn't particularly like the harsh Eden-like tone in the statement, but the declaration was one of his friend's familiar mantras. He lifted his beer again, almost in a mock toast to Eden St. Claire and her life lessons. "Took me until we finally solved Chloe's case and found her killer that I finally accepted that."

"But the answers, they had to have helped you a little at least. Didn't they?" Was that hope in Lana's voice?

"I stopped spiraling, if that's what you mean. I didn't feel caught up in the vortex of what-ifs and if-onlys." He took another drink. "I don't dream about my sister as often," he admitted. "At least now when I do, she's not pleading with me to find her killer." Or accusing him of not doing enough. "She's at peace now. That's something." Instead, he heard the ghostly sounds of her laughter on the air or in the wind chime hanging on the balcony of his San Francisco apartment. No, Chloe had been able to move on.

Now, instead of being driven by anger, he found himself amused by having earned himself a mischievous guardian angel who continuously attempted to remind him there was more to life than work. He could remember her with fondness and affection now, rather than guilt and grief. "Answers are great, but Chloe's still dead, Lana. Nothing is ever going to bring her back." His sister was eternally nine years old, with crooked pigtails and mismatched sneakers. A brief life but one that had impacted so many of those she'd loved. Was that a legacy? Eamon blinked slowly. He liked to think it was.

"So, what's going on with you, Lana? You're a ways from Seattle. Once upon a time you told me it would take something close to a truckload of C-4 to blast you out of the station house for anything remotely resembling a vacation."

"Seattle PD finally made me take all that time off I had stored up." Her smile flickered as if her own nerves were attacking. She pulled her hand free from his and tucked a loose tendril of hair behind her ear before she sat back. "You look good, Eamon. Whatever else you say, I can see putting those ghosts of yours to rest has helped. I'm hoping maybe you can help me do the same. If you have the time."

"I've got a few days while the internal affairs board clears me for active duty." Eamon's response was tempered by the knowledge Vince had been right about her sad eyes. He remembered her spark, Lana's zest for life that seemed superhuman and brought out the best in everyone around her. "What's going on, Lana?"

"I've been working on a special case. A closed case. For a while now. Months." She ducked her head but not before he saw her flinch. "Almost a year, actually."

"A year?" Eamon's eyes widened. What special case could she be talking about? "You're sniffing around someone else's work?" Didn't matter which law enforcement agency one worked for; cases were sacrosanct even after they were put to bed.

Agents, cops, they knew to stay on their side of the fence or risk ruffling more than feathers. He'd meant to tease her, to coax something close to that amazing smile of hers that he used to dream about. But no hint of a smile emerged; only a stoic hanging on to hope by a spider's-web-thin thread shone in her eyes. "Lana?"

"They didn't leave me any choice." Both her hands fisted and she knocked them against the table. The defiance in her whisper sent a chill down his spine. "I didn't remember at first. Everything was so…loud in my head after Marcus died. But I know what I heard, Eamon. I've had so much time to think now. Before, I was too caught up in having lost him, but…they've tried to convince me otherwise, the investigating officers, my superiors. My partner. Make that former partner," she added with another wince, filling Eamon's head with even more questions.

"But I know, I *know* I'm right," she said, her voice low. "If I tell you…" She broke off, her brow furrowing as if in a silent argument with herself. "I don't think I have anyone left I can talk to about this. If you say no—"

"Hey." He grabbed her hand again so he could surrender to temptation and slip his fingers through hers. "I made you a promise after we first worked together, what was it, three, four years ago? I said then that if you needed me for anything, *anything*, all you had to do was ask." It had been an easy promise to make to a woman he had no business caring for.

"I know. I kept telling myself that on the flight down." Her lips twitched as if he'd triggered a spark of humor. "The truth is I can't keep doing this on my own. I'm out of ideas. Out of leads. Out of anyone who will talk to me. If I don't get to the bottom of this, I'm really scared I'm going to lose my mind."

"That isn't going to happen." Especially if he could do anything to stop it. "Whatever it is, you've got my help." He refrained from mentioning that if she'd burned as many bridges as she was alluding to, chances were he wouldn't be able to rebuild them.

"You say that now," she hedged with a disbelieving shake of her head.

"There's nothing you can say that'll change my mind." He squeezed her hand to help her focus. "When I make a promise, I keep it. Let's have it, Lana."

She let out a long, controlled breath. "I need you to help me find out who murdered my husband."

Chapter 2

It took Lana all of five seconds to kick herself for not coming to Eamon months ago. Doing so might have stopped her continued spiral that, honestly, had yet to slow. The second she saw him head toward her in the bar, the part of her that had been existing purely on adrenaline and speculation had finally calmed.

Every single facet of her life had shifted on its foundation since Marcus's death eighteen months ago, but nothing was on shakier ground than her faith: faith in her surroundings, faith in her abilities as a cop, faith in the few friends she had left.

But seeing Eamon felt like a first step in rebuilding it.

She should have believed he'd be the stand-up man she'd always known.

He could have easily done what so many others had: shake his head in disbelief or, worse, humor her. Attempt to convince her she was reading too much into memories that probably weren't reliable. Persuade her she hadn't heard what she'd heard. Insist she was making something more out of the "accident" that had left Marcus Tate, her husband of three years, dead.

Out of habit, she reached up for the necklace on which Marcus's and her wedding bands now resided, along with the key pendant Marcus had given her as an engagement present. Feeling the cool gold against her fingertips centered her most of the time. It reminded her not of what she once had, nor even of what she'd lost, but of what she had to do.

She held her breath, still expecting Eamon to look at her with abject confusion and disbelief, shake his head and walk away.

But FBI special agent Eamon Quinn didn't do any of those things. And this was where her faith, tenuous as it was, began to reknit. Not only did he not do any of those things, but she would bet every penny she had that the idea never even occurred to him.

He was a man of honor who kept his friends—however estranged—close and protected.

A very handsome man of honor, she found herself noticing. Not that she hadn't made note of it before. Of course she had. Eamon Quinn was the kind of man no one could ignore or miss in a crowd. Tall, broad-shouldered, steady, and built to masculine perfection, thanks to the workout routine she remembered he'd stuck to since he'd been a recruit at the FBI academy. The red hair and sharp hazel eyes spoke to the Celtic roots of his ancestors. A man from another century, possibly more suited to wandering the Highlands in a kilt with a sword strapped to his back than wearing a suit with a gun at his side.

Her cheeks warmed at the thoughts slipping through her mind. Marcus had often teased her that Eamon looked at her as definitely more than a friend, but she'd never particularly seen it. She wondered if she was seeing it now, however, with the way Eamon held on to her even as his eyes searched her face for what she suspected were questions he now had himself.

There was something unsettling yet empowering about having his entire focus trained on her. Her fingertips tingled with the impulse to reach across the wooden table and stroke the lines of concern marring his brow.

The calm, unreadable expression on his face left her mentally scrambling, but only for a few minutes. He didn't speak. He didn't nod or give any indication he'd heard—or misheard—her. He merely pushed himself out of the booth, headed over to the bar to surrender his drink. She quickly tucked the rings and chain back under her shirt. A few minutes later Eamon accepted an oversize paper sack and returned to the table.

"Let's go."

"Where?" Not that she wasn't going to follow. The fact he hadn't told her she was out of luck with him was cause enough for her to go wherever he led. And, of course, she had nowhere else to go. She'd meant it earlier when she'd said she was out of options.

He stepped back as she climbed out of the booth, large satchel tight against her side. Eamon kept a gentle hand on her back as he guided her around the tables and customers toward the staircase at the end of the hallway where the restrooms were.

"Third floor," Eamon murmured as she grabbed hold of the railing. "Although I have serious doubts you have enough stamina in you to make it past two."

The same grit and determination that had put her at the top of her police academy class kicked in and, despite her churning, empty stomach and slightly shaky legs, she made it to the landing without fully collapsing. "Shows what you know," she told him as he walked around her, digging his keys out of his pocket.

"Yeah. Silly me, challenging your capabilities so I didn't have to throw you over my shoulder like a sack of potatoes."

Lana's lips twitched before they twisted into a scowl as he unlocked the door and pushed it open.

Once again, he stood back and waved her ahead of him. "After you, Detective."

How the man could make her professional title sound like the beginning of a seduction was beyond her. A full duffel bag sat inside the door of the tidy, practically furnished space. She bent down almost immediately and picked up an embossed white envelope that had made its way halfway into the room. "Special delivery. Fancy."

"Thanks." He plucked it out of her fingers with a quick smile, set it on the edge of a computer desk over in the corner. "Wedding invitation for the end of June. This is their subtle way of reminding me to write it down on my calendar. Don't suppose you're free to be my plus-one."

She blinked, a bit shocked at the question but even more astonished at the color that flooded his cheeks. "Um…"

"Kidding." He held up his hand, shook his head, but the frown she caught on his face before he turned his back on her had a load of new questions landing on her. "You know me. Just getting all the awkwardness out of the way before we get to work."

"I'm not in a position to plan anything for tomorrow, let alone three weeks from now."

"No problem. It's more about me fending off my friends' continued attempts to fix me up. Showing up alone at a wedding may be the final straw they've been waiting for."

She heard the affection in his voice when he spoke about his friends. More importantly, she heard the ease with which he embraced them. The last time she and Eamon had gone out to dinner more than a few years ago, Eamon had lamented the fact he'd only stayed in touch with a few people from his childhood. The fact he now, at least by comparison, had what appeared to be a wide circle of friends eased some of the concern she'd always felt for him. Especially now that she'd become well acquainted with living a very solitary life.

She was all out of friends at this point. She'd gone about things in the wrong way, caused too many problems, and hadn't considered the risks others might be taking. She'd ignored all the warnings and advice, so much so she literally had no one left she could call on. Except Eamon.

All that said, she didn't think he'd appreciate hearing he was her final option.

"It's nice up here." The view from the windows overlooked downtown Sacramento with an illuminated view of the golden Tower Bridge. It was a skyline she wasn't familiar with and it certainly didn't come close to rivaling that of her beloved home city of Seattle. With the cloudless, late-spring-plunging-into-summer night sky kissing the tip-tops of a mishmash of architectural feats, she could understand what continued to draw Eamon back to the River City.

The apartment didn't seem completely his. She didn't see any personal mementos out in the open. Not that she knew whether he was a collector or displayed such things. Their interactions really hadn't delved that deep. It wasn't that the apartment wasn't cozy and lovely. But it didn't scream Eamon Quinn either.

"Left upper cabinet by the sink," he told her as he carried the paper bag over to the table between two windows. "Vince added a second burger to my order, so grab some plates and napkins, will you?"

She didn't have the heart to tell him the thought of food had been making her queasy for the better part of the past year. But as she sniffed the air and caught the telltale promise of bacon, onions and oil-hot fries, she could feel her salivating glands activate. Maybe she could eat.

The magic of Eamon, she told herself. He'd always had a way of setting everything right.

She pulled out a chair and sat. He grabbed a couple of bottles of water out of the fridge nestled at the far end of the galley-style kitchen, then detoured to the desk and popped open the invitation. "Looks like Kyla won the first battle," he said as he skimmed the information. "She got the venue she wanted for her wedding. I bet Simone had something to do with that," he added with a chuckle, a sound that took her a bit by surprise. "That woman has contacts. Jason said that vineyard was booked up months ago." He set the pair of insert cards aside and joined her at the table to unload the cardboard containers. "I'm assuming your tastes haven't changed so much you'll refuse what I ordered for you."

"Food is food." She shrugged and, given the expression on his face, surprised both of them by snagging a steaming hot fry and popping it in her mouth. Her stomach immediately growled, as if being reminded of food for the first time in forever. "Are we going to wait for dessert before you begin interrogating me?"

"What makes you think I have dessert?"

"Because you're you." It felt good, oddly so, reminiscing on tidbits of information she probably should have forgotten years ago. "Your one constant whenever we worked together. Carbs and sugar."

"With some occasional protein thrown in," he added as he folded up the bag and set it on the counter. "For the record, I don't plan on interrogating you, Lana."

"Why not?" She focused on the food, because it gave her something to do other than feel nervous whenever she looked at him. "You wouldn't be the first."

Eamon was supposed to be her safety net. Her one reliable option left in a life gone roller-coaster wild. She wasn't supposed to be feeling, well, anything other than at ease around him. Instead, her insides buzzed as if she'd dragged an entire nest of bald-faced hornets with her from Washington.

"All right, then." He sounded almost resigned. "What changed your mind about Marcus's death? When we spoke at the funeral, it seemed pretty cut-and-dried that it was an accident."

"A hit-and-run." She dropped a knife into the burger and cut it in half. "At the time I didn't see how it could be anything else. Not with how it happened. I was in a fog back then, Eamon. His death knocked me sideways. I wasn't thinking straight for months." The drinking hadn't helped. It had been a fast and easy way to dull the pain, and then it had been the only way she could get through the day.

And then through the nights.

"I shouldn't have gone back to work so fast. I see that now. But what else was I going to do?" She knew she didn't have to explain herself to Eamon. "Without Marcus, the only thing I had left was my work."

"What happened?" Eamon's tone remained light. Calm. As if they weren't discussing one of the most intimate and devastating events of her life.

"I had this…" She blew out a breath. "I guess you could call it a flashback. I'd only been back on the job for a couple of weeks. My partner and I were called to the scene of an accident." She hesitated, took a bite of her food, mainly because she knew that once she got into the details of what she'd been chasing, she'd probably lose whatever appetite she had. "It was a hit-and-run and I reacted…badly."

"No one could blame you for that," Eamon said.

"Actually, yeah, they could." She swallowed hard. "But it was my own fault. Because I'd never said anything. Didn't tell anyone..." She looked over his shoulder, at the stunning seascape painting mounted on the wall behind him. The interplay of colors and imagery of jagged cliffs overlooking a stormy ocean niggled something in the back of her mind. "Is that a Renault?"

Eamon glanced around, lifted one shoulder. "Sure is. Is this a stalling tactic or do you follow Greta's work?"

Both. "Greta. You call her Greta?"

"I tend to use people's names when I speak with them." His lips twitched as he refocused on his meal. "Greta Renault is a friend. She's also married to a local detective I've worked with on and off. If you stick in town awhile, I can get you in for a sneak peek at the gallery she's going to be opening by the end of summer."

"That might be worth enduring a notorious Sacramento summer for," she murmured, enjoying the normal conversation. She'd missed normal. "She had a show up in Seattle a couple of years ago." Lana neglected to mention it had been one of the last events she and Marcus had attended together. "I only spoke with her briefly. The place was packed, but I must have walked around looking at her work for hours. It felt like visiting another world. I can't believe you have one just hanging there like it's—"

"Art?" Eamon grinned. "Funny how that happens when you put a frame around something. I haven't had the heart to take it to my apartment in San Francisco yet. It seems at home here."

"Marcus refused to buy one. He said he wasn't open to the competition." The comment slipped out so effortlessly and without so much as a stab of pain that she wondered if she'd imagined she'd said it. "He was teasing, of course. He actually did make a bid on one, but it was already sold. Sorry." She sat back, pressed her fingers to her temples. "I'm all over the place. I've been on my own with all this for so long I think maybe I've forgotten how to have an actual conversation."

"You're doing fine." He reached over and nudged her plate closer. "You'd probably do better if your brain had something to work off. What is it you didn't tell anyone before?"

She was standing on the precipice of a moment. This was usually when things went in one of two directions. Either the person listening interpreted her statement as being trapped in the circle of never-ending grief and guilt or that she'd been imagining things and her mind was only trying to help her heal. At this point, Eamon was her last shot at making sense of the entire situation.

"I was on the phone with Marcus when it happened. When he was hit by that car." She said it rip-the-bandage-off quick. "I heard the entire thing. It wasn't an accident."

Eamon swallowed, set his burger down and picked up his napkin, wiped his mouth. She watched him, her own pulse hammering in her throat to the point she could hear it pounding in her ears. She could only imagine what he was thinking. The same thing her former partner thought. Her bosses thought. The investigating officers she'd browbeaten a few short weeks ago into finally showing her the accident report thought. Each of those responses had been expected and, in a way, motivating. But she wasn't sure she could bear it if Eamon jumped on that thought train along with them.

"I'm not lying."

He frowned. "I don't think you are."

"I'm not imagining things either. Marcus was walking back to his car after a late dinner meeting with his boss when he called me. He'd had to reschedule his return flight and was due to fly back first thing in the morning. He was worried I'd be angry."

"Why would you be angry?"

Now was not the time to be stingy with the details. "We'd had a huge fight before he left. I didn't like how often he was away, all these last-minute out-of-town meetings he got called to. All of a sudden he'd be gone days or even weeks at a time. Of course, he countered by reminding me he wasn't thrilled about the hours I spent at the station and with murder victims." She hesitated. "I think we were both terrified at the idea of starting a family and that was just our way of trying to hash things out."

"Ah." He nodded. "I understand."

She gave him credit for not sounding completely shocked. It had been a decision she'd struggled with for months, but when she'd finally made it, it had just made sense. "I thought I was pregnant, a couple of months earlier. For those few minutes, before the test results come in, you see all the directions your life can go. When I found out I wasn't, we were both, I don't know, sad. I told him when he called that night that I was willing to make some changes, transfer departments if we really wanted to give it a shot."

"You were going to leave Homicide?"

"I know. Impossible for me, right? I mean, I know a lot of women can make it work, Homicide and having a family, but you know my history, Eamon. I grew up a latchkey kid. My parents were always working, hardly ever around, and when they were—"

"You wished you were anywhere else," Eamon finished. "Yeah, I remember you telling me."

"He grew up in foster care. He didn't really have any stability or direction until he was a teenager. Still, I believed in Marcus, in us. So I was ready to make a go of the kid thing, which is what I told Marcus when he called. I'd initiated the necessary changes so we could start our own family." Her heart twisted at the ghostly memory of her husband's laughter ringing over the phone. "Turns out his last-minute meeting with his boss was his idea so he could let her know he was going to take some time off, reevaluate his priorities." For a future that would never come to pass.

"We were laughing about our similar plan when I heard this horrible thump." She heard that sound every time she closed her eyes. "Then the tires screeched and there was an odd crackling sound before another thud." That sound bodies made when they hit the ground without any resistance. After almost a decade in Homicide, she'd finally experienced something that had horrified her to the point of emotional paralysis. "I don't think I realized I was screaming his name until…" Until her head had stopped spinning and she'd all but yelled herself hoarse.

Eamon stretched his hand across the table, caught hers and, for the second time that night, steadied her to the point her lungs relaxed and the memory slipped back into the dark places where she stored it up tight. "Why didn't you tell me?" he whispered. "That you'd heard it all happen?"

"Honestly? At the time, I thought maybe I did imagine it. That I was just looking for some way, any way, to cope."

"And later?"

She shook her head. "I didn't think you'd believe me." Now that she'd started, she couldn't stop. Especially when she had someone willing to listen. To hear her. "There was someone who picked up his phone after he was hit. A woman. She told me he'd been hurt and she'd seen it happen, and that she'd called 911. They were waiting with him until they got there. She…" Lana took a shaky breath. "She held the phone up to Marcus's ear so I could talk to him and I tried to. I tried so hard to tell him everything was going to be all right, but I think I knew. From the second I heard that thump, I knew he wasn't going to come home. The next thing I remember is his phone went dead. When my phone rang again, it was the Boston police telling me what had happened." She took a long, deep breath to relax even as her hold on Eamon's hand tightened. "I've had eighteen months to come to terms with all this, Eamon. I've spent a good chunk of that time focused on what I heard that night. I was not imagining things. It wasn't an accident. I know it wasn't. You need to believe me."

"I do."

She couldn't have heard him correctly. She'd hoped. Even prayed. But she'd also spent the past few days preparing herself for the fact that any conversation with Eamon might very well end just like the others had. However, her tenuous faith in him had been proved right... Her breath shuddered in her chest and her lungs expanded for the first time in months. "You do?"

"Based on what you've told me. You said the tires screeching came after the thump. Makes me think no one hit the brakes ahead of time to avoid him."

"Exactly." Her throat constricted around the word. Her heart beat so fast it was as if it were trying to catch up with her breath. "That's exactly what I told my boss, Captain Davis, but she said the local police back there had numerous eyewitness accounts that contradicted that."

"Cops will always accept eyewitness testimony over ear testimony every time. You know that."

"Especially when said witnesses are unbiased observers." She sighed. "My commanding officer suggested I was looking for new ways to cope. To find answers where there weren't any questions. If I had a nickel for every time she said 'accidents happen'..."

"Accidents do happen," Eamon said. "But I'm not going to say that's definitely the case here. Not without doing a bit of investigating myself."

It hadn't occurred to her how freeing it might feel to have someone listen to her and actually hear what she'd said. Suddenly her growling stomach's insistence wasn't nearly the nuisance it had been. She almost didn't have time to process the actual taste of the food before she'd eaten the first half of her burger, then reached for the second. If Eamon's expression told her anything, it was that he was tongue-tied due to amusement and self-satisfaction at having been proved right.

"You just made the last few days of waiting around worth it." She made herself slow down, give her stomach time to adjust to functioning fully again. "Where do you think we should start?"

"We can start with what you've done so far to prove your theory about the hit-and-run."

"What I've done?"

He closed his take-out container and stood up to stash it in the fridge. "You admitted you've been working on this for the past…what? Year? Eighteen months? Who have you talked to?"

"About that." One of the things that made him a stellar agent was the fact he remembered every little thing he ever heard or learned.

"You also hinted at the fact I'm one of your last options moving forward. So." He washed his hands, set the paper bag in a bin by the door for recycling. "How many people involved with Marcus's case have you ticked off?"

All of them. From the Boston police commissioner, to the on-site detectives, right down to the patrol officers who had been first on scene. "I'm sure there are some who would be willing to talk to us. To you," she added. "If you don't mention my name."

"Seattle PD didn't tell you to take your vacation days, did they, Lana?"

"There are all kinds of ways to tell someone something." She couldn't quite meet his gaze. "I've been honest about his case, Eamon."

"Now you need to be honest about your actions. I can't go into this blind, Lana, or worse, misinformed. If you want me to dig in, I need to know what roadblocks are waiting for me. Preparation is going to be half the battle."

Whether she was full or his warning killed her appetite, she couldn't be certain. Either way, she was done eating. "I've got a list of everyone I spoke with. I've got notes about those conversations." So many notes that didn't make any sense. "As far as my vacation is concerned, I might have been a bit too loose with the word. I'm on indefinite leave."

"You mean you've been suspended."

She shrugged.

"And when did that leave start?" he asked.

She found it amazing how high she could feel one minute before plummeting to the bottom of the barrel. She stood, shoved her hands into the front pockets of her jeans and rocked back on her heels. "A little over four months ago." She could feel the sobriety chip slip between her fingers where it provided both comfort and pressure. Eamon wasn't dumb. He could put two and two together.

"So, was it your investigating Marcus's death or your drinking that triggered your suspension?" He didn't sound angry. In fact, he didn't even sound disappointed.

More like he was gathering pertinent information to move forward with. It should have come as a relief, but instead it annoyed her.

"One has an awful lot to do with the other," she said. With disturbing ease, she pushed aside the doubt that statement brought up. "Heading home to an empty house every night was tough, and the only way I could stop obsessing about how he died was to have a few drinks at the end of the day." And then the days had gotten longer. The drinks more plentiful. "I took some short-cuts I shouldn't have. Didn't pay attention as closely as I maybe once did. I'm better now." She could only hope he didn't pick up the doubt in her voice.

"But your obsession with these questions of yours has kicked in."

"I need answers," she said flatly. "I came to you because I know you know what that's like. I don't mean to make it sound like what happened to Marcus is in any way as horrific as what happened to Chloe."

He shook his head. "For you, it is. You don't owe me an apology for that. I'll do what I can to help, Lana. But there are only two outcomes here, right?"

It took all her energy not to cringe.

"We either discover you're right, or we find out you're wrong. At the moment we're at fifty-fifty. You get that?"

"I know what I heard." She wasn't about to entertain the notion she was wrong. "My reputation as a detective might be ruined, but I can't stop trusting what few instincts I've got left. Marcus was murdered. If I give in to doubt, I may as well walk away right now."

He looked at her for a long moment. And she looked

back. She saw a friend, a man she knew she could rely on. And she saw doubt shining in those tranquil, albeit determined, eyes that held fewer shadows than they once did.

"All right." Eamon picked up his plate and carried it over to the sink.

"Yeah?" She felt a jolt of excitement charge through her system when he glanced over his shoulder and nodded. "You'll help me?"

"Of course I'll help you."

"Okay." She breathed out air she had been holding for months. "All right. So, what's the plan?"

"The plan is to make a plan. Tomorrow," he said quietly as he washed and set the dishes into the rack to dry. "As much as I'd like to dive in right away, I haven't slept more than three hours a night for the past week. I've got to get some shut-eye."

"Right. Of course." She winced. She should have paid closer attention. He did look wiped out. But just the sight of him had been so welcome she hadn't let herself notice just how exhausted he must be. "I'll head back to my motel, see if I can get some sleep myself." Fat chance. She was as wired as she'd been on her first undercover assignment.

"Or." He indicated the sliding doors into the bedroom. "You could crash in there and I'll take the sofa."

"What? Absolutely not." She shook her head.

"Then you take the sofa," he insisted. "We both know you're going to work off this energy you have on that laptop I'm sure you've got set up wherever you've bunked into."

"For the record, my laptop is in the trunk of my rental in the parking lot, and the motel I found near Old Town is perfectly satisfactory." Overstatement of the decade, but given her threadbare finances these days—four months without an income was proving more difficult than expected—the cheap, fifty-buck-a-night motel had been what she could afford. It had also been the first one she'd come across when she'd hit downtown Sacramento. "But I'll take you up on your offer of the sofa." She needed the added incentive of his presence to keep her on the straight and narrow. She recognized the energy zinging through her system. It was a boost that made her feel invincible, and that feeling was rarely a good thing for those in recovery. But there were other ways to burn off that energy. "Truly, the sofa looks great."

"Hang on." He disappeared into the bedroom, returned with a stack of sheets, a lightweight blanket and a selection of T-shirts and boxers.

She grinned and plucked up a plaid pair of said shorts and dangled them in the air. "Guess that answers the question as to whether you're a boxers or a briefs kinda man."

"I'm too tired to laugh." He set the rest of the stack on the edge of the plush sofa with a pull-out strap that would instantly transform the sofa into a bed. When he turned, she was standing right behind him.

"Thank you, Eamon." She was close enough she could feel the warmth of his body, smell the remnants of aftershave drifting off his heated skin. "You'll never know how much it means that you listened. That you're willing to help."

The sudden tension in his body had her inclining her head, her mind filled with new puzzles tempting her to solve them. She lifted a hand to his face, and her fingers tingled at the sensation of red stubble on his cheek. Lana rose up on her toes, just enough to put their mouths at equal level, but before she leaned in, his hands caught her shoulders.

"Don't, Lana."

"Oh." She blinked, embarrassment flooding through her like a dam had broken. "Jeez. Of course. That was… Wow." She tried to step back, but he tightened his hands and kept her in place even as she squeezed her eyes shut so as not to look at him. "I guess I let gratitude cloud my judgment. Overstepped those friendship boundaries. Won't happen again."

"Please don't say that."

His murmured plea had her questioning her hearing once more. It almost sounded as if… "Don't say sorry?"

"Don't say it won't happen again." He took what she interpreted as a reluctant step forward. "We're both exhausted. It's been a long few days for each of us. Now isn't the time to be making decisions we can't change after the fact."

"So…" She frowned, confused. "You're not saying no. You're just saying not right now."

He lifted his hand, cupped her face in his palm and very gently brushed his mouth against hers. "I'm saying sleep on this and let me know if you feel the same in the morning."

She pressed her lips together, trapping the spicy taste of him. The butterflies in her belly, the zinging in her fingertips as she touched his bare arm, left her speaking before thinking. "What time in the morning?"

He chuckled, ducked his head and pressed his forehead against hers. "I want you clearheaded and thinking straight when you come to my bed." He stood up straight, just enough to put a hair's-breadth distance between them. "Lest you think this is me being chivalrous and levelheaded, I'll tell you that this might be the most difficult decision I've made in my life. My bed, any bed, is where I've wanted you for a very long time. I just want to make sure you're there for the right reasons."

"I can think of a couple of reasons off the top of my head," she teased, unwilling to dwell on the fact that his statement had just thrown her into an entirely new level of confusion. Eamon wanted her? *Wanted her* wanted her? As impulsive as her attempt to kiss him had been, she honestly hadn't considered...

"How about we keep the changes in our relationship to a minimum until we get you on the other side of Marcus's death, yeah?" Eamon suggested.

Curse the man for making sense. He knew grief had brought her to his door. He wasn't going to take advantage of that. Or of her. Surprising? Not at all. Irritating? Only so far as she now realized the sofa was not going to be particularly comfortable for her for very long.

"As I've reached my politeness quota for the day," Eamon said, "I'm going to grab a quick shower. I'll leave you plenty of hot water." He pressed his mouth to her forehead, but only increased her frown lines by doing so. How had she managed to spin the one remaining stable part of her life off its axis? "Good night, Lana."

"Yeah," she whispered as he disappeared behind the bathroom door and left her churning with new regret and longing. "Good night."

Chapter 3

The mattress dipped behind Eamon and he shifted, rolling onto his back as Lana's silhouette moved. The curvy outline of her frame was all too familiar even in the darkness. He'd imagined this moment so many times, longed for reality to call and place her in his arms, a place he'd tried desperately for years to tell himself she didn't belong.

"Eamon." His name on her lips had him reaching out his hand, brushing his fingers against the warm softness of her cheek, down the side of her neck, over her rounded shoulders. Her scent, an intoxicating combination of subtle floral and the barest hint of citrus, wafted around him, drawing him up even as he pulled her close.

He shouldn't be doing this. He shouldn't even be thinking this. She'd come to him for help, not only to solve the supposed mystery of her husband's death, but to push her through the grief that was as prominent as the staccato beating of his heart.

Her name sat poised behind his lips, lips that could only search out hers to quell the building desire inside him. A desire that, for the first time in his memory, felt as if it might actually be abated by her touch.

The moment his mouth brushed hers, she evaporated. Her entire being vanished in a shimmering burst of mist that left his hands filled with nothing but unfulfilled promise and his ears ringing with a constant beat he couldn't tune out.

A ringing that grew louder by the moment.

Eamon's entire body jerked as he pulled himself out of the dream. His fingers tingled, as if the sensation of being with her was still pulsing through his system. He groaned, dropped an arm over his eyes as he rolled onto his back and tried to ignore the frustration and disappointment crashing through him.

He sighed, dropped his arm and stared up at the ceiling, frowning as that incessant ringing continued, only now it had an added buzzing he soon realized possessed the power to drive him over the edge.

Eamon sat up, reached for his cell he'd plugged in on the nightstand, only to find it completely dormant and, if he had to guess, a bit cranky at having been disturbed during its charging sequence.

He shoved himself up, adjusting his drawstring black pajama bottoms as he pried open the sliding door into the living room. The buzzing and ringing intensified as he identified the culprit.

Lana's cell phone vibrated against the glass coffee table scant inches away from where she slept, burrowed so deep in the cushions of the sofa he suspected he'd need an excavation crew to get her out. No wonder she hadn't heard her cell. But even as he lifted the phone, he felt reassured she felt safe enough with him to sleep so deeply. Only a small part of him hoped she was having as good a time in dreamland as he had been. He could only imagine how often he'd regret declining her offer.

There were fewer things he wanted in life more than Lana Tate in his bed. But he'd meant what he'd told her earlier: he wanted her there clearheaded, doubt-free and for the right reasons.

At least now there was hope of it happening. That thought lifted his mood considerably as he checked the screen of her phone.

It had gone quiet, but only for a few seconds before it started up again. He walked back into his room and lifted the blinds to look out over the alley between the Brass Eagle and the independent bookstore that had opened a few months ago. It always amazed him how eerily quiet those midnight hours could get, even in a major city the size of Sacramento. So quiet he could hear the buzzing of the streetlamps, one of which streamed far too brightly through the now unobstructed pane.

"Detective Tate's phone." Whoever was calling clearly was determined to reach her, and seeing as he couldn't reach through the phone and strangle the caller, answering seemed the lesser of two evils.

"Lana Tate?" The squeaky, uncertain voice on the

other end left Eamon wondering if this was a pip-squeak of an informant.

"She's unavailable at the moment." He scrubbed his free hand over his eyes, longing for the sleep that had proved anything but restful. "Can I help you with something?"

"Uh." The hesitation sounded couched in uncertainty. "Sorry. This is the number she left at the front desk."

The background noise pushed its way through Eamon's foggy mind. He could hear sirens and car engines and more than a number of voices bellowing and shouting.

"Front desk where?" Eamon snapped on the bedside table lamp and was instantly alert.

"Shine A Light Motel. I'm the night clerk. She checked in three days ago but I didn't see her come back tonight. The officers on scene—"

"Back up. Slow down," Eamon ordered in his practiced, calm tone. "What's your name?"

"Myron. But my friends call me Skates."

It sounded as if Myron, aka Skates, was younger than the cell phone Eamon was currently holding. "Skates, I'm FBI special agent Eamon Quinn. I'm a friend of Detective Tate's."

"FBI? She's a cop? Whoa, man, I didn't get that from her at all when she—"

"What's going on?"

"Right. Sorry. I've never had anything happen like this. I mean, take a name, a credit card and phone number. That's all I'm supposed to do, but I'm not cut out for—"

"Skates?" Eamon's voice sharpened.

"Sorry. You should see what's going on around this place. It's like I'm in a movie or something. There's a fire. They think it started in room 113. That's Ms. Tate's room."

"Anyone hurt?"

"Nah, man. I don't think so. We evacuated the entire place."

"Who's the officer in charge?" Eamon demanded as he walked over to his duffel and pulled out the last set of clean clothes he had.

"Officer Bowman and his partner. I didn't get her name. Should I have? I can go ask—"

"No. But I need you to go to Officer Bowman and tell him you spoke with me and that I'll be there with Detective Tate shortly. Can you do that, Skates?"

"Yeah, man. I can. He's standing right there by his patrol—"

"I'll speak to you when I get there. Thanks, Skates." He hung up, tossed Lana's cell onto his bed and got dressed. He was still pulling a black T-shirt over his jeans when he brought her phone out to her. Even as he stood over her, he hated to wake her. But he didn't have a choice. "Lana." He set her phone down, reached out a hand and touched her shoulder. "Lana. Wake up."

It shouldn't have surprised him, the force with which she shot out of a dead sleep. In the dim glow from his bedroom, the gold rings dangling from the chain around her neck glinted in the light. He stepped back and held his arms up and stared down at the sidearm she'd whipped out from beneath her pillow. The panic and fear in her eyes told him a number of things first and foremost. Most importantly that she clearly hadn't told him everything that had been going on.

Cops, law enforcement people in general, could wake at an instant and be on alert; power naps were second nature and vital to maintaining control over long cases especially. But there was a ghostly shadow in her gaze that had Eamon going against his training as he very carefully, very gently reached out and grasped the barrel of her weapon.

"You're okay, Lana." He pushed the gun down, pressed his fingers against hers to loosen her grip as he pulled the firearm free. It had to be her backup piece. They'd have taken away her sidearm along with her badge, thanks to the suspension. "I'm sorry I had to wake you." It was a lie. Now at least, since he'd seen just how skittish she was. "The manager at your motel called. There's been a fire. They think it started near your room." He walked around, turned on the table lamp. "You didn't leave a curling iron plugged in or something, did you?"

"What?" She shoved her long hair out of her face, frowning up at him as her eyes cleared. "Sorry. Fire? At the motel? I don't own a curling iron."

It was then he saw the bottle of Scotch he'd bought a few weeks ago next to the lamp. And the empty tumbler next to it. Something inside him twisted. He picked up the glass, held it in his hand. And looked at her.

"Don't look at me that way, Eamon. The glass is clean," she muttered, shaking her head. "I'll admit I got thirsty, but I didn't take a drink. I went to sleep instead. Happens all the time."

He shook his head, attempted to quell the disappointment churning inside him. Not necessarily in her, but in himself for not having realized how far off-kilter their earlier discussion must have pushed her. "You need to get dressed."

"Right. Fire at the motel. I heard that." She nodded, shoved up, then dropped back down. "My room?"

"Seems so. I know the officers on scene. We need to get there. Now."

"Ever wonder if the universe has it in for you, Special Agent Quinn?" She snatched up the jeans and T-shirt she'd tossed over the back of one of the chairs and, after turning her back on him, stripped out of the sleepwear he'd given her. "I don't know how I got the gigantic Kick Me sign on my back, but I want it off."

Speaking of her back, the sight of Lana's bare skin glistening against the soft light from the living room lamp had his hand tightening around the gun he still held. She made stripping down and getting dressed look like a choreographed ballet straight off the Met stage. The fluidity with which she moved, the efficiency as she whipped her hair out from under the collar before she jammed her long legs into her jeans, had him memorizing the sight for what he knew would be the stuff of dreams for years to come.

"You want to know what I'm thinking at the moment?" Lana demanded as she held out her hand for her gun, shoved it into the back waistband of her jeans. "I'm thinking what I wouldn't give for you not to have believed me last night when I told you about Marcus. Someone setting my motel on fire would give me one major reason to say how right I was."

Nothing to argue about there. "Who knew you were coming to see me?"

"No one." She spun around, zipped up her jeans and, after digging into her back pocket, pulled out an elastic for her hair. "I left on impulse, for the most part. My social calendar hasn't exactly been filled, so there was only one dinner I needed to cancel. I asked my neighbor to water Marcus's plants. She's done a better job at keeping those things alive than I have. Even if I had mentioned you, as far as I knew you were in San Francisco. And I told you, I didn't even decide where I was going to stay until I got off the freeway."

"You didn't notice anyone following you?"

"No." She frowned. "But I wouldn't have really thought to look, would I?" She scrubbed both hands down her face. "I probably should have."

Eamon wasn't about to pile on to her self-realization. "You said you've been looking into Marcus's accident for months. You talk to anyone recently?"

"I called his former assistant at the law firm a few days before I left." Her sigh betrayed her exhaustion, but now that he'd started asking questions, he couldn't stop. "I might have asked if she had a list of Marcus's clients I could see, but she's a kid, Eamon. Twenty-three, just out of college. She was trying not to cry while we spoke. She only wants to help."

"Doesn't mean she didn't tell anyone she spoke with you. What about the list you asked for? Did she send it?"

"Yeah." She nodded. "I haven't gotten around to looking at it in detail yet. I've got it on my laptop, though."

In her car, thankfully. "And I need you to make a list of—"

"Everyone I've spoken to since I started digging around?" The strained patience in her voice actually made him feel better. "I haven't lost all my policing abilities, Eamon. I know not to leave a laptop in a motel room. Not only does it stay with me, I've got cloud access to it on my phone." She motioned to her cell on the coffee table, then frowned. "How did you answer it?"

"Answer what?"

"My cell. It's facial recognition or a code. FYI, you look nothing like me. How did you answer it?"

"Thirty-three-oh-eight."

Her eyes narrowed.

"You're a 49er fan living in Seahawk country." Eamon was grateful to be able to tease her about something. "Roger Craig and Steve Young's jersey numbers. You have signed ones hanging in your house."

"Remind me to change that code to my backup when this is over," she muttered.

"Sixteen-eight-seven." His grin widened at her glare. "Montana and Dwight Clark. You told me once your dad used to watch 'The Catch' on a loop to gear up for football season."

"Your memory terrifies me," she said as she headed to the door. "Your car or mine?"

They took his SUV, but not until after Lana made a pit stop and grabbed her computer bag out of the trunk of the rental and stashed it in the back of Eamon's SUV. It might have taken her a while to get fully conscious, but now that she was, she felt like she'd been zapped by yet another energy beam. Sitting still for any length of time was going to be an issue. She could just tell.

Which meant she regretted the decision to ride shotgun within seconds of him exiting the parking lot at the back of the Brass Eagle. Staring out at the night sky punctuated by glaring streetlamps only gave her time to think. And all those thoughts spinning untethered only made her begin to spiral and feel as if she might suffocate.

She'd been a cop for eleven years. It was all she'd ever wanted to do after spending most of her childhood watching old cop show reruns. She was a good cop. A really good one. She rubbed hard fingers across her forehead. At least, she had been. Unlike a lot of officers, she'd loved her time on patrol. She'd built up a good communications network working the streets. People knew her and she made it a point to know them. Situation, status, even criminal tendencies didn't define a person—but knowing someone's name, on the other hand, went a long way to building trust. Whether they gave it or she remembered it, there was something powerful about that exchange that kept her reputation solid among the people she'd sworn to protect.

As good a patrol officer as she'd been, she was an even better detective. She prided herself on looking outside the box, examining angles that might otherwise go unnoticed or ignored. Every investigation was different, just as every person was. It was her responsibility to be open to absolutely everything.

But that was before she'd been on the other end of an

investigation. Before she'd come up against the stone wall of instant "it was an accident" mindset that had never, from the second she'd heard the words, rung completely true. Of course, that was hindsight telling her this.

Instinct was as vital to a detective as evidence. She couldn't follow one without the other, and every instinct, even as it had lain dormant beneath the grief of losing her husband, had screamed at her that something was very, very wrong.

By the time she'd been able to hear those screams, she was so far beyond a reasonable time frame that there was no one left to believe her. Or advocate for her. Instead of being listened to, she'd been humored and tolerated and, later, if the attitude of her fellow detectives back in Seattle was any indication, pitied.

"I can hear you thinking all the way over here." Eamon's voice broke into her thoughts before they turned to the dangerous coping mechanism that had gotten her suspended from the force. "Want to talk it out?"

"Not really. Pity parties are best attended solo."

He frowned, made a left turn and headed for the plumes of gray-tinged smoke in the distance, blocking out what few stars twinkled above. "There's nothing self-pitying about you, Lana. We cope how we cope at the time. Right or wrong. Hasn't your sponsor taught you that?"

"I don't have a sponsor." She'd gone to meetings, off and on, for the past few months. She'd listened to others, empathized and sympathized, but she hadn't been able to take that final step and open herself up with her own experiences. Heck, she hadn't even been able to bring herself to utter that sober-life confirming line *Hi, I'm Lana and I'm an...*

She shook her head to clear it. It had taken her three tries to make it past thirty days. Stop and start. Strengthen, then fall off the wagon. Where was the power in sharing failure like that?

Every time she'd made the decision to get sober, she got stronger. At least, that was what she told herself. She'd gone back occasionally, most recently to claim her ninety-day chip. But she didn't share. She didn't... confess and purge. All she'd needed was the physical reminder of what was possible. "Sometimes it's difficult to remember I need to take things a day at a time."

"Sometimes it's an hour or even a minute at a time." He glanced at her. "Friend of mine reminded me of that on more than one occasion. He still goes to meetings when he feels the need."

"How long does he have?"

"Not really sure," Eamon said. "Years at least. He only looks at the day he's living in, not the past. But he'll be the first to admit some days are harder than others. It helps he has a lot to live for now. Second chance with his wife. New baby. And by *new* I mean the little guy's just over a month old."

Envy slipped through her like midnight fog on the bay. What she wouldn't give to have that life. That mindset. Instead, she seemed to get a perverse kind of pleasure challenging herself to see how long she could stare into a bottle before she decided whether to drink or not.

"It's strange, to hear you talk about your friends and their families," she said, more to herself than to him. "I don't think we ever really talked about that kind of stuff when we worked together." Doing so now seemed a better solution to regaining control.

"You liked to keep your personal life separate from the job," Eamon said. "I understood that. For the record, I'm honorary uncle to not one, but three little'uns, thanks to Eden, Allie and Simone."

"Those were your sister's friends." Lana recalled him mentioning them when he'd told her about his sister. They'd been with her the night Chloe had disappeared, when the girls had been camping in one of their backyards. Her body had been found a few days later in a field of flowers. "You mentioned them a few times. Three kiddos, huh?"

"Make that soon to be five, actually," Eamon boasted. "Eden's expecting her second girl in a few months. Chloe Ann is looking forward to being a big sister. Or so she thinks," he added with a quick smile. "And then Greta's due... What is it?" He scrunched his brow. "Around Halloween? Getting hard to keep track."

"Chloe Ann?" Lana's throat tightened around the familiar name. "Eden named her daughter after your sister?"

"Yeah." There was no mistaking the tinge of sadness in his voice. "The three of them—Eden, Simone and Allie—had an agreement. First girl born among them got the name."

"You love it, don't you? The big family bit."

"I really do. Surprising, right? Turns out I always

had it, even when I didn't realize it." He stopped at a red light and farther along she could see spinning lights. "After Chloe was murdered, my parents couldn't take staying here. Then my father couldn't take staying, period. It was just me and Mom for a lot of years in the Bay Area. She tried to start over, but she was stuck. Couldn't move on. A good part of her died with Chloe, I think. It just took another twenty years for her body to follow." His hands tightened on the steering wheel. "She passed three weeks after we found the person responsible. Mom's with her now. At least, that's what I like to believe. I miss my mom a lot, but she wasn't meant to be here without Chloe. And now I have another family, here in Sacramento."

"Family is what you make, not always what you're born to," Lana said more to herself than to him. Something else to be envious of. "You haven't married, though, have you?"

"Me? No."

An odd wave of relief washed over her. "Why not? Never found the right woman?"

"Right woman wasn't available."

Her eyes went wide before she ducked her chin and berated herself for slipping into the role he'd assigned. He'd said something about having wanted her in his bed, but that was entirely different from wanting to be in someone's life 100 percent. Not that being involved with Eamon would be a bad thing. Quite the contrary. Now that she thought about it, it almost felt...

"Well, this is interesting."

"What?" She glanced up as Eamon pulled into the

parking lot of the two-story motel that, at this moment, looked as if it had been reset in a war zone.

"Familiar faces. Detective faces. They must have found something." He parked near the office beside an almost identical dark SUV. "Coming?"

"Yeah." She unbuckled her belt, pulled out her side-arm and stashed it in Eamon's glove compartment, then double-checked that she had her phone before kicking her purse under the front seat.

When she caught up to him, she nearly missed a step. The front of the motel was singed and smoking, black soot covering most of the facade. Smoke continued to billow into the sky, but whatever live flames had licked the building clean had been extinguished by the two fire trucks parked haphazardly in the lot.

A couple of the cars had taken hits as well. Hoods had black splotches and piles of ash floating away in the breeze. Windshields were blown out and scorch marks littered the asphalt. And there, in the center of it all, room 113.

She coughed, choked on the smoke and ash in the air. "Was anyone hurt?"

"Not that I'm aware of," Eamon said.

"There's the good news, at least. That place is a total loss," she said to Eamon, who nodded in agreement. "Guess I'm going to have to go shopping for some clothes. And shoes. My favorite pair of work boots were in there." She planted her hands on her hips, stared at the destruction, even as she felt slightly ill at the thought of being the potential cause. She blinked quickly and tried to get her eyes to stop burning. "Tell me there was a gas leak or something."

"Afraid we can't do that." She turned at the voice and found a pair of plainclothes detectives nearby. One was taller than the other, a bit ganglier than the other, but both were fit. The one who spoke had dark hair while the other was blond, with a charming grin she suspected stayed permanently in place. "Eamon," the dark-haired cop said. "The night manager told Bowie you'd be stopping by. This her?"

"If by *her* you mean Detective Lana Tate, then yes." Lana offered her hand. "I am her. Detective?"

"Cole Delaney," he said easily. "This is my partner, Detective Jack McTavish."

"Pleased to meet you, Lana," Jack said. "We've heard absolutely nothing about you." He aimed that widening smile at Eamon, who rolled his eyes in a way that actually had Lana chuckling. "And it's Jack, please. Sorry about your room and your belongings."

"Hi, Jack. Thanks." Lana felt instantly at ease with both men, no doubt because she knew Eamon considered them friends. "Eamon said only uniforms were on scene. What changed and brought in two detectives?"

"Night manager mentioned someone had set a fire in Lana's room when I spoke with him earlier," Eamon supplied.

"Night manager got it partially right," Cole said. "Arson investigators can't get in until the morning, but the crew found beer bottle remnants right near the bed."

"Well, I know that wasn't from you," Eamon said. "She hates beer," he added at Cole's blank stare.

A chill raced down Lana's spine despite the warm night. "Molotov cocktail?"

"That'd be my guess," Cole said with a nod. "We'll get a full report in a day or so. In the meantime, the entire motel's been evacuated. Bowie and Clarke are working with the local Red Cross to find alternate housing for the displaced customers and residents. Not much else we can do here except get in the way."

"Residents." Her stomach dropped straight to her toes. "I should have… Where will they go?"

"Local motels have been working with the city to get the homeless off the streets," Eamon said. "A lot of them get subsidies to offer temporary housing to assist in helping them use addresses for employment and benefits. They'll find a place. Don't worry."

"It was literally the first place I saw when I hit town." Guilt had her swallowing hard. "Now they're back on the street because of me."

"No," Jack said. "They're displaced because someone threw a bomb through your window. This isn't your fault, Lana. But you can bet we're going to find whoever is responsible. Both for you and for them."

"An optimist detective," Lana said with a tight smile. "Didn't realize those still existed."

"Why don't you come by the station later today, give a statement?"

"And fill us in on the case you've been working," Cole said, rather than suggested.

Eamon's light touch on the base of her spine stopped her from tensing at the request. "We'll do that. Give you time to get a little shopping in first, right, Lana?"

Lana glared at him. Her idea of shopping was one-clicking to fill her closet. But that wasn't here nor there. She had come to Sacramento to ask Eamon for help, not get anyone else involved. She glanced toward the burned-out motel, nausea churning in her stomach.

"Works for me," Jack agreed. "I need to pick up a case of soy sauce on my way home. Greta's putting it on everything. Have to say, though, soy sauce on vanilla ice cream? Not half bad."

"If you say so," Cole muttered. "Beats Eden's cravings for milk and Doritos."

"The trials of soon-to-be fathers." That earned Eamon a slug on the shoulder before the detectives moved off to their cars. "What are the odds the firefighters let us anywhere near your room?" he asked her once their tail-lights disappeared down the street.

"I'd say somewhere between nil and nada," Lana said.

"Better to ask forgiveness than permission."

She stayed close, stepping over fire hoses and around equipment set out for easy access. The water was still spewing from overhead as the firefighters continued to keep the flames from reigniting. Rivulets of water soaked her shoes and made her toes squish against the dampness. They made it as close as a car that was parked a few doors down from Lana's room before they were stopped.

Eamon had his badge out so quick it was as if he'd blinked it into existence. "Agent Quinn, FBI," he said to the female firefighter who had stepped in front of him. She was on the short side, definitely the stout side, and had *Harvelle* spelled out along the front of her helmet. "Detective Tate," he added with an incline of his head toward Lana. "We were hoping to get a look at the point of origin."

"No can do, Agent," the woman said. "I let anyone pass, I'll be on KP duty for a month. Trust me, no one wants that." She kept her tone light, but the determination in her gaze told Lana this wasn't her first go-around in this kind of situation. "I'm happy to talk to my captain, see if he'd be up for giving you a briefing, but this is as far as either of you goes."

"Got an ETA on that possible briefing?" Eamon asked.

"Ten, maybe fifteen minutes? He's on his way down from the roof now." She pointed behind them. "I'll send him your way when there's a break."

"Sounds good. Thanks."

"Were you expecting them to tell us more than Cole and Jack did?" she asked as he steered her toward the manager's office.

"Not even a little bit," Eamon said. "Just thought it was worth a shot." He scrunched his nose. "Hate fires. That stink stays in your nose for days."

"We could try to replace it with the stink of the coffee they have at the reception desk," she suggested.

"Caffeine would not be a bad idea."

"Is it ever?" She hugged her arms around her torso as they made their way across the parking lot to the office with the bumped-out window paralleling the street. "You ever wonder why they haven't started a caffeine anonymous group? CAG. Cag. Has a good ring to it."

Eamon's lips twitched. "Talk about a group the majority of the human race would have a need to join. Nice to hear your sense of humor is still intact, Tate."

"I aim to entertain, Special Agent." A sense of humor in this job was vital. "Since we've got time, I'm going to grab my laptop out of your car. Start getting those lists together you want to look at. Keys?"

He dug into his pocket and tossed her the fob. "I'll be inside talking to Skates."

"Who?"

"You'll find out," he warned before he headed inside.

From a distance, Lana beeped the alarm off and hit the release on the back hatch. She leaned in, grabbed for the strap of her bag, but it was caught in the seam between the back seats. She leaned farther in just as the side window exploded.

She yelped, pulled her legs in behind her and tucked into a ball as she was showered in glass. She heard the distinctive sound of a bullet hitting the side of the car, then another, and a third.

Automatically, she reached behind her for her weapon. She cursed. She'd stashed it in the glove box. Lana lifted her head slightly, guesstimating her odds of making it not only over the back seat, but all the way to the front. Another shot hit, this time coming through the open door, angling toward the gas tank. Her heart pounded in her ears as she considered her options. Outside, she'd only be a bigger target. Inside, she had to move. She needed to do something before one of those bullets hit the tank.

She only had to make it over the back seat to wedge between the driver and passenger...

Lana reached up, grabbed the top of the back seats

and began to haul herself up, but another shot took out not only the second side window, but the one across from it. Air whooshed in through the car as she ducked back down.

She heard shouts and cries from all around her and the squeal of brakes before she felt firm hands wrap around her ankles and pull.

"No! Don't!" she cried as jagged fragments of glass cut into her arms and through her shirt. She could feel a deep scrape form up her right side. She was instantly released and she sat up. "Sorry," she said to a shocked-looking Eamon. "There's glass everywhere." She plucked her shirt away from her body. Her blood dotted and bled through the rips and tears. "I don't have any other clothes at the moment."

She hadn't meant it to be funny, but the darkness in his gaze lifted. He held out a hand and she shoved herself forward and out of the car. Once her feet hit the ground, she breathed a bit easier. At least until she felt Eamon's hands on her again, skimming over every bit of her for injuries. She was trying to remind herself to breathe when he caught her face between his hands, peered down at her with such abject concern she barely saw a trace of the agent she knew.

"You're okay?" he demanded as three firefighters made their way over. "You're sure?"

"I'm okay. Nothing a few tubes of Neosporin won't fix." She laid her hands on his arms and squeezed a couple of times to get his attention. "Eamon, I'm fine. They missed." She glanced behind her, to the pile of glass on the floor of his car. There wasn't a window left other than the cracked windshield. "Well, they missed me, but oh, man. I am so sorry. Your car is totaled."

"Company car," he said stiffly. "I'll get another."

"Everyone okay?" It was the man Harvelle had identified as her captain who reached them first.

"Yes," Lana insisted. "I ducked in time," she said in a loud voice, noticing Eamon's skeptical expression.

"Best check the manager's office," Eamon suggested. "Bullets took out a couple of windows before Skates hit the floor."

"Right." The captain nodded. "We've got EMTs onsite. I'll send them over."

"Where are you going?" Eamon demanded when she pulled out of his hold and hurried to the passenger-side door.

She had her sidearm in her hand in seconds, double-checking the load and the chambered round before she shoved it into the back of her jeans. "Last time I leave it behind," she said as he stepped up beside her. She returned to the back, grabbed her laptop case and slung the strap over her shoulder. "You get a look at the car?"

"Late-model sedan. Dark blue or black. Partial plate."

"Anyone hurt?" she demanded.

"Other than you?" He grabbed her arms, held them out. "You're covered in cuts." He plucked out a shard of glass from her hair.

She dismissed his concern even as his touch warmed her. "What about the motel guests and residents? No one was hit, were they?"

"Not as far as I know," Eamon said. "The shooter

seemed to know where they were aiming. And who they were shooting at."

"Yeah." She bent over, pulled her hair out of the elastic. Glass fragments rained onto the pavement as her hands began to shake. "Looks like that target on my back's getting bigger. Think maybe I asked someone the wrong questions about Marcus's death?"

"No," Eamon said slowly as he drew her close and slipped an arm around her shoulders. "I think you asked the right ones."

Chapter 4

"Here." Eamon's offer of a filled mug of coffee earned him an irritated, albeit reassuring, glare from Lana. She'd settled herself at the square table closest to the door in the break room at the Major Crimes division of the Sacramento Police Department with unsurprising ease. "Trust me, it's better than what was back at the motel. What I drank of it before the bullets started flying," he added at her smirk as he resupplied the coffee condiments out of the bottom cabinet.

Lana sipped her coffee, looked surprised, then sipped again. "Not bad for cop coffee."

"Eden gave the department that fancy coffee machine for Christmas a couple of years ago," Eamon told her. "She said her husband's safety was reliant on his caffeine intake being sustainable and continuous. But truthfully? I think it's because she spends a lot of time here herself," he added at Lana's arched brow. He was on the edge of babbling. Something he rarely did except when he got scared.

Hearing those bullets hit the car where he knew Lana was inside might just qualify as the most terrified he'd been in a very long time. Given his profession and his own close calls, that was saying something. Normally, compartmentalizing things like this came easy, but then he'd learned early on that nothing was easy when Lana Tate was involved.

There were parts of him still quaking even as re-awakened parts were already working on figuring out the fastest way out of the mess they found themselves in. He wanted to be on the other side of whatever this was, to get those answers she was so desperate for. He was keeping an open mind, or at least trying to. Lana needed someone to believe her. Believe in her.

Normally he'd be anxious to close a case to do just that: close it. But this time, it was what potentially waited for him on the other side of that case that drove him. Would there still be sparks between him and Lana outside of a professional environment?

There had been plenty of sparks last night. The second she'd touched him in the bar—let alone what had almost happened in his apartment—he'd been engulfed by a desire he'd long denied himself. A desire that was back in full force and in a way that put the motel flames to shame.

The sooner they put any questions about Marcus Tate to rest, the better. For Lana's own safety, most of all.

That said, before the call from the motel, he wasn't entirely convinced her stalwart belief in her husband's death being anything other than an accident wasn't manifested grief. But since then her motel room had been torched and she'd been shot at like a plastic duck in an amusement park gallery.

That gave her story more than enough credibility.

On the other side of the door, the dulled voices of the ending night shift echoed in the distance. The changing of the guard, so to speak, was upon them with uniformed officers and detectives finishing up their rotations and readying themselves to head home. Eamon exchanged pleasantries with a number of them as they came in and out and earned a knowing expression from Lana that told him she was more than a little impressed at his friendliness with the local department.

If TV and movies were to be believed, the competition and animosity among and between law enforcement agencies made working together virtually impossible. The truth was that anger and resentment were rare. On more than one occasion, his arrival on scene to take over an investigation from local law enforcement had been welcomed and heartily accepted. But reality like that didn't make for good script writing, he supposed.

Everyone who swore an oath to serve and protect, be it local, state or federal, had one priority: to make things right and get the job done. If that meant working together, that was what they did. Egos rarely entered into it. That wasn't to say there weren't problem agents. Eamon had run into too many of those, but more often than not, the working relationship was smooth and mutually respectful.

Which was why Eamon often found himself at the Major Crimes division here in Sacramento. ADA Simone Armstrong-Sutton laughingly stated this was his office away from his office. Fair enough. He'd worked on more than a couple of cases with this department, with cops he respected and admired. While the local FBI office suited him fine and he got along well with his fellow agents, he couldn't help but be pulled toward the camaraderie he felt with these detectives and cops.

"Eamon." A short, compact Latino man rapped his knuckles on the door frame and stuck his head in as Eamon poured himself a second cup of coffee.

"Lieutenant Santos." Eamon glanced over the older man's shoulder. "I didn't realize you were in already, sir."

"Yes, well, an overnight motel fire and an out-of-state detective getting shot at in the parking lot of the same motel meant my phone was ringing earlier than normal. You two okay? Detective Tate, is it? Lieutenant Santos." He stepped inside, stretched out his hand in greeting, then handed the mug he was holding over to Eamon for a refill. "Delaney and McTavish are on their way in. I told them you were waiting for them."

"It made more sense for us to hang out here than to go driving around after the fact, Lieutenant." Eamon didn't have to spell out his concerns. Whoever had targeted Lana could very well still be keeping tabs on her to try again.

"Agreed." Santos nodded. "Incidentally, just got the report Patrol found an abandoned car fitting the description you gave as the one used in the shooting. It's being taken in for processing."

"I'll be stunned if it produces anything," Lana said, rubbing her temple as if staving off a headache.

"Looks like you two really got caught up in something. Care to explain?"

Lana's suddenly guarded expression had Eamon choosing his words carefully. "Uh, with all due respect, Lieutenant—"

"Let me rephrase." Lieutenant Santos's dark eyes sharpened. "As a professional courtesy, I'd like a report, please. Or should I put in another call to your superior?" He looked at Eamon for a long moment before turning his attention on Lana. "Captain Davis is who you report to, isn't it, Detective?"

"Yes, sir." Lana took a deep drink of coffee and uncurled from her chair. "At the best of times, at least. I'm currently on suspension for…various reasons."

"Yes. I know."

"You do?" Eamon asked as Lana cringed.

"Early morning phone calls often result in me making some of my own. They do provide one with a wealth of information."

"Ah." Lana turned concerned eyes to Eamon. "I see."

"Normally we're advised when an out-of-town law enforcement officer is here to work," Lieutenant Santos said.

"Yes, well, I'm not exactly here in an official capacity," Lana admitted. "But then I suppose you know that as well."

"Captain Davis suggested as much. She had some interesting things to say about you, Detective," the lieutenant said. "She didn't sound particularly surprised to hear you'd gotten into a spot of trouble down here."

"I would imagine she wasn't." Lana's smile was fleeting. "Am I to assume she filled you in on my...situation?"

Eamon's heart hurt for her. It was always difficult to own up to professional shortcomings and personal foibles. In law enforcement, especially for a woman, it could be even more complicated and rife with potential consequences.

"I got the gist of it." Lieutenant Santos's expression shifted to unreadable. "I'm sorry about your husband."

Eamon saw Lana visibly swallow. "Thank you, sir."

"I've seen what happens when detectives take on cases that are so incredibly personal. Complications often arise." The lieutenant came inside the break room, rested his back against the wall, arms crossed over his chest. "I understand you and Agent Quinn have worked together previously."

"On a few cases up in Seattle. A missing person. One kidnapping. He's a friend," Lana said in a way that put a big ding in those growing hopes of Eamon's. "I came to him for help. I thought his perspective might be useful."

"Then clearly, despite your captain's claims to the contrary, your judgment remains intact," Lieutenant Santos said. "Given the morning's events, I'm going to assume you've agreed to assist, Eamon?"

"Yes, sir." It didn't matter that Santos wasn't his superior. The man's rank and experience, as well as his past support of Eamon, demanded Eamon's professionalism and respect. He'd worked with the commanding officer enough to know Santos looked beyond rules and regulations to see the people behind the badge and the curveballs life often gave them. "I plan to stick with this, with her, until it's resolved."

"I'd expect nothing less." Santos turned an assessing gaze on Lana. "Captain Davis said you're convinced there's something more to your husband's death. That it wasn't an accident."

"That would be accurate, sir."

"Given the events of the past few hours, I think it's safe to say you might be on to something," he observed.

"I do seem to be the common denominator," Lana stated. "And given I haven't been working any other cases for the past few months—"

"Clearly you flipped someone's switch," Santos said. "Will this be an official federal investigation, then?"

"To be determined," Eamon said and ignored the frown of surprise from Lana. "I've already spoken with my superior back in San Francisco." Not a great idea to wake said superior up before dawn, but the hail of bullets had dampened his usual caution. "I'll be extending my post-case leave with some of the vacation and sick days I've accrued in the past—"

"Lifetime?" Santos said. "Rumor has it you can barely spell *vacation*, let alone apply for it, Special Agent."

"Yes, sir." Eamon's smile eased.

"I have no doubt you can find outside assistance with your investigation," Santos said. "Still, I'll make arrangements for Detectives McTavish and Delaney to have some flexibility with their caseload. If you need their help, just ask. Provided—" he raised a finger "—you keep me in the loop and updated as to your progress. Both of you," he said with a pointed look at Lana before the ding of the elevator had him pivoting toward the windows looking out into the bullpen. "Speaking of my two best detectives."

Eamon snorted behind his mug of coffee and Santos shot him a look that warned Eamon that comment was not to be shared.

"Here they are, loaded down with a healthy amount of sugar." Santos's amusement was fleeting as Cole and Jack approached. "Detective Tate, suspension or no suspension, you're still a sworn law enforcement officer. I ask that you remember that," Santos warned as Jack, big pink bakery box in hand, entered the break room. "But I also ask that you come to me if you need anything while you're here."

"Thank you, sir. I appreciate that," Lana said with a nod as the lieutenant moved toward the counter to doctor up the coffee Eamon had fixed for him.

"This is my version of a shield," Jack said to his commanding officer before setting the box on the table and facing Eamon. "We were gone from the motel, what? Three minutes? Before the bullets started flying. That has got to be a record."

"It was eight minutes, actually," Lana said. "Personal best for me. Usually it's at least a half hour before someone starts using me for target practice."

Eamon wasn't surprised Jack didn't laugh. The man might be more easygoing than his partner, but he took his job and responsibilities seriously. Eamon had no doubt Jack was second-guessing his and Cole's decision to leave the scene.

"And here I was wondering what could have possibly gotten you suspended, Detective Tate." Santos approached, napkin in hand, and flipped open the box to grab one of the half dozen apple fritters tucked inside. "I would like a briefing on your unofficial case within the hour, please," he ordered before leaving them alone.

"That was…unexpected," Lana said to Eamon as she watched the lieutenant return to his office across the bullpen.

"He trusts us," Jack said with a glance at Eamon. "All of us. That earns us some leeway."

"Not too much, however." Cole, having changed into a clean shirt and tie, hefted an oversize, reusable shopping bag toward Lana. "Eden, my wife, sends her regards in the form of clothes," he told Lana. "She doesn't anticipate fitting into any of these in the near future, so keep what you like."

"She sent these for me?" Lana rose and accepted the bag with overly wide eyes. "She doesn't even know me."

The surprise in Lana's voice triggered a wave of sympathy inside Eamon. How lucky he was to have the friends he did.

"Yeah, well, blame this guy." Cole jerked a thumb in Eamon's direction. "Guy goes and earns himself bigbrother status back when we were young, so you're accepted by default."

"I'm not that much older than the rest of you," Eamon grumbled and eyed a maple bar.

"You're pushing forty faster than we are." Cole's dry tone felt surprisingly warm. "In any case, Eden's ready to rock and roll as soon as you give her something to work with."

"Rock and roll with what?" Lana asked.

"Right." Eamon ran a hand across the back of his neck. "That unofficial assistance Lieutenant Santos mentioned earlier? Eden's part of it. She has a talent for digging up information people don't want found. Or accessed."

"I've got a call in to Jason, too," Jack said. "He's carrying a full load of classes now that he's going for his psychology degree, but he said he can jump in when and if we need him. He thinks in different ways than the rest of us," he added at Lana's continued blank stare.

"That's Jack-speak for saying that once upon a time Jason worked on the other side of the law," Eamon explained. "He's better now."

"I don't…" Lana's voice hitched. "I don't know what to say."

"Eamon asked for our help," Jack said matter-of-factly.

"I had some favors to call in," Eamon said with a shrug at Lana's disbelieving look. "Why don't you go get cleaned up and changed? I'll get these two filled in on the recent developments."

She plucked at her holey and torn shirt and winced. "Good idea." Her low voice suggested she was having difficulty processing this. But then her head snapped up and suddenly she was on the move. "Please tell Eden thanks from me. I'll be back in just a sec, yeah?" She grabbed a chocolate-sprinkled doughnut on her way out to change.

Eamon stood where he was, coffee in hand, trying not to notice the two detectives looking at him as if they expected him to self-combust in the next ten seconds.

"That's her, isn't it? The woman you couldn't forget,"

Jack said as he took Lana's vacated seat. "And before you answer, please consider I have fifty bucks riding on this answer with Greta. Rumor is you've never been serious about anyone because you were already hooked."

"Please." Cole shook his head. "You even have to ask? Look at him. He's not just hooked. He's sunk."

"It's not what you think," Eamon said, not quite certain why he felt the need to deflect. Immediately, the temptation she'd offered last night leaped to mind.

He cringed, drank more coffee. Okay, maybe he did know.

"Oh, I think it's definitely what we think," Jack teased. "The after-fire target practice just ups the ante. You want to give us the short version of what L.T. already knows?"

"Lana's been asking questions about her husband's death that was almost two years ago." It seemed best to just be honest about things. That it had the added benefit of shutting his friends up? Bonus. "There's a lot going on. A lot I'm not even in on yet, but she came here looking for help. I've said I'll give it to her." He eyed the two detectives. "And I think we'll need your help."

Chapter 5

If Lana ever met Eden St. Claire, she'd shower the woman with enthusiastic thanks. After gobbling down the doughnut like a starving woman, Lana found two pairs of practically brand-new jeans in the bag, along with a rainbow of tanks and T-shirts that, while a bit brighter on the color spectrum than Lana was accustomed to, fit almost to a tee. The sleepwear was practical and the simple black knee-length dress reminded Lana of one she had in her closet back home. The fact there wasn't anything frilly, sparkly or overly feminine made Lana suspect she'd found a kindred spirit in the clothing sense.

The waist-length, black lightweight zip-up sweatshirt seemed perfect for the indecisive weather, which had yet to take that final plunge into summer.

There was also a pair of flip-flops with tags attached,

and a pair of hiking boots that came pretty close to re-placing the ones she'd lost in the motel room fire, and slightly scuffed black flats Lana suspected were meant to go with the dress.

All in all, she'd hit the jackpot when it came to reset-ting her clothing supply. The dreaded shopping excur-sion she had on her mind for later had been reduced to a quick stop for underwear and socks. Score.

The fact Eden had also included a zip-top cosmetic bag filled with various toiletries and personal prod-ucts told her Eden was a sensible woman who planned for various contingencies, proved by the fact she'd also included a box of condoms in the bottom of the bag. Cheeks blazing, Lana folded and stuffed everything into the zipper duffel Eden had tossed in. Obviously Eamon's friends, Eden at least, believed they were more than work buddies. The idea didn't unsettle her exactly, but it did add to her rising confusion. She'd come out to ask for Eamon's help, not start something...personal.

She took a slow, shuddering breath. Last night had been revelatory. Eamon had feelings for her. Dread and uncertainty spiraled around each other and lodged in her lungs. He hadn't been pushy about it. To the con-trary, when she'd made her intentions regarding their physical attraction obvious, he'd firmly put some dis-tance between them just in case she wasn't thinking clearly.

Except, she had been. Maybe more clearly than she had in months. Maybe that was part of the problem. And, okay, perhaps he was partially correct in that she'd been looking for a quick, no-ties tumble to serve as a distraction for everything that had thrown her off course. There was nothing wrong with that. But there was something wrong with her thinking Eamon Quinn was the quick-tumble kind of man.

This was a dangerous path to go down. Trying to shake herself free of the increasingly unsettling thoughts, she went over to the sink to splash water on her face. She hadn't felt anything remotely sexual since Marcus had died. It was as if losing him had made that side of her disappear, but moments after being in Eamon's presence, feeling his touch, his simple, hand-to-hand touch, she'd felt that long-dormant fire ignite almost to a full burn.

She stood up, stared at herself in the mirror and wondered, not for the first time, what Eamon saw in her. She stripped off her shirt, wadded it up and tossed it in the trash, then dabbed at the scrapes and cuts the EMTs had done their best to treat. Her stubbornness, her tenacity, it was all etched into a rather angular face that carried little softness even when she smiled. She wasn't a conventionally pretty woman, she thought, but she was a woman who knew what she was and what she was good at. It was what Marcus had always said he saw in her.

Maybe Eamon saw that, too.

She pulled her necklace free from between her breasts, looked down at the pair of rings that, at times, called out to her as if from a different life. The rings and key pendant acted as both anchor and memory personified. The good and the bad. Happy and...

Part of her waited for the guilt to descend, but that wasn't going to happen to a realist like her. Marcus was gone. There was nothing to cling to that would ever bring him back and he, more than anyone, would have wanted her to get on with her life. Heck, they'd had this discussion about what if the worst happened. The only difference was the conversation had been triggered by Lana's dangerous profession.

She wasn't clinging to the rings as a reminder of their marriage. She didn't need that. She was wearing them as a reminder that Marcus's life had meant something. Even now she could practically hear her husband teasing her for attempting to usurp sentimentality, something she wasn't particularly known for.

"Who are you kidding?" she muttered to herself as she tucked the rings back into the center of her bra and quickly put on a raspberry-colored T-shirt and a clean pair of jeans. "He'd be seriously outraged at how you've handled this whole thing." Except, neither of them could have predicted Marcus's death would leave her with so many unanswered questions and suspicions.

If it wasn't guilt getting in the way of seeing the potential with Eamon, what was it? She pressed a hand against the bare skin over her heart. No. She frowned, shook her head. She wasn't a romantic. She had never let herself become so lost in the fantasy of what she and Marcus had shared that she couldn't consider what else might be out there for her.

Her heart skipped a beat. Up until recently, this was when she'd be taking a shot—or more—of whiskey to calm her nerves. But while the nerves might settle, the booze would also dull her reactions, not to mention taint the emotional wherewithal she needed to make full use of Eamon's expertise and investigative connections. She closed her eyes, took a long, deep breath.

Eamon.

Before she'd seen him again, she'd considered him a bit of a life raft in very choppy waters. One that she was fairly convinced she could grab hold of and feel safe.

Now? She lifted shaky fingers to her lips that still felt warm from his kiss. Now she had unexpected images of things that hadn't happened, had never been in her realm of possibilities. And not just the potential sex. Emotional promise. And risk.

Doubt of an entirely different kind crept over her with the stealth of a midnight shadow. She didn't have it in her to love again. She'd given it a chance to work with Marcus and she'd been left broken. She never wanted to give that big a piece of herself away again.

But Eamon…

Even as the thought passed through her mind, she found herself rationalizing.

There wasn't a better man she could think of to take another risk on than Eamon Quinn. It could be the distance, the years that had passed, making her think such things. They'd had little to no contact after the last case they'd worked on together, other than his brief appearance at Marcus's funeral, and even that existed only in foggy memory. And yet…

And yet it was as if no time had passed at all.

"Gah." She ducked her head and splashed more water onto her face. Stupid close calls and near-death experiences. She should be used to them by now, but somehow they always messed with her head and left her dwelling on things she had no business addressing.

Eamon Quinn wasn't asking anything of her. He sure wasn't demanding anything close to love. But he should. Eamon needed love in his life. He *deserved* love, love she wasn't in any position to offer. She was way too messed up for a relationship. She probably always would be.

She gripped the edges of the slightly stained porcelain sink and dropped her chin to her chest. How arrogant of her to believe he was thinking about anything near happily-ever-after or happily-for-now. He was a man who returned the desire she'd finally acknowledged she felt for him. That was all.

The rap of knuckles on the door had her swiping the tears from her cheeks. "Lana?" Eamon's voice didn't bring quite the amount of comfort it usually did. "You find something that fits?"

"Yeah," she croaked. She cleared her throat and grabbed a handful of paper towels to dry her hands and face. "Yeah, I'm good. Out in a minute."

"We've moved to the conference room."

Conference room. Perfect. The more people around, the better. It was being alone with Eamon that was likely to get her into trouble. She needed to get her head on straight. She hadn't come down here to pursue a relationship or give in to a surprising and distracting physical attraction. She'd come for help to find out the truth about Marcus's death. That was what she had to focus on.

Which was what she did as she gathered up her new duffel and headed out of the bathroom. The second she

was out in the hall and heard the familiar clamor of
cop talk and muted conversation, the doubts instantly
vanished.

There was a universal truth among law enforcement
personnel that said any serving officer could step inside any dedicated building and instantly find their way
around. It was as if some kind of invisible homing beacon had been implanted in their brains the second they
graduated the academy.

She did consider that this particular division of the
Sacramento Police Department had a bit more polish
than most she'd been in, her own Seattle offices included.

Not wanting to interrupt, she quietly closed the conference room door behind her.

"Six, six thirty." A woman's voice came over the tablet screen set up in the center of the conference table.
"We've got the food taken care of. All you have to do is
show up. Oh, hey, there. You must be Detective Tate."

"Sorry to keep you all waiting." Lana set her bag
down. She wasn't entirely sure what to think about the
fifth face reflecting back at her from a tablet screen. The
woman on the other side of the screen had her straw-
berry blond hair messily knotted on top of her head.
The expression on the woman's round face appeared
to be part skepticism, part excitement. Behind her sat
a pile of file folders, one very old printer and a one-
eyed, ragged stuffed bear perched precariously on the
edge of a stack of storybooks. The wall that served as
a backdrop to her video screen was covered in news-
paper clippings and printed-out articles circling around

various disappearances, unsolved murders and suspicious deaths. The pieces of the puzzle came together in one simple answer.

"I'm betting you're Eden." Lana approached the tablet as if walking up to a friend. "Thanks for the survival package," she said and earned a smile of approval from the other woman. "I'm not sure I'll need everything you included, but—"

"Better safe than sorry." Eden dismissed her embarrassment. "Nice to meet you, Detective."

"Lana, please." Lana couldn't have missed the ever-so-there hint of disapproval at the title and neither, it seemed, had Eden's husband. Cole was sitting back in his chair, a few fingers covering his now curving lips as something akin to admiration and amusement flickered in his eyes.

"Eden's going to take notes, do research you might need. That kind of stuff," Lieutenant Santos said. "What she will not be doing is any gathering of information via asking questions in person. Correct?"

"You've turned me into an admin." Eden's animated grumble had Lana's lips twitching. "Not that there's anything wrong with that."

"Strangely enough," Lieutenant Santos replied, "Molotov cocktails and flying bullets tend to make me leery about putting a pregnant civilian front and center of a case."

"Yeah, yeah." Eden grumbled more. "For the record, I would have agreed had I been consulted. If I can't find my feet, I can't very well be useful on them."

Detective Cole Delaney, Eden's husband, didn't look

entirely convinced. "She works better ticked off—don't worry," Cole told Lana. "You want to get us up to speed on your late husband's case?"

Lana took a deep breath and sat in the chair beside Eamon. "What do you already know?" Santos got comfortable in a chair at the far end of the long table.

"Eamon's given us the outline," Jack said from his seat across from her. "Marcus Tate was killed in a hit-and-run eighteen months ago in Boston." He ran through the metadata of the accident: time, location, basic report details. "Officers called to the scene closed it pretty quickly. Detectives followed. Witness statements, of which there were five, all pretty much said the same thing. Mr. Tate was cutting across the street from a local restaurant. It was dark. At least one of the streetlamps was out and a silver SUV clipped him just as he reached his car." Jack glanced up. "He died at the scene shortly after the ambulance arrived."

Lana wished, more than anything, for the level of detachment Jack possessed while reciting the details. But as she'd learned the last few months, some wishes were never meant to be granted.

"What the report apparently doesn't say," Eamon said in a tone that had Lana's attention snapping his way, "is that Marcus was on the phone with Lana when the accident occurred."

Eden swore. "You heard it happen?"

Lana swallowed hard. "I did, yes."

"There was a woman who picked up Marcus's cell shortly after the accident," Eamon said. "She told Lana what happened."

Jack flipped through the printed-out pages. "I'm not seeing any mention of any witness who said they spoke with you, Lana."

"That was one of the first things that struck me when I finally got hold of the reports." She hadn't liked hounding the detectives and officers, nor did she enjoy going over their heads to their superiors. But she'd needed to see for herself what the official record stated. If only to prove she wasn't losing her mind.

"Can you fill in some of the blanks, Lana?" Eden asked. "You and your husband lived in Seattle, correct? Obviously you work for the Seattle PD, but what did Marcus do?"

"He was an attorney. Business contracts and acquisitions mainly, for a company called A&O Solutions." Lana tapped restless fingers on the table. "They're part think tank, part consultancy. They recruited him when he was still in college, thanks to his mentor. They covered his tuition and housing cost, and once he graduated, he went to work for them. A couple of years later he passed the Massachusetts State Bar. He had to travel a lot and most of the times his trips were last-minute. He always said he loved his work. He said it made him feel important. Like he was making a difference." And it had paid well, which, after growing up in the system, had been a plus for Marcus.

"I'm betting his job probably covered a wide range of responsibilities," Eamon said. "The few times I met him, he never went into particular detail about his job. Any idea of the particulars? Any problems he was having with clients or accounts?"

"None. As far as I knew, everything was fine." Lana shrugged. "He didn't complain about anything work-related."

"The *A* and *O* stand for Alpha and Omega," Eden read off her computer. "Subtle. Their client list is a who's who of the rich and powerful. Businesses, private individuals, other multimillion-dollar companies."

"Takeovers in play? Political agendas?" Cole slipped in. "If Marcus was working on something like that, it might explain why someone would have wanted him—"

"Dead," Lana finished for him even as she steeled herself. "Don't worry. I'm past breaking down at this point." One thing about not having any answers was that there were no wrong suppositions. "Marcus and I didn't talk a lot about work." She hesitated. That wasn't entirely true. "We didn't talk a lot about *his* work. Most of his clients required NDAs, and he was never entirely sure what he could talk about, so we agreed early on we wouldn't discuss any of it."

She glanced at the screen where Eden was glaring and typing furiously.

"That's her transcribing face," Cole told her. "She's making note of everything we say."

"The devil's always in the details," Eden murmured, then kinked her head to the side. "Better speed this up. I hear signs of life from Chloe Ann's room. Our girl's Little Miss Cranky Pants until her first glass of juice."

"Like mother, like daughter," Cole muttered.

"So Marcus didn't tell you what he was working on for this particular trip to Boston?" Eden asked.

"Not at first, no. Turned out to be more personal

than business-related," she added and only hesitated a moment before saying, "He was going to take a leave of absence so we could start a family."

"What a shame," Jack said without the expected look of pity masking itself as sympathy. "Did he go to Boston a lot?"

"Often enough he kept an apartment there. It's where the company is based." She glanced at Eamon, uncertain how much detail she should share. "He'd flown there the day before to meet with his boss, Felice Covington. She headhunted him back in his college days, but he first met her when she visited one of the youth centers he attended as a foster kid. They were close. Not that kind of close," she clarified at Jack's raised brow. "Marcus was in foster care from a very young age. Felice belongs to a number of charities that focus on children's issues. It's her pet project with A&O. If she saw promise in someone, she took them on. Sponsored them, both financially and in their education. She considered it a good investment for the future. I think, in a lot of ways, she served as a mother figure for him. For a lot of young people, actually."

"That must make for a very loyal workforce," Cole observed.

"I met her at Marcus's funeral," Eamon said. "Very posh. Very polished, with an underlying hint of steel. Wicked sense of humor, too, if I recall."

"I would consider that an apt description," Lana agreed. "She also has infinite patience until she doesn't. The woman can burn through ice with a quick look alone."

"She has an impressive résumé and portfolio." Jack scanned the screen of his own laptop. "I'm seeing dozens of offices and properties all over the world. She's this successful and yet I've never heard of her. Or A&O Solutions, for that matter. Interesting."

"She likes to fly under the radar. But she's very generous." Lana nodded. "She arranged for us to stay in one of her homes for our honeymoon."

"Where was that?" Eden said as her fingers continued clicking.

"British Virgin Islands." Lana was grateful for the good memories. "Marcus said it would give me a taste of what he was hoping to achieve for us. He had expensive dreams." It was one way they were completely opposite to one another. Lana's dreams were more practical and down-to-earth. She'd have been happy with a white picket fence. Marcus wasn't going to be satisfied until he had an iron gate. Ordinary, Marcus had teased, referring to her choice. It had become a kind of joke between them. One she hadn't found particularly amusing.

"How often did he travel overseas?" Eamon asked.

"Pretty regularly." She shrugged. "He was high up the food chain at A&O. Honestly, I was too focused on my work to pay that close attention. I knew when something big happened, if there was a problem that cropped up or something was bothering him, not that he offered any details. Otherwise…"

"What kind of problems?" Santos asked.

"There were a few issues with employees. People not pulling their weight. Oftentimes Marcus was called in to fire them. It was a talent of his, apparently." Lana frowned. "I remember him having to take a trip to Tokyo because one of A&O's board members died while on vacation with his family. Marcus is who they sent to make sure all the arrangements were made and the family assisted with getting back home."

"When was this?" Cole asked, glancing at his wife, who was nodding in approval.

"Um, a couple of months before Marcus was killed. When I asked Felice if there was a possibility Marcus might have been killed because of his work, she assured me she didn't see how. Nothing he—or the business—was involved in was dangerous."

"So you've been to Felice with your suspicions?" Eamon finished his coffee and rose to get another.

"She was the first one I spoke with, actually." Lana had hoped to be convinced she was wrong, that there was nothing worth pursuing, but Felice had not put her mind at ease. "Like I said, she and Marcus were close. Honestly, I think I'd have been lost without her right after Marcus died. She took care of everything for me. The funeral arrangements, the life insurance coverage that paid off the house. She probably would have sold his apartment in Boston, except for some tax reason he put my name, not his, on the title." She barely remembered him telling her about it when he bought the place.

She'd planned to stay there when she'd gone back to Boston the one time to ask questions, but all she'd gotten was the runaround from the Boston PD. She'd also attempted to go straight to the police commissioner and made it as far as the lobby door before she'd lost the nerve to go inside. In the end, she'd ended up going back and booking a room at the airport hotel. "It was a relief, letting her deal with it all," Lana admitted.

"When was the last time you spoke with her?" Eamon asked.

"Right before I left Seattle." She pulled out her cell and checked her call records. "She's the dinner I had to cancel that I told you about," she added to Eamon. "I said I'd let her know about rescheduling."

"She's based in Seattle?" Eamon asked.

"No. Boston. She was coming out for business," Lana explained. "That's usually when we get together."

"What about Marcus's work stuff?" Cole asked. "Did he have a home office?"

"Yes." Again, she'd seen it more as a status symbol than a practicality. "Not that he used it very often. He kept work out of the house as much as he could."

"Did you find anything in his office when you went through the room?" Jack asked.

"No." She frowned. "No, Felice and one of her assistants went through his office shortly after the accident. Those NDAs aren't anything to play around with." Now that she was being questioned, Lana could see all the mistakes she'd made handling things. Mistakes she never would have made had this been one of her homicide cases. "Hindsight," she murmured. "I'm feeling like an idiot talking to you all right now. There's so much I'm seeing. I should have gone through his office before she got to it. Maybe there was something there."

"More likely you'd have ended up violating an NDA and gotten yourself into trouble," Eamon suggested.

"I managed to get in trouble anyway," she attempted

to joke. "That's my talent. The least I could have done is actually produce something because of it."

"You've never been one for breaking the rules, Lana," Eamon said. "Don't try to convince yourself otherwise or feel guilty for being who you are."

It was on the tip of Lana's tongue to tell him that breaking the rules was one of the reasons behind her suspension, but that wasn't an admission she wanted to make in front of the group. Right now they seemed willing to help her. They didn't need to know about... the rest.

"No one thinks clearly in the middle of a storm." Eden continued tapping on her keyboard. "And that's what grief is. A storm. Sometimes it's a fast-moving one. Other times it's molasses-slow. You have to wait until the worst of it passes. Beating yourself up about something that could have opened a whole other can of worms is only going to weigh you down. Letting stuff like that go might even help clear up other things that feel muddled."

"She knows what she's talking about," Eamon murmured.

Lana smiled, grateful for the sentiment. And the support.

"Trauma is tricky. Just when you think you've gotten over the worst of it, it'll start eating away at you again," Eden added.

It hadn't helped, having the people she thought she could trust accuse her of making things up in order to cope with her loss. But rather than make her back off and rethink things, their disbelief had driven Lana even harder, which had definitely put her in a precarious position, professionally at least. "I don't care what all those witnesses said," she told the people surrounding her now. "There was no sound of brakes before the car hit him. I know that as certainly as I'm sitting in this chair right now."

"No one here is going to argue with you, Lana." Eamon reached across the table and covered her hand with his, curled his fingers around hers until she felt the warm comfort of his touch seeping into her skin. "I promise, you don't have to fight us about this."

Considering she'd been fighting with just about everyone involved so far, she found that difficult to believe. "Boston PD closed the case. Everyone in this room knows what that means. We also all know how we'd each react if someone came at us with questions about a case we'd closed."

"Maybe," Cole said.

"Probably," Eamon agreed.

"Could depend on the case," Jack tossed in and earned some raised brows. "Each of us have had cases that left questions open. Loose threads, for want of a better term. Cases we didn't have the luxury of spending more time on, but enough answers were found that we moved on. Could be these officers had questions that didn't go anywhere at the time or they didn't feel they were in the right position to ask."

"That's an opening to use to stick your nose back in," Lana observed.

"Yes, it is." Lieutenant Santos sat back, stretched out his arms and tapped his fingers on the table. "I'm friends with Eleanor McKenna. I can reach out, see if she'd be willing to take another look, give me her thoughts."

"Maybe find out if the officers on scene didn't put in something they wish they had?" Eamon suggested. "Hindsight being what it is."

"You know Commissioner McKenna?" Lana asked as her stomach dropped to her tingling toes. The McKenna family was legendary in law enforcement circles. Their lineage traced back to the early days of Boston and the first organized police department in the nation. The commissioner hadn't only solidified her reputation as a premier figure of law and order, but her children had kept the legacy going by joining various branches of federal agencies, including the Secret Service and the ATF.

"Ellie and I go back a ways," Santos said. "A number of years ago she gave a series of lectures on law enforcement career options beyond the norm. It was geared toward young women, seeing as at the time she was one of the first female police commissioners in the country, but we struck up a friendship. Let me see what I can find out."

"Ah." Lana swallowed hard as regret clogged her throat. "Just so you know, my name might set off a few warning bells with her. Suffice it to say, I don't think I made the best impression."

Out of the corner of her eye, Lana saw Eamon glance at her. It took all her effort not to meet his gaze.

"Noted," Santos said with a quick nod before he left the conference room. "Keep me apprised of your progress."

"Wow." Some of the knots Lana hadn't realized were there loosened inside her. "I guess maybe I finally made the right decision about something. Coming here." She finally looked at Eamon. For the first time in what felt like forever, hope sprang to life. She should be wondering why these people, who didn't know her from a stranger on the street, were willing to stick their necks out for her. But she knew the answer.

They were doing it because of Eamon. Because Eamon trusted her. Believed in her. Lana pressed a hand against her fluttering stomach. She could only hope that trust wasn't misplaced. "I don't even know what to say."

"I do," Eden said. "Lana, can you put together a time line of everything you've laid out for us? Seeing as you're focusing on things you might not have paid attention to before, maybe start before the hit-and-run? By the way, did they ever find the car?"

"Not that I know of," Lana said. Hit-and-run. Not accident. That turn of phrase alone would have made the trip down here worth it. Appreciation and gratitude washed over her like a warm tide from the Pacific. It wasn't only Eamon who believed her.

"We've also got a list of Marcus's clients, thanks to his assistant," Eamon said.

"Fab. I'll mark that off the to-do list, then," Eden said. "What's his assistant's name, Lana?"

"Cynthia Randolph."

"She didn't argue about confidentiality?" Eamon asked.

"No," Lana said. "Now that I think about it, I remember being surprised at how quickly she sent the list."

"Does strike me as odd." Cole nodded his thanks as

Jack took his mug for a refill from the machine on the back counter. "Considering the NDAs."

Lana's stomach twisted into a new knot. Maybe if she'd been paying closer attention, she might have connected these threads earlier. Even as she thought it, her hands trembled. She snatched them back into her lap.

"Cynthia," Eden murmured as she narrowed her eyes at the screen. "I'm not finding her listed on the A&O Solutions website. I'll check her on LinkedIn. Go around that way."

Lana frowned. "I have her phone number—"

"Eden'll ask for it if she needs it," Eamon assured her. "Woman can find a needle in a needle stack with those programs of hers. Plus she loves a challenge."

"She also has exceptional hearing," Eden said without looking at them.

"All reasons I married her," Cole confirmed. "She also has the uncanny ability to attract the wrong kind of attention."

"What kind of attention is that?" Lana asked.

"The serial-killer kind," Jack announced and earned a glare from Eden. "Oh, come on, E. It's been years. You can't still be upset about it."

"They chained me up in a meat locker and left me to freeze to death," Eden mumbled. "Not to mention I never could wear my favorite boots again. What's not to feel bitter about?"

"Hang on. The Iceman." Lana balked. "That was you? You're Eden on Ice. Oh, man. I should have put that together sooner. The entire Seattle PD reads your blog. You really need to turn that into a podcast."

"Please don't give her ideas," Cole ordered.

"Way ahead of you," Eden announced. "Seeing as I'm going to be tied closer to the house now that number two is on the way, I need to find a way to... Hey, Sunshine. Good morning!" Eden bent out of view for a moment, and when she popped back up, her arms and lap were filled with a snuggly, still-sleepy-eyed toddler. "There's Daddy and your uncles."

"Hey, Chloe Ann." Jack shoved Cole out of the way so he could take up most of the bandwidth. "How do you like that keyboard Uncle Jack got you?"

"Musical instruments as gifts for toddlers are *e-v-i-l*," Eden spelled out with a sharp look at her husband's partner. "Unfortunately for us, she loves it."

"Of course she does," Jack teased.

"Ack!" Chloe Ann covered her eyes with her hands, then threw them out to the side. "Peek ah you!"

"Kid's going to be thirty and still calling you Ack," Cole teased.

"It's better than Amu," Eamon said and earned a squeal of delight from the little girl as she grabbed for and dislodged the camera, her sleep-tousled curls bouncing around her face.

"Okay, when she goes for the hardware, it's time to say goodbye." Eden struggled to get the camera back on straight while keeping Chloe Ann settled on her lap. "I've got a lot to run with. Dinner, our place, remember, Eamon. Six thirty-ish. I hope you'll join us, Lana. It would be nice to meet you in person." Eden aimed a pointed look at her husband. "Cole, please be careful. Maybe let Eamon take the lead on this one? No offense, Lana, but I'd prefer he not get caught in the line of whoever is firing at you."

She'd prefer no one got caught in that line of fire, but Lana nodded. "Noted and agreed. Thanks for your help, Eden."

"Haven't done anything yet, but I love a good mystery. Say bye to Lana, Chloe Ann."

"Bye, Lala!"

"Oh." Lana blinked as the screen went dark. Unexpected tears blurred her eyes, but she blinked them back. "Well, that's just delightful."

"More than delightful," Eamon said as he got to his feet. "It means you're officially part of the family."

Chapter 6

This was getting to be a habit, Eamon thought, when he found Lana asleep on his sofa much later that afternoon. This time, instead of being burrowed into the cushions and blankets like a hibernating hedgehog, she had one hand thrown over her eyes and a humming laptop resting on her gently rising stomach. The scrapes on her arms weren't quite so angrily red, but they were still there. A reminder of how close some of those bullets had come.

And yet…he frowned. And yet they'd missed.

He was trying to not get ahead of himself, to not embrace the comfort and excitement he felt at having Lana in such close proximity. While he'd thought of her often over the years, he'd purposely buried himself in work so as not to have to think about the fact he should have called. Reached out and checked in. It was difficult, being in competition with a dead man. There was no winning against Marcus and the life he and Lana had had together. As much as Eamon had been tempted to pursue something romantic with her, the idea of being turned away, turned down or slipped firmly into the friend zone was a chance he hadn't been willing to take. Better to stay safe than sorry.

Now?

Now she'd been the one to take that first step that had terrified him to his core. Somehow she'd tapped into his dreams of them walking the same road together and set them on it herself. The road wasn't cemented with certainty by any means. There were plenty of obstacles to overcome if this was going to be something long-term and serious. But her sleeping on his sofa was definitely progress in what he'd all but given up hope on.

Funny how things worked out.

Eamon glanced at his watch, buttoned his cuff. They had more than an hour before needing to be at Eden and Cole's, but he wanted to give Lana plenty of time to try to worm her way out of having dinner with his friends. He wouldn't let her, of course, but still.

The last thing he wanted was to leave her alone in the rather spartan apartment. She did not need alone time with everything that was going on. Especially after she'd spent the day typing nonstop on her laptop, putting that time line together for Eden. He'd been relieved when she'd crashed a little while ago. The woman needed a serious recharge.

He had a secret weapon in his back pocket, should she put up too much of a fight about going out. And enough verbal bombs to lob back at her should she throw excuses his way. He was as prepared as he was ever going to be.

"You look like you're going to a movie premiere in Hollywood."

Eamon blinked, not having noticed her watching him as he stood in the middle of the living room staring at her. "Thanks. You think?" His smile was quick. "It's always nice when your work attire doubles as formal wear for a party."

She snorted. "Like you've worn that suit to work. And a party? I thought it was dinner?"

"It's a bit of both. And it's not just me. It's we, remember?" He walked over, clicked her laptop closed and set it on the table beside her.

"Eden was just being polite inviting me."

"Shows how much you know. Eden doesn't do polite." Eamon heard the expected sigh of resignation escape her lips. "And it's not a party by its usual definition. More of a get-together for a common celebration."

"I'm not really in a party get-together mood." She scowled and pushed herself up on her arms, looked up at him. "What's the occasion?"

He hesitated. "If I tell you, you'll think I'm guilting you into coming."

"Try me," she challenged.

Suddenly his collar button felt too tight. "It's Chloe's birthday."

"Oh!" Lana swung her legs around. "Well, that's different, then, isn't it? What is she, two? Did you get her a… Oh." She went a little pale even as her cheeks tinted.

"Oh, not Eden's Chloe Ann. You meant your sister Chloe. Today is your sister's birthday?"

"It was a few weeks ago, actually." His smile felt forced, but the pain didn't last nearly as long as it once did. "We were supposed to have the celebration earlier this month, but I got called in on that case. As soon as we closed it, Eden threw it together. Simone is usually our organizer, but with Caleb just being born, Eden took the lead this time. Just as well. Security in Eden's building is top-notch. Nothing to worry about, you being out in public." He was preemptively negating any argument she could come up with.

"Eamon, this is family stuff. You don't want me there."

"On the contrary." So far she was not disappointing him with her protests. "I would very much like for you to come."

"What, like as your date?" She snort-laughed before catching his expression. "Oh. You do actually mean…"

"Only if you're okay with it." He walked over to the fridge, his loafers smacking smartly against the hardwood floor. Withdrawing a chilled bottle of water, he twisted off the cap and drank, more to calm his own nerves than to give her time to consider his request. "We can look at this as a test run of sorts, for when we're on the other side of—"

"The off-book investigation into my late husband's murder?" She suddenly seemed quite interested in the blanket she'd tossed over the back of the sofa. "I just made things awkward, didn't I? Always bringing Marcus into things."

"No, you didn't." He clasped the bottle in one hand

and returned to sit in the low leather chair near the sofa. "I don't mind you talking about Marcus, Lana. It doesn't bother me. And I don't want it to bother you." He was a man used to putting all his cards on the table. He wasn't about to change now on the one topic that could drive a wedge between them. "He's always going to be a part of you. But if it's too soon—"

"It's not." He took the fact she cut him off as a very good sign. "I'm just…a lot to take right now. I'm a mess, Eamon. Between my job being in jeopardy, not to mention my reputation, I don't understand how I can be remotely appealing."

"And yet you are." He could have joked and told her he liked a challenge, but now wasn't the time for humor or teasing. "Circumstances and life's obstacles aside, I see you as I've always seen you, Lana. As a woman I like very much. I'd like to see where things go between us, and not just in there." He gestured to the bedroom. "We've both been witness to some pretty dark events. I think maybe we can agree that life's too short to waste an opportunity simply because the timing might be inconvenient."

She closed her eyes. "You really are a dying breed, Eamon Quinn. I had no idea you were such a romantic."

"I endeavor to continue to surprise." Never in his life had he felt so strong an urge to wish away the tension and worry he saw on her face. The semipermanent wincing. The way she carried herself, as if she was going to take a step in the wrong direction and set off a chain reaction of pain. Those aspects faded from time to time, but he wanted them to disappear. Forever. "You came looking for me to help pull you out of what you've been buried in alone for so long. Coming with me tonight will most definitely help you do that."

"Well, I did like Eden. And Cole and Jack."

"See? You already know four of us. The rest'll be easy. It's not an inquisition, you know. It's just good people, good food and good memories," he pressed. "And did I mention Greta Renault will be there?"

"Seriously?" She sank back in the cushions and went wide-eyed. "You're not just saying that to get me to leave this apartment?"

"I am not." His secret weapon deployed, he felt a zing of delight that it had worked. "She owns the building where Eden and Cole live. And it's where her private gallery is being built. You know—" he took a long drink of water "—in case you wanted that sneak peek I promised you."

"You do not play fair." He could see the doubt battling against desire. "All right. I'll come."

Eamon feigned offense even as his plan fell into place. "I should have known the art would be more of a selling point than yours truly. So if that's a yes, maybe try to relax and enjoy yourself."

"And what happens tomorrow?" Now she opened her eyes and looked at him.

"What do you mean?"

"You know what I mean," she warned. "Between us."

"What would have happened today if last night had gone as you'd planned?"

She only stared at him, her expression unreadable, for

once, despite him being able to almost see the thoughts spinning in her head.

He knew what he'd like to have happen, but he wasn't going to press the issue. He'd meant what he'd said about not wanting to dismiss or ignore the fact Marcus had existed. But he also wanted to make sure there weren't any ghosts following her into his bedroom.

"How about we make a deal? We won't try to predict tomorrow, nor will we dwell on the past. And you can focus on trying to have a good time." He set his water down. "Why don't you go get changed? If I know Eden, she stashed something appropriate in that bag she sent you."

"She did, actually. It's not fancy or anything."

"Neither is the dinner. Go on. Bathroom's all yours. Just one thing." He pushed himself up as she rose, caught her hand and tugged her against him. Before she could speak, before he could breathe, he lowered his mouth to hers.

It was one thing to have thought about, dreamed about, kissing Lana Tate. It was another to actually do it. The instant his lips caught hers, it was as if he'd been on life support and suddenly zapped back to life. Every cell in his body sang as he tasted and teased and dived in. Capturing the moan that escaped her mouth in his own had him releasing her hand so he could slide his arms around her back and bring her in closer.

He knew the instant her shock wore off as her mouth opened and she took a tentative taste of him before her arms encircled his neck. His entire body tightened; parts of his body hardened, and he relished the sensation of her breasts crushed against his chest, even as he struggled to draw in breath and stay on his feet.

When he tilted his head back, her fingers tangled in the hair at the base of his neck, clearly wanting to begin again. Her breath came in short, surprising gasps as she raised her chin, dark eyes filled with dazed confusion and surprise as they met his gaze.

"Guess that answers that question." She drew her hand forward, down his chest, then back up to brush her fingers against his swollen lips. "Probably a good thing we never tried that before, yeah?"

Definitely a good thing. "I'm thinking, all things considered, our timing is pretty great." He couldn't resist. He kissed her again but resisted the tug of her arms to take it further. "And if this were any other night, I'd say forget dinner and take you to bed."

"But it isn't any other night," she whispered. She stroked a finger down the side of his face. "I'll go get dressed, yeah?"

He almost changed his mind. "Yeah." Eamon stepped back and watched her pull out something from her bag by the sofa, pick up her cell phone, then walk across the room to the bathroom. She turned in the doorway after clicking on the light, faced him with the glow behind her. For the first time since he'd seen her in the bar last night, she looked almost…happy.

"I won't be long." Her cell buzzed. Lana rolled her eyes, glanced at the screen and sighed as she answered. "Hi, Felice. You know, I was just talking about you today…" She closed the bathroom door.

Eamon remained where he was, staring at the door.

She could take as long as she wanted. Because he'd be waiting for her. No matter what.

"What did Felice have to say?" Eamon asked as he pulled into a parking spot across the street from a four-story building with enough architectural interest to tell Lana it had been constructed almost a century before.

She'd debated answering the call from her late husband's boss, but the truth was, now was not the time to cut ties.

"She came across some photos of Marcus she thought I'd want to see. From when he was a boy." Lana waited for the wince, or the cringe, or the grief to pool in her stomach, but it didn't. Another one of those steps forward, she supposed. "I got the feeling she wanted an excuse to call, so she made one up." She glanced at Eamon, saw him frown. "I'd seen the pictures before. We have one of them framed at the house. She misses him, I think almost as much as I do."

"Ah." He nodded. "Good talk, then?"

"I guess." It wasn't that she didn't like talking to Felice. She did. And she appreciated everything Marcus's boss had done for her, but she couldn't help feeling the call was... intrusive. As if maybe there wasn't the room for Felice in her life as there had once been. Did that mean she was moving on?

Oh, she hoped so. She was tired of feeling as if she was stuck neck-deep in quicksand, slowly sinking into darkness.

Eamon climbed out of the car and came around to open her door.

"I think I've forgotten how to do this." Lana turned and dropped her feet out of the replacement SUV Eamon had picked up earlier that afternoon at the FBI depot. She stared at his outstretched hand, slightly confused as to what to do. Taking his hand felt as if she was taking that final step into a different world. A world where she and Eamon were more than just friends.

"Forgotten how to do what?" Eamon asked far too innocently.

"You know what." She accepted his hand and stepped out of the car. While he locked up, she quickly adjusted the simple black wraparound dress that, honestly, was something she could have pulled out of her own closet. The shoes were a little snug, but she could manage for a few hours. She scrunched her toes. Hopefully.

As he lifted her hand, the butterfly charms on the bracelet she wore caught the last bit of sunshine. Other than her wedding set, it had been one of the few pieces of jewelry she frequently wore: a memento of a trip she and Marcus had taken to Butterfly Harbor on their first anniversary. The small coastal town situated near Monterey had become one of their favorite vacation spots. She'd fallen in love with the shops and the Victorian Inn, situated at the top of the cliffs, and looked forward to the morning greeting of monarch butterflies that flitted past when they opened the balcony shutters.

"Do you really think we can do this?" she whispered.

"What? Have dinner?"

She arched a brow at him.

"Oh." His grin returned. That amazing, surprisingly boyish, teasing grin that made her stomach flip over.

"You mean do we want to push the boundaries of friendship?"

"Not that either." She chuckled. He really was determined to put her at ease. "Do you think we can forget what happened last night at the motel?" It certainly hadn't escaped her thoughts that not so long ago she'd been shot at and her motel room had been burned to a crisp. "Even for a little while?"

"I'm darned sure going to try. On the off chance I didn't mention it before, because I have been thinking it…" Eamon pocketed the car key, took a familiar assessing look around them, before slipping his arm behind her and guiding her across the street toward a four-story building that took up a good half of the downtown city block. "You look beautiful."

"No wonder you get so many confessions. You could charm the spots off a giraffe." She smoothed a nervous hand over her hair, which she'd left down for a change. It felt odd, going to a dinner party when the rest of her life felt as if it was spinning off its axis, but with Eamon beside her she felt steadier. Stronger.

Irritation slid through her. Her confidence and inner strength shouldn't be so dependent on anyone else, but…it was Eamon's confidence in her, his affection for her, that made her feel as if everything was going to be all right. For the first time in a very long time, she was believing in herself again. What a remarkable gift for him to give her.

As they approached the rather elegant front door of the building, Lana spotted a couple striding their way. The man was tall, with dark hair and perfectly trimmed

beard, and his attention—all his attention, it seemed—
was directed to the beautiful Black woman tucked securely under one arm.

"Eamon! You made it." The woman broke away from
her partner and hurried forward, her flowing dress
matching the long scarf woven through her curly black
hair. The second she reached him, she stepped into a
welcoming hug and kissed his cheek. "Seems like every
time we see you someone's in trouble. You don't come
around often enough just because, you know."

"I know. I'm working on it. Jason." Eamon nodded
to the man who joined them. "Thanks for coming."

"Glad to be here. You must be Detective Tate. Jason
Sutton. This is my fiancée, Kyla."

"Oh." Lana exchanged handshakes with them both
as her stomach fluttered with nerves. Give her a murder scene or a hostage standoff and she managed great.
Strangers and socializing? She was way out of practice.
"Of course. Kyla and Jason of the wedding invitation
under the door," she joked. "It's a pleasure to meet you
both. Congratulations."

"Thanks." Kyla reached for Jason's hand. "Eamon,
I've finally figured out what your job should be for the
wedding. Other than groomsman."

"Yeah?" Eamon grinned as he climbed the three
steps to the double-glass, brass-handled doors. "Something other than picking up the kegs for the bachelor
party? What's that?"

"Help him pick out a suit. He's dragging his feet."

"My best man—" Jason rolled his eyes.

"Is at a loss suit-wise," Kyla said, cutting him off.

"Vince has it easy. Marine uniform, bam, he's done," she said to Lana. "I'd appreciate it if you'd lend your expertise, Agent Fashion Plate Eamon. You wear a suit every day of your life and yet this one tonight puts you in an entirely different league. That's what he needs. If only for as long as it takes for photographs."

"Comments like that make me wish we were eloping," Jason teased.

Lana had to side with Kyla on this one. At least as far as Eamon was concerned. There was no way Eamon had ever worn this particular dark suit to the office. The neatly pressed black slacks and jacket were perfectly tailored, nipped in at the waist, and, with the crisp white button-down shirt he'd left unbuttoned at the collar, made him look as if he'd just stepped out of one of those TV commercials for men's cologne. One of the good ones.

"Consider him taken care of," Eamon said as the door was pushed open from the inside by a fortysomething man wearing a simple black suit of his own. His jet-black hair displayed slight hints of blue in the overhead light. "I've got some connections. Good evening, Estavo."

"Agent Quinn, hello. Ms. Bertrand. Mr. Sutton." He stepped back to let them all enter, and once they were all in the foyer and the door was closed and locked behind them, he glanced at Lana. He made his way to the small curving desk in the center of the lobby. "May I get your name, please, ma'am?"

"Detective Lana Tate." She opened the purse she carried. It was larger than she'd have liked for an event like this evening, but she wanted enough room for her gun. "Do you need my—"

"No ID necessary, but thank you," Estavo assured her. He lifted the receiver to the antique-style phone on the desk. "I'll call ahead and let Eden and Cole know you're on your way up."

Lana couldn't stop her mouth from falling open as she looked around the lobby that could have been transported out of a 1940s hotel from New York. The floor was white marble flecked with gold and gray, the walls painted in alternating stripes of the same colors. Elegance personified, from the multiple groupings of comfortable, cushioned gold chairs to the large round table situated between the security desk and another pair of glass doors that mirrored the ones leading into the building. Atop the table sat a tall and wide vase filled with a huge spray of beautiful spring flowers.

"Is that the gallery?" She wasn't sure why she whispered and felt a bit embarrassed that she had.

"It will be," Eamon said. "You want that peek now?"

Even before she answered, he gave Estavo a quick look. "Why don't you two go ahead?" Eamon told their companions. "We'll be up in a bit."

"Okay." Kyla looked a bit confused as she and Jason headed toward the wrought iron elevator that reminded Lana of something out of an old movie. It wasn't the way the steel clanged as Jason closed the elevator door, but the jarring grinding of metal as the car disappeared up and out of sight.

"You remembered," Lana murmured.

"That you hate elevators? Hard to forget," Eamon

said as they followed Estavo toward the locked doors of the gallery. "I had to climb fifteen flights of stairs because of you not so long ago. I still think I left half of my right lung in that building."

"It was only ten flights," she argued. "And it was just as well. Those kidnappers didn't expect a flood of agents to hit from both the elevator and the stairwell."

"I believe Ms. Renault left a surprise for you on the western wall, Agent Quinn," Estavo said as they stepped inside. Then he quickly returned to his desk.

"So, a doorman. In Sacramento." Lana was tempted to toe out of her shoes for fear she might mar the marble floor. "That's different."

"Private security masquerading as private security, actually," Eamon said. "A friend of ours recently contracted out as the West Coast representative of a private security firm. With Greta opening her gallery in the building and some previous events that have taken place, it's bringing her some peace of mind. Someone's at that desk twenty-four seven. There's also security cameras covering just about every angle of this place. At least if she starts sleepwalking again we can track her."

Lana barely heard a word he said. The stark white walls might seem cold and sterile, but as a future display area for Greta Renault's paintings, they were the perfect backdrop. A maze of walls, some higher than others, most of which had fabric swatches of different measurements hanging as if testing frame sizes, created a walkway and experience that made the gallery seem far larger than the actual space.

"Originally Greta was only going to showcase her

own work," Eamon said as they made their way to the west wall. "But since she's been pregnant, she hasn't been painting as much. Plus she's sold off a lot of her collection. She's sponsoring a number of artists' shows in between her own showings. And she's not limiting the mediums. Photography, sculpture, and she's particularly fond of mosaics at the moment. She's also working on arrangements with some of the local high school art departments to display their students' work as well. Ah. Here it is." They took one last turn to the left. "Looks like she finally finished it."

Lana stared, frozen in place, at the enormous painted canvas. The trees of the forest had been painted in such a perspective as to make onlookers feel as if they'd stepped into the trees. The light shimmering from above cast a glow about the solitary figure in white, a woman with long silver hair in a robe that, while painted, appeared to be as soft as silk. She had one hand cradling her stomach, which was full with her child, while her other hand brushed against the ray caressing a nearby branch. Beyond her, a waterfall tumbled from far above and plumed up in mist that sprayed her feet.

"I can see her face." Lana moved closer, mesmerized. "Every other painting I've ever seen of hers, the woman's back has been turned toward us. But this one? She's smiling." Something akin to joy burst through Lana, as if something had broken open and hope had spilled out. "I always thought her paintings carried this hint of sadness. Of longing and grief."

"They did." Eamon rested a hand on the small of her

back. "Greta spent a lot of years trapped in her past. I don't know how much of her history you know—"

"Nothing beyond what she's talked about publicly." She knew Greta's parents had been a powerful couple in Hollywood back in the day. A troubled noir actress and her filmmaker husband. They'd died tragically when Greta was just a little girl. But it was an event that defined a good portion of her life since. In recent interviews, Greta had been open about her struggle with various issues, including agoraphobia and, for a while, paranoia. The latter, fortunately, had been proved to be an outside manipulation in an attempt to steal her money. The agoraphobia? Jack McTavish had helped with that. A lot. Perhaps even more than her art. "She's happy now." Tears burned the back of Lana's throat. "That's what this painting shows. That she's happy. With Jack. And the baby they're going to have. *Transformation*." She read the description card on the wall beside the work.

"She said we'd be the first to see it. Besides Jack," Eamon said. "Life can change when you want it to. At least, that's the message I'm getting from it."

"One of the messages," Lana said. "Thank you, Eamon." She turned, lifted her hands to his face and drew his mouth to hers. She kissed him. Not in the way she longed to, but in a way that she hoped conveyed both gratitude and the promise of making the changes she wanted to. "I think I'm ready to go upstairs and meet the rest of your friends."

Chapter 7

"I take it as a good sign we haven't overwhelmed your girlfriend."

Eamon glanced as Eden St. Claire nudged his arm and grinned at him. Her face was a bit rounder than normal, her hair a bit messier. But the color in her cheeks and the smile on her face erased the final fragments of the tragedy that had bonded them as children. He'd lost Chloe, his sister, but along the way he'd gained a few others, if not by blood, certainly by affection.

"You're going to get every bit of mileage you can out of that, aren't you?" Because he knew it would annoy her, he lifted that same arm and slung it around her shoulders. From where they stood, just outside Eden's kitchen, he could see the breadth of the vast loft apartment that was filled with everyone Eden considered family. Glancing over his shoulder to the line of windows behind him, he saw a more modern building that had, in the last year or so, become a major employment hub for Sacramento.

He'd had absolutely no doubt about Lana fitting in with his friends. She might not have been overly anxious to dive into the pool of his social circle. It gave him some satisfaction to know she'd agreed to come because of him. Not that she would have been walking into a lion's den. There wasn't a more gracious, welcoming group of people, as far as he was concerned. She'd stayed close at his side through the initial welcome and the first round of appetizers. She'd happily acquired a bottle of sparkly, flavored seltzer water that Eamon himself couldn't stand. Within moments of their arrival, however, Lana had been swept away by Simone Armstrong-Sutton, who somehow managed to make a soft gray lounge suit look as if she were having tea with the Queen.

Dr. Allie Kellan, sporting her usual dark-haired pixie cut and a sweater set that reminded him of a summer sunset, pulled both women onto one of the well-broken-in leather sofas situated in front of the fireplace. The three of them had had their heads together ever since, with the sound of Lana's genuine laughter lightening his heart.

She fit. With them. With him. As precisely and perfectly as he'd allowed himself to imagine.

Eamon sipped his beer, tried to smother a chuckle at the sight of Detective Cole Delaney, PI Vince Sutton and former firefighter turned private investigator

Max Kellan huddled in the corner of the room, arms filled with offspring of varying ages. Cole caught Chloe Ann's hand in his before she could bop baby Caleb on the nose, while Max jostled back and forth to calm a four-month-old Sabrina, who was clearly demanding something her father could not provide.

"Lala!" Chloe Ann yelled loud enough to drop the room into instant silence. Cole, clearly used to doing his daughter's bidding, especially when she was kicking him in the stomach, bent down and released her into the wild. She hit the ground running. Kyla and Jason stepped back while water rescue specialist turned DART instructor Darcy and her husband of five months, Riordan Malloy, lifted their glasses to avoid spilling as Darcy spun around like she was caught in a tailwind.

Eamon watched, a bit surprised, as Chloe Ann propelled herself straight into Lana's arms. He held his breath, but not for long. Lana immediately set her soda down and reached to pick Chloe Ann up to settle her in her lap. The conversation started up again, this time with more smiles than had been in place before and with Chloe Ann reaching up and patting Lana's cheek.

"Well." Eden put a hand over Eamon's heart and cleared her throat. "If I'd had any doubts about her, they'd certainly be gone now." She looked up at him. "I like her."

"Yeah," Eamon whispered. Pride filled whatever space love hadn't taken up in his heart. "So do I."

"And now I understand why I could never convince you to let me set you up on a date."

"I admit nothing." He wasn't about to give her more

than necessary. Eden St. Claire collected information the way most people collected dust bunnies. "She came with me tonight even though she didn't want to."

"Why didn't she want to come?" Eden frowned as the doorbell chimed and Cole, standing nearby, opened the door to let Dr. Ashley McTavish-Palmer and her husband, Slade, in. Seeing the two of them together always triggered a niggle of unease when Eamon thought how close they'd come to losing them last year when Ashley had found herself caught in a planned prison break. Slade had been undercover in the prison at the time, fortunately, and had managed to get both of them out alive. But only barely.

"Sorry we're late!" Ashley called out in greeting and waved at Eden. "Couldn't get out of the ER."

"We've got a house full of workaholics," Eden grumbled.

"Takes one to know one," Eamon teased.

"I'm coming around on that front," Eden admitted. "And you just changed the subject. Why didn't Lana want to come? We're a fun group."

"What you are is family," Eamon said. "That's a big thing to step into when you weren't expecting it." Or when you didn't know how to deal with it. Lana's upbringing hadn't been exactly picturesque, which had made the peace she'd found with Marcus all the more precious. "She argued with me before she agreed."

"But she did agree." Eden rocked back on her heels. "Interesting."

"She knew tonight was about Chloe," he said simply. "That's all it took."

Eden scrunched her face. "Well, doesn't that just move her up the ladder of acceptability. I did a background search on her."

"Figured you would." Eamon took another sip. "What is it you think I don't know? She was open about everything, including her suspension."

"So you know that came as a result of her drinking on the job and that she assaulted a fellow officer?"

He swallowed hard, did his best not to cringe. "I've not been made privy to the exact details of that event, actually."

"Hmm." Eden's approval seemed to have slipped a notch.

"I'm going to go out on a limb and say he deserved it," he said easily even as his stomach knotted.

"But you knew about the drinking."

"I know she's got a sobriety chip in her pocket and that she clings to it when she's stressed." He didn't think Lana would appreciate him having picked up on that behavioral pattern. "She's got four months sober, Eden. She's trying."

"Not saying she isn't. Just wanted to be sure you knew what you were getting into."

"None of us is perfect, E."

"I am well aware," Eden said and rested her head on his shoulder. "You know we love you, right? We don't want to see you getting into something that's going to get you hurt. That's all we were doing. Protecting you."

We? Eamon glanced over to Cole and Jack. Yeah, no way Eden would have gone poking around in Lana's record without sharing it with the dynamic duo. "Getting hurt is part of the risk. Otherwise what's the point? I appreciate having a lookout." He glanced down and swore he saw tears in her eyes. "Eden? Are you crying? Did I make you cry?"

"Please." She swiped at the tear that escaped. "These days the laundry makes me cry. Leave me alone," she laughed when he kissed the top of her head. "This big-brother thing makes me weepy."

"Good to know how to get to you. Hey, Ashley, Slade." Eamon greeted the newcomers as Eden made her way back into the kitchen to see to dinner. "Hard day in the ER?" he asked Jack's sister, who worked at Folsom General supervising the emergency room.

"I've had worse." Ashley pulled the bottle they'd brought out of her husband's hand. "And I need some wine. Slade?"

"Nothing right now, thanks." Slade held on to his wife's hand until she walked away. "So." The former undercover FBI agent shifted position to scan the room. After years of being undercover, he never ever kept his back to a room. Even one filled with people he knew. "Heard you were on scene of that fire downtown last night. And that there was an after event to close out the morning?"

"Private security has definitely aided your sense of humor," Eamon said. "All that was missing were the marshmallows and graham crackers. Could have had ourselves a real s'mores fest."

"Even with the flying bullets," Slade added.

"Who blabbed?"

"I wouldn't call it blabbing, exactly," Slade added

at Eamon's doubtful expression. "Eden ran into a few walls where A&O Solutions and that client list is concerned. She thought maybe I might have some insights. The details as to your early morning activities came shortly after." He glanced over his shoulder as Ashley emerged with a large wineglass filled halfway with red in one hand and an open bottle of beer in the other.

"In case you change your mind." She brushed past him, handed off the beer to Slade and gave the latter a look that suggested to Eamon their tardiness had nothing to do with the emergency room being overcrowded.

"Your new job provide you with insights?" Eamon asked.

"Let's just say I don't miss all the rules and regulations that come with a badge." It wasn't just Slade's humor that had lightened, but his tone and the way he carried himself. He would never be rid of the intensity he naturally exuded, but the tension Eamon had seen from the first moment they'd met had abated. Eamon glanced toward Ashley, who was admiring Kyla's engagement ring before she beelined right for Vince and a baby fix thanks to Caleb and Sabrina.

"Okay. Do you have any insights you care to share with me or do I need to wait for Eden's status report?"

"I do hate to steal Eden's thunder." Slade ducked his chin, his lips curving. "Suffice it to say, I did a little poking around. And the firewalls protecting A&O Solutions' servers and systems? They're no joke. Could probably hack into the Pentagon more easily. Apparently A&O Solutions has been on the feds' radar for quite some time."

"Seriously?" Eamon frowned. "Why haven't I heard anything?"

"Above your pay grade. Above most everyone's. Just asking questions was enough to set off alarm bells."

"I get the hinky part where A&O Solutions is concerned," Eamon mused. "Most businesses that cloak themselves in subterfuge and mystery have something untoward going on, and it's obvious they're making a ton of cash, but—"

"Uh-huh. I don't think there's a way to finish that thought that won't disturb you," Slade said. "I ended up on a phone call with my boss. The second I mentioned A&O Solutions, he told me to hold my questions until he got out here." Slade eyed Eamon. "He didn't want any discussion over the phone."

This conversation definitely wasn't making him feel better. "Wouldn't it have been easier for you to go out to DC?"

"I don't like venturing too far from home," Slade said. "Part of the deal I made when I signed on with Minotaur Security. But if my boss is getting on a plane tonight? He's spooked. And you and your Detective Tate have stepped in something big. He wants to meet with you. The sooner, the better."

Chills raced down Eamon's spine. "So much for hoping you would put my mind at ease." His gaze wandered back to Lana, sitting with his friends, bouncing little Chloe Ann on her knee as the tyke shoved a miniature cupcake into her mouth, frosting and all. "When is he getting in?"

"First thing in the morning. I'm meeting him around

ten at the Hyatt Regency on L Street." Slade met his gaze. "You two want in?"

Lana glanced up just then, met Eamon's eyes, her brow furrowing slightly as if asking him what was wrong. He instantly relaxed his face, offered a smile and toasted her with his bottle.

"Yeah," he told Slade. "We'll be there."

Chapter 8

Lana blinked her eyes open and, for a moment, had to puzzle out where she was. Even after a short time, she'd gotten used to sleeping on Eamon's sofa. The idea of waking up somewhere else, like in his bed, was going to take some adjustment.

She tucked her chin into her chest, rolled over just enough to peer through the slight opening of the sliding barn door. She could hear the tap-tap-tap of a keyboard in the living room and Eamon's low voice holding a conversation with someone on the phone, she assumed. She inhaled the familiar aroma of continuously brewing coffee emanating from the kitchen. The sunshine streaming through the windows was somewhat of a surprise, or maybe she was just allowing herself to notice some of these things for a change.

She frowned, laying gentle fingers over the gray comforter. Funny. She didn't remember falling asleep in here. In fact…

She sat up, shoved her hair out of her face and glared at the door. She distinctly recalled crashing on the sofa after coming home from Eden's. It had been late. Far later than she'd expected to be. By the time 1:00 a.m. rolled around—with the under-three sect having long since crashed, either in their beds or in their carriers— she and Eamon had made their way back to the Brass Eagle and his apartment.

She'd been tired. A good kind of tired for a change. Not the she'd-run-herself-into-the-ground-so-she-didn't-have-to-think exhausted.

She hadn't been so tired, however, that she hadn't wondered if perhaps this was the perfect evening to finally breach the barriers of their friendship and venture into more carnal territory.

But Eamon had seemed… She wasn't sure if *off* was the correct phrase, but it seemed to fit, even now. Something was on his mind. Something he either needed to or didn't want to discuss with her.

Which was no doubt how she found herself alone in his bed.

She threw back the covers, scooted to the end of the mattress and, as she swung her legs over the edge, found those personal mementos and pictures she'd thought lacking in the rest of the living space. A trifold brass frame sat on the nightstand beside her cell phone. Three photographs that made her heart break.

One image was of a teenage Eamon—apparently he

hadn't gone through the same awkward, geeky stage every other teenager on the planet had. She could see the man's face in that of the boy. His smile was brighter, his eyes lively, his posture relaxed. He had his arm slung around the shoulders of an overall-clad young girl with crooked pigtails and an overly wide smile as they goofed in front of the camera.

"Chloe." The name came out almost like a prayer even as Lana let her gaze slide to the center photograph of the same little girl, at around the same age, only this time she was surrounded by three friends—friends Lana had met last night. Rough-and-tumble, cautious-eyed Eden. Elegant, protective Simone. And wide-eyed, analytical Allie.

The four of them stood arm in arm beneath a fantastic tree house that, to Lana's roughened heart, seemed impossible to envision, let alone experience.

Lastly, the third picture had her reaching out and lifting it off the nightstand.

A larger group this time, as large as the gathering last night. Taken in a setting similar to that of Eden's apartment, with the Sacramento skyline as their backdrop. Greta Renault, barefoot and in an ethereal white dress reminiscent of the frequent figure in her paintings, was embraced by her groom, Jack McTavish, and surrounded by their friends. Correction, Lana noted. Their family. The fact the group included Eamon lightened her heart. He stood a good two inches taller than the rest of them, and those hazel eyes of his displayed at least a fraction of the joy reflected in the first photo.

She traced a finger over his face, smiled. He looked

happy. The shadows she remembered in his eyes were gone even then. After he'd left the ghost of his sister's death in the past. How she envied that. Even as she thought it, she realized that last night—the time she was in the presence of these people—she'd felt the same. As if the group provided a kind of magic that healed hearts. And souls.

Lana set the frame back where it was, unplugged her cell and made her way to the door to slide it open.

Eamon glanced over, a cell phone up to his ear. He held up a finger, offered a quick smile, then lowered his voice as she set her phone on the table beside his open laptop and made a beeline for the coffee machine and her morning jolt. While the coffee finished brewing, she dug around in the cabinets and fridge for something to eat, finally settling on a banana that was more than ready to be turned into bread or muffins.

"That's right, no, I appreciate you letting me know," Eamon said. "I agree. It's not information we were hoping for…Yes, sir. I'll get to work on it as soon as I'm back in the office." He glanced up when Lana, having finished her banana, brought the pot over to refill his mug. "Yes, sir. You, too." He clicked off but the smile curving his lips didn't come close to reaching his eyes. "Morning."

"Morning." She faced him, leaned back against the cabinets. "Was that Lieutenant Santos?"

"No. My supervisor at the Bureau," he said, clearly working through his distraction. "A case I've been on for the past year is about to blow up. Judge we went to for a warrant won't sign off. Says we don't have enough evidence yet. Guess there's a reason they call him Iron-clad Cahill." He scrubbed both hands down his face. "Guy doesn't sign a warrant until he knows it'll lead to a conviction. And we can't get that without the warrant."

"What about a different judge?"

"Burned through them already. The sad thing is, Cahill's right. He's a good check for what we do have and it's just not enough."

"I'm sorry." She cringed. She knew only too well the difficulties red tape could often cause. Sometimes it felt as if their hands were tied when it came to helping people. "What more do you need?"

"Don't know, actually." The defeated expression on his face hurt her heart. No more than his own was hurt working in the Crimes Against Children division. "Guess when I'm back in the office, we'll have to start over. The hope was this guy could be the loose thread we pull to unravel the organization, find out where the photos are being distributed from, hopefully trace the source of who's taking them."

He shook his head as if trying to clear it. "Sorry to lay all this on you. Not what you came out here for."

"Don't be sorry." She'd never been so grateful to be a listener for someone else. She turned, doctored up her coffee and sipped. "After everything I've thrown at you the past couple of days, I'm more than happy to lend whatever meager expertise I can." She'd dealt with her share of child sex abuse cases and she'd hated every single one. There was a certain vile toxicity that came with that kind of work. Some people, like Eamon, seemed to have an immunity to it. Others? Well, most cops couldn't deal with it, certainly not for any length of time. Eamon had been working cases like these his entire FBI career. She forced herself to turn back around and look at him. "How do you do it?"

"Do what?"

She could tell by his response he knew precisely what she was referring to. "These cases. Deal with these children, what's been done to them? The people responsible. Day after day. Eamon, it has to get to you."

"Of course it does." A shadow passed over his face before he ducked his head, grasped the handle of his coffee mug but didn't drink. "But how do you walk away from something you're good at?"

It was a fair question. One she'd asked herself frequently over the past few months. She'd been a cop all her life. She didn't know how to do or be anything else. "I guess maybe you don't until you become so self-destructive or dangerous that you aren't given a choice."

"You know, it's strange," Eamon said. "I joined the FBI because of what happened to Chloe. I wanted to stop what happened to her from happening to any other child. To any other family. I figured I couldn't find or stop him, so I'd focus on doing the next best thing—stopping others. Making those responsible face justice for their crimes and the damage they do."

"I hear the *but.*"

"But." His eyes looked almost pleading when they met hers. "Sometimes I can't help but feel as if I'm trying to empty an ocean of ugliness with a teaspoon."

"Maybe it's time you think about handing off the teaspoon to someone else."

"And do what?" His smile was quick, but not quick enough to cover the grief in his eyes. "I've considered that a lot since we closed Chloe's case. And then I remember how many other Chloes are out there. How do I walk away from that, Lana? How do I walk away from them? How do I ask someone who has a family, who probably shouldn't be bringing all this home with them, to take over for me because I'm, what, tired?"

She wouldn't say he was tired. There were only so many times a heart could be broken before it refused to heal.

She opened her mouth, wanted to tell him it was okay to put himself first, to find a new path and walk away. But no response formed. It wasn't any of her business how he continued his career, the decisions he made for his future. That said, Lana could only imagine how his job ate away at him. She worried that someday there wouldn't be anything left of the Eamon she…

"Okay, enough psychoanalyzing the agent," Eamon announced and clicked his laptop closed. "You sleep okay?"

Recognizing deflection, she let him have his distraction since she wanted him to avoid spiraling down that dark tunnel she was all too familiar with. "Better than I have in a long time." Lana once again rested her back against the cabinets and held her mug in both hands as she sipped. "Having trouble recalling how I ended up in there, however."

"Oh, that was me."

"No." She gasped playfully and earned the delightful

reward of seeing Eamon blush. "And here I thought the nighttime fairies carried me into your room."

He sat back in his chair looking, Lana thought without a second of remorse, something like a hero out of a medieval romance novel with that red hair and fit biceps that had her insides warming. All that was missing was a kilt and a sword strapped across his chest and that unbeatable dragon he continued to attempt to slay. She had a general idea what those arms felt like when they embraced her, but she wanted a more complete picture. A more complete experience. An experience that would only create new complications she couldn't afford. Complications and worry she wasn't in a position to responsibly deal with.

That said, what this man did for a simple white T-shirt really should be deemed illegal.

"I had some work to catch up on and I didn't want to take the chance of waking you up," he explained.

"So I gathered with that call," she murmured, waiting for additional information that didn't come. "So. You were up all night?"

"Pretty much." He sighed, raised his arms over his head and stretched. "Got out of the chair around three this morning and did some push-ups to wake myself up."

Catching a glimpse of his bare torso as his shirt lifted away from the hem of his jeans made her feel as if there was a blast furnace coming to life inside her. "Sorry I missed that," she said. "So, you weren't very chatty last night on the way back here after the party at Eden's." Time to try to push open that door he seemed determined to keep closed.

"No. It looked as if you and Greta hit it off," he said. "Was she everything you expected?"

"Everything and more." Lana couldn't help but smile fondly at the idea of having become friends with one of her favorite artists. "She gave me a tour of her art studio and put my name on the guest list of the official opening of the gallery."

"That was nice of her."

"She also showed me the nursery and the mural she's painting." The fairy-tale-inspired forest scene reminded Lana very much of the painting she'd seen in the gallery last night.

"At least she isn't painting the ceiling." Eamon chuckled. "Jack was convinced he was going to have to talk her out of building a scaffold à la Michelangelo. I know it's indelicate to say, but I think her due date must be off. She's showing a lot more than Eden, Simone or Allie did at five months."

"Her due date is accurate." Lana hid her smile behind her mug.

"Everything's okay, isn't it?" Eamon's instant shift from amused to concerned had her wishing she'd kept her comment to herself. "There's nothing wrong with Greta or the baby, is there? Not that she'd have said anything—"

"She's fine. She was just super excited to share something she hadn't told Jack yet. Although, to be fair, I'm shocked he hasn't figured it out for himself." She hesitated, waited to see if he'd catch on. "She's having twins."

"Twins," Eamon repeated. "Jack's getting two babies

at once?" He threw back his head and laughed. A sight and sound that lightened her heart considerably. "This is the best news I've heard in ages. He's going to freak out. In a good way," he added quickly. "So you're in on the secret, huh?"

She shrugged. "Greta's been dying to tell someone, but she's afraid everyone else is going to spill the beans before she can surprise Jack. She probably figured I'm safe since I don't know everyone as well as everyone else does." One benefit of being an outsider, she supposed. It made her privy to some fun information. "You can't tell him. Or let on you know."

"Don't worry. Her secret's safe with me. Aw, man. Twins." He shook his head. "I don't know if there's a better way to start the day than with that kind of news."

"I completely agree." And now that he was in a better mood… "What were you and Slade talking about so intently?"

"When?"

She eyed him as he shifted into familiar protective mode. It was a mode she recognized mainly because she had the tendency to do the same thing herself. Whenever she didn't want to share something disturbing with Marcus about a case or an investigation or a victim, she'd danced around his inquiries as if she were a lifelong ballerina who had earned her prima status.

"Last night when Chloe Ann shoved that whole cupcake into her mouth and got frosting up her nose," she said in an attempt to keep the mood light. "What's going on, Eamon? You're evading. What don't you want to talk to me about?" She narrowed her eyes. "That wasn't

Lieutenant Santos you were just talking with but did he call earlier?"

"He did, actually."

"And are you going to share whatever information he told you or do I get to play twenty questions this morning?"

"I don't think your questions are going to come close to the right answers."

"Fair warning—there isn't enough coffee in this apartment for either of us to survive my irritation, Eamon. Spill."

"He was able to speak with Commissioner McKenna yesterday afternoon. Suffice it to say, your suspicion was correct and she did remember you."

She stared into the depths of her coffee. "I'd be surprised if she didn't."

"Mmm-hmm."

Lana pressed her lips together. She knew that tone. It was Eamon's version of sliding into DEFCON 1. Her stomach churned around the banana she now knew she shouldn't have eaten.

"You said you'd reached out to the commissioner for help with Marcus's case," Eamon said. "You didn't tell us you flew back to Boston and camped out in her office waiting room for more than half a day. And then came back the next day. And the next. Apparently Security had to escort you out every time."

"Security should have stopped me before I hit the elevator after the first day." Her attempt at humor fell as flat as the floor beneath her feet. Humiliation wound up from her toes all the way to the top of her head. That sick, ashamed feeling she'd worked so hard to suppress these past months twisted into an even bigger knot of regret. "Those few weeks are a bit fuzzy," Lana admitted. "I remember more about the seedy hotel and airport bars than I do visiting her office. I'm sorry," she said on a sigh. "I should have told you."

"You should have told me a lot of things."

She could feel his eyes on her, but resisted the temptation to glance over. She didn't think she could bear seeing disappointment on his face. Disappointment she would completely understand.

"Was this trip to Boston before or after you punched your partner and broke his nose?" Eamon asked.

"Before." Her entire body went hot. Her hands tightened around the mug and she set it down before it shattered in her hold. It was difficult enough, admitting to herself that she'd hit bottom. How did she admit it to a man she cared for?

"What did he say? Your partner," Eamon clarified at her look of confusion. "What did he say that made you punch him?"

It helped that he asked. It helped that he understood she had to have been pushed awfully far before she struck back. "He told me to get over it. Marcus's death." Her voice caught and she cleared her throat. "He told me to just get over it and move on."

"Ah."

"He didn't know I'd heard Marcus die. No one did." She could sense the nod he gave. She wasn't one to scare easily, but the idea of turning around and seeing disapproval on his face terrified her more than she cared to admit. But she did it anyway, because there was no moving forward with him, with this investigation, as long as the past stood between them. "Not that it would have changed anything if he did know. The guy's always been a jerk."

"Sounds like. I was right, then," he said as he met her shaky gaze. "I told Eden he'd probably said something to deserve it. I'm surprised you only broke his nose."

"So was my captain," Lana admitted. "The fact he said what he said in front of a room full of detectives worked a little in my favor." A very little. That her partner already had reports filed against him for disrespectful behavior also helped.

It still burned, though, that it was those reports and not her own, up until then, exemplary record that had left her suspended rather than fired. Still, it did take three of her fellow detectives to pry her off him and that, to this day, felt like a badge of honor of sorts. "I don't have any excuses for what happened," she told him. "It just confirmed what I already knew. I'd gone back to work too soon. Hadn't processed any of my feelings the way I should have. And I wasn't particularly eager to seek counseling." Counseling for cops was a double-edged sword at times, especially for women in law enforcement. Any signs of weakness could be easily exploited.

The main miscalculation she'd made was how much worse the drinking made things. "I accepted my suspension without question," she continued and turned her back. "And I'll accept whatever consequences remain to be handed down, but in the meantime, I did what I needed to do to get myself straight. I needed to in order to think and work this through. So I could..." She trailed off before she admitted something she hadn't even admitted to herself.

"So you could what?"

His hands gently rested on her shoulders, squeezing as she let out a shuddering breath. She hadn't even heard him get out of the chair. The man moved like a shadow, quiet, stealthy and just a little bit intimidating. She wanted to reach up, to take hold of his hand and not let go, but instead she splayed her palms on the counter.

"Lana, there is nothing you can't tell me. If you don't understand that by now, then what are we doing?"

What were they doing? She hated the tightness in her throat, the way the tears burned. Tears she knew to be useless and ridiculous. "I needed to get straight and sober so I could come to you. I didn't want to give you any excuse to turn me away. To make you doubt what I knew to be true." She stopped short of admitting the rest: that she never ever wanted to be the object of his pity or sympathy.

"You were my plan," she told him. "I knew if I was going to find out what really happened to Marcus I would need your help, and I couldn't do that until I stopped drinking. It took me some time, after my suspension, to make it happen, but I did it. I made mistakes on my way, but I got to where I needed to be, Eamon." She lifted her chin and took a deep breath. "I got to you."

"We didn't finish our conversation, you know," Lana said as she emerged from the bathroom after her shower.

"What conversation was that?" Eamon asked from his place at the small square kitchen window. He wasn't standing directly in front of it, but off to one side, where the occupants of the dark-colored SUV across the street couldn't see him. He'd jumped in the shower first, got dressed in four minutes flat so he could retake sentry duty while Lana took her time.

Eamon glanced over his shoulder, saw she'd chosen a bright pink beacon of a T-shirt that no doubt could be seen from space. Her hair was still damp and hung around her shoulders. Her face, makeup-free as usual, carried some actual color in it this morning. He didn't like to take the credit, but wondered if she was feeling more stable around him. Or maybe he was just imagining or seeing what he wanted to.

"Our conversation about Lieutenant Santos calling." She picked up the gun she'd left on the sofa side table and slipped it into the back waistband of her snug jeans. "Have you been standing there the entire time I was in the shower?"

"Yep." He sipped his coffee, waited for the return call from Jason Sutton with the results on the plate trace. "Good shower?"

"Lonely," she said in a way he knew was an attempt to get a reaction.

"All you have to do is ask," he said easily when she popped up on her toes to look over his shoulder. She grabbed hold of him, one hand on his back, the other on his shoulder. Both warmed him all the way to his marrow. "See them?"

"Dark SUV, rental car, across the street? They're hard to miss."

"Especially when we got back at one in the morning with no one else around." He'd kept an eye on them every hour on the hour since then. "They followed us from Eden and Cole's. Been parked there ever since we got back."

She swore with such magnificence he had to grin. "You think those are the ones who firebombed my motel room? The ones who shot at me?"

"I'm going to assume so." If they weren't, they were part of a bigger team, and that wasn't something Eamon was happy to consider. Still, he wasn't ruling anything out.

"What's with all the cloak-and-dagger stuff?" she demanded and, to his chagrin, fixed yet another pot of coffee they didn't need. "If I have something they want, why not come right at me?"

"They did come right at you, actually. Email's up on my computer. Initial report from the fire department on the motel fire."

"And?"

"You don't want to read it yourself?" He debated about pulling an Axel Foley and sticking a banana up the SUV's tailpipe, but he had yet to see that work in real life. Now wasn't the time to experiment. But it might be an opportunity to turn the tables and get some information. He'd already worked out a plan on that front. All it was going to take was a couple of people for backup and one perfectly timed phone call.

"I think we're past the point of either of us keeping

secrets from one another," Lana said. "Let me have it. What's in the report?"

"The lock on your motel room door was busted in. Handle and door frame, too." He couldn't help but replay that first night she'd arrived and feel grateful she'd accepted his invitation to use his couch.

"They came in looking for me first, then torched the place when I wasn't there." She sat at the table with her coffee. "Why? To scare me?"

"Didn't work, did it?" Whoever was trying to intimidate her didn't have the first clue who they were dealing with. Or they were underestimating her frame of mind. Maybe because they'd been told what to expect by someone familiar with her recent erratic behavior. Someone who didn't realize she'd gotten herself together. "Hired help," he said as his cell phone vibrated. "That's Jason." He answered the call. "You find anything?"

"At six thirty in the morning you're lucky I can find my phone. Car's rented under the name of Steve Stark. Someone's been watching too many superhero movies."

"Criminal masterminds they are not," Eamon muttered.

"The card he used at the airport agency is a business account registered to Klein Technologies, but their website? It's a facade. Nothing deep or informative, just a showpiece should anyone go looking."

Which they did. "It's a shell company."

"More like a matryoshka company. You know, those Russian nesting dolls with a doll in a doll—"

"I am familiar."

"Right. Well, halfway down the rabbit hole, I found what you suspected. A&O Solutions pulls the strings. You want me to dig deeper?"

"No, thanks." Jason was good, but the last thing Eamon wanted was to alert anyone at A&O that they were on to them. "I've got the rest handled. Appreciate the quick assist, Jason. Next Thursday, ten a.m. I'll pick you up."

"For what?" Jason asked.

"Your suit fitting. I know you didn't want to go tux—"

"I'm not a tux kind of guy."

But Kyla was definitely a tux kinda woman, and by now Eamon had been to enough weddings to understand keeping the bride happy was the most important thing. "Ten a.m. Thursday. Be ready." He hung up just as a white panel van pulled up beside the SUV. Windows opened, a package was handed over and the SUV's driver glanced up and nodded.

"Breakfast delivery?" Eamon inclined his head for Lana to join him. This time she stepped in front of him. He could smell the bath gel from the shower drifting off her skin in tempting, sea-inspired waves. It was all he could do to keep his hands to himself and not slip his palm down the soft curve of her hip.

"Doubtful. No plates. What did Jason say?"

Exactly what Eamon had anticipated, but wanted confirmed. "If they followed us from Eden's, that means they've been on our tail for a while." And he hadn't noticed. Not something that was sitting well with him. "Who all have you spoken to since you got to Sacramento?"

"Just you. And your friends." Lana glanced over her shoulder at him. She was close. So close the heat of her body warmed his. He was almost distracted enough to miss it, but he didn't. The realization of what he'd accepted hours before. "Felice." The woman's name came out more like a curse than an answer. "She called me before we left last night."

It wasn't disbelief or dismay he heard in her voice, but irritation, disappointment. And more than a touch of anger. "That car out there was rented by a shell company Jason traced back to a nonexistent entity." He chose his words carefully. "It's A&O Solutions."

"Seriously? You think someone there is behind this?"

Eamon bit the inside of his cheek. Well, she'd almost gotten it right. He couldn't exactly blame her for wanting to cling to the notion that her husband's boss, his mentor, was someone she could count on and trust.

"But that doesn't make sense." The anger remained as she looked back out the window. "If I had something of Marcus's, something they wanted, all they had to do was ask. Why didn't Felice just ask?"

"Maybe she did? Or maybe she couldn't." Eamon had yet to land on an answer. "Or perhaps she might have, had you been anyone or anything else."

He could almost hear her frown before she turned and faced him.

"You're a cop, Lana. Even worse, you're an honest cop. She probably can't take the chance of you coming across whatever it is she thinks you have."

"You make it sound as if she's some kind of criminal mastermind or something."

"For the record, I'm leaning more toward the former, not the latter."

"Stop leaning at all. This is my life we're talking about, Eamon. I don't have anything they want."

"That you know of." He was already ten steps in front of her, but for now he could wait for her to catch up. And accept the truth of what was developing in front of them.

"I hate this. I detest not knowing what's going on in my own life."

At least she was thinking straight. He could use that, use her anger and her determination to prove his suspicions wrong to both their advantages.

"I know. And this news probably won't help clear anything up. Lieutenant Santos's conversation with Commissioner McKenna went beyond her passing interactions with you and her familiarity with the hit-and-run file. She checked in with the officers who reported on Marcus's accident. One took his vacation time almost immediately after, then resigned before coming back. She can't find him."

"And the other?"

"The other told the commissioner he had nothing to add to the official report and that if she had additional questions she could speak with his union rep. The detectives? Same exact response."

She grimaced. "Not a normal reaction if you don't have anything to hide."

"No," Eamon agreed. "It's not." It was, in fact, a big red flag. One he suspected the Boston police commissioner was not going to accept lightly.

He could imagine seeing the wheels turning in Lana's

mind. Eyes that flashed between confusion, dismay and back to confusion. "What is going on? What was Marcus involved in, Eamon?"

"Apparently those were Commissioner McKenna's questions as well. Lieutenant Santos said she's not opening a formal inquiry, but that she has one of her best people already handling it."

"Well, I guess that's something. Is that all Lieutenant Santos said?"

"Not quite." Eamon looked over her shoulder as the second car pulled away. "Commissioner McKenna did some checking of her own, ran all the names associated with Marcus that were on record just to see if anything popped. One thing did."

"Yeah?"

"Cynthia Randolph."

"Marcus's assistant at the law firm?" Lana's eyes went wide. "What about her?"

"There was a car accident the day after she spoke with you, after she sent you Marcus's client list." There wasn't any other way to put it… "I'm sorry, Lana, but she's dead."

Chapter 9

The back door of the Brass Eagle closed behind Lana as she stepped out into the parking lot. Without casting a glance to the surveillance van she knew was waiting to follow her, she took a moment to inhale a lungful of early morning air before she made her way around to the front of the building. No sooner had she reached the locked front door than her phone rang.

Heart skipping a few beats, she stopped to answer the call. "Don't tell me—you decided you wanted coffee after all."

"Been practicing that line, haven't you?" Eamon's voice carried the strained smile she had no doubt was on his face. She glanced up, pretending he wasn't in the surveillance van but still upstairs waiting for her to return.

She stopped, tucked the cell under her chin and bent down and retied her shoe. "Just staying in character."

"Remember," he continued, "all you have to do is take a walk to the coffee shop. We just want to confirm you're the target and then draw them away from here. Cole and Jack are on standby if we need backup."

There was no determining where her nerves started and her anxiety ended, and it was taking a lot of her energy to conceal both. She chose to believe Eamon's repeated "reminder" was him being extra cautious; the alternative was admitting he was concerned about her. Eamon Quinn didn't do worried, as far as she knew. She didn't want to be the reason he started now.

"Max is monitoring communications from the Eagle," he continued.

"Copy that," Max confirmed over her earpiece.

"You won't be alone for a second," Eamon stated. "We'll be right there with you. In your ear the whole time."

It was on the tip of her tongue to remind him she could take care of herself, but she supposed, after the past year, she needed to prove it. So she slipped right back into the role she'd written for herself as caffeine-supplying girlfriend.

"You know espresso makes you jumpy." It wasn't difficult, making sure her voice carried toward the SUV that was still parked across the street. The same two men still occupied the front seats. Honestly, if she didn't know better, she'd have thought someone stuck two mannequins inside as a practical joke. "Okay, here we go." She stood up, brushed her hands on the back of her jeans and headed off down the street.

Her and Eamon's thrown-together plan to draw the car away from the bar and the surrounding businesses and homes made sense. He hadn't been thrilled with the idea of using her as bait, but what other choice did they have? Collateral damage had to be considered, especially now that the body count was rising.

The last thing she wanted was any more innocent people to get caught in whatever cross fire she caused. Their best chance at drawing them out and giving them an opportunity to approach was to put her out in plain view. Alone.

That was assuming, of course, that an approach was their priority. The other night at the motel it seemed they'd had other ideas about what to do with her.

Lana purposely didn't look in the SUV's direction as she walked. The truth was, she was grateful to be out on her own for a while, away from Eamon and his increasingly confusing, distracting presence. She'd gotten used to not caring about anyone, not wanting to care, but after even a few hours in his company, she was so deep into caring she could feel herself slipping into emotions she'd sworn she'd never embrace again.

She pinched her lips tight, remembering that talking to herself wasn't an option unless she wanted to have a full-on confession session. How stupid to have thought she was beyond being able to be shocked. Wrong yet again. Learning her late husband's assistant had been killed, possibly as a result of Lana's reckless questions, added a weight to her soul.

Guilt made her thirsty, and not for water. She should have been grateful he'd stuck that bottle of Scotch of his back in the cabinet. If it had still been out...

She shook herself free of that thought. Quenching that thirst was only going to mess things up even more, but she'd appreciated the excuse to get out of the building that was filled with her greatest temptation. She should feel lucky Eamon and Vince were trusting her enough to make this play and draw out the men surveilling the apartment. Besides, throwing herself into work she hadn't been able to do for months was a good way to push herself through the cravings.

Part of her wanted to believe it was just a car accident, a coincidence, but who was she kidding? She'd been a cop long enough to know coincidences like that weren't likely. Cynthia Randolph's death was tied to Marcus's, which tied it directly back to Lana. It was up to her to get answers—and justice—for both of them.

Her stomach knotted hard enough to make her wince. People like Eamon, people who trusted her, were poised to get hurt. And what about his friends and their families? If she didn't get to the bottom of this soon, she'd just be acting as an anchor dragging them all down. That was not something she planned to be responsible for. No matter what she had to do.

As far as those men in the SUV were concerned, however, she had one simple plan in mind. There was little she liked more than proving someone wrong.

Unless it was making them regret underestimating her.

"You've got this, Lana." Eamon's voice brought her back to the present. "And we've got you."

Her chin inched up. His confidence in her was the shot of adrenaline she needed. Now wasn't the time to play it safe. Now was the time to go full bore and confront whatever monster she'd awakened. As anxious as she was, she kept her pace slow and casual, as if taking a Sunday morning walk with two potential killers on her tail was an everyday occurrence.

She flexed her hands that were shaking as if she was a rookie out on her first assignment, even as she could feel the muscle memory begin to return.

It was all coming back to her. Not in drips, but in subtle waves that built upon one another. The energy surge, the way the plan ran through her mind, over and over as a kind of mantra, even as she reminded herself to stay fluid and be ready for anything.

The focus on keeping her actions completely normal and predictable was helping tame that guilt that continued to threaten her. "I'll be back before you know it," she said to Eamon. "Keep the sheets warm for me."

"She does know you aren't the only person on the line, right?" Vince Sutton's deep voice had Lana's lips twitching.

"All part of the fun," Lana said before Eamon could respond.

Eamon had found himself a really great group of people to surround himself with. People who were there for him the instant he called. Neither Max nor Vince had cast any looks of doubt or concern her way after Eamon filled them in on their plan. Vince had set her up with the special two-way ear pods while Max cut a small hole in the seam of her right sneaker to place an infinitesimal tracking device into her shoe. Any temptation she might have felt to protest would have been silenced by Eamon's warning expression.

Instead she'd rolled her eyes and offered a ghost of a shrug of acceptance. It had been the only indication he was concerned she was up to the job.

She *was* up to this, she told herself. She *was* okay.

Had it been anyone else in the van other than Eamon, however, she might not have been so easily convinced.

Lana straightened her ear pods as she kept her sights focused on the hole-in-the-wall coffee shop that, according to Eamon at least, gave a certain chain a definite run for its money. She was barely a block into her walk when she heard an engine start up and rumble to life.

"Okay, we're on," Eamon said quietly. "They're pulling out now, Lana. Be ready for anything."

"Copy that." Hands tucked into the pockets of her borrowed zip-up hoodie, she kept her gaze straight ahead even as the anger percolated in her blood, hotter and stronger than any coffee machine was capable of brewing. She was either bait or a target. Or, worst case, she was both. It wasn't easy, accepting Eamon's supposition that Felice Covington was behind all of this. It was a bitter pill to swallow, that a woman Lana considered a friend had ulterior motives where maintaining their relationship was concerned. Lana thought of Felice as someone to lean on while Felice thought of her as…as what? A pawn? A tool? A source of information?

The idea that their get-togethers were nothing more than surveillance check-ins made her slightly sick and eroded the already fragile trust Lana still possessed.

"Crossing over to 8th Street." She caught sight of the SUV as she glanced down the street before crossing against the light. They wouldn't be able to follow, as it was a one-way street. Instead they'd be forced to circle around and approach from a different direction—one that should be easy to see coming.

In the distance she could hear the church bells ringing at the Cathedral of the Blessed Sacrament, calling worshippers to Sunday service. A homeless woman pushed her overfilled grocery cart along the sidewalk on the other side of the street. A pair of joggers came to a quick pause at the corner, glancing both ways before continuing on their way. The white noise of the jumble of freeways reminded her of the sound of the ocean roaring.

Lana kept her pace steady and casual. Three blocks down, another four blocks over. Now was not the time to get anxious or get ahead of herself or obsess about what came next. One step at a time. One day at a time.

Jumping to conclusions and fixating over possibilities rather than responsibly looking for answers and following a plan had been partially responsible for getting her suspended.

She had to be careful. If for no other reason than Eamon was a part of this now and the last thing she wanted to do was put his career—or his life—in jeopardy. If someone was going to have to take chances, it was darned well going to be her. She wouldn't survive anything happening to him.

Her stomach swirled at the very idea. She wouldn't want to.

"Okay, Lana. Looks like they're going to circle around to catch sight of you again. Stay alert."

"What else would I be?" Probably not a question she wanted an answer to. "Max? You got me on your screen?"

"Sure do." Max Kellan, Vince's partner in his private investigation business and Dr. Allie Hollister-Kellan's husband, sounded like the epitome of calm. "One nice big green blip."

"Not too big, I hope." The back of her neck prickled. She stopped, looked behind her, but found only an empty street. "You still have that SUV in your sight?"

"That's affirmative," Vince said. "Why? You see something?"

"No." But she felt something. Or did she? Her instincts weren't exactly firing on all cylinders these days. "No, I'm good. Just felt like someone…" She didn't finish that thought for fear Eamon would pull the plug. "Where are you exactly?"

"Close. They're coming up two blocks in front of you, Lana."

"We've got a couple of delivery vans between us and them right now," Vince said. "But we've got them."

"Right. Okay." The sign to the Jumped Up Café hung overhead in the distance and reminded her to get her bearings.

She counted nearly every step of the remaining blocks and forced herself to glance into the small shop windows as she passed. A dry cleaner. A yoga studio. A number of papered windows that promised new businesses opening soon. The remnants of an old pet store took up a corner space while next door, Sir Barks-a-Lot, a dog grooming business, was clearly a recent addition to the area, with its brightly painted windows featuring a Jack Russell terrier wearing a suit of armor.

She splashed through a puddle caused by an over-watered patch of grass as an older man walking his dog passed and offered her a bright good morning.

"Okay, we're circling back in your direction." The relief in Eamon's voice didn't make her feel better. She shivered, still unable to shake the sensation that she was being followed. "Lana? You okay? What's wrong?"

"I don't know." The traffic light changed as she pulled open the door to the coffee shop. The van that drove past had her glancing over her shoulder, frowning.

"Eamon, that van we saw with the SUV this morning, the one that passed off a package to the SUV? I just saw it again." Was she imagining things, or had the driver looked at her?

The hesitation was brief but enough to get her blood pumping. "You're sure?"

"Yes." She caught a flash of a shadow out of the corner of her eye and turned, scanning the empty street behind her. "No plates, same as the one this morning." Driving around without plates was a sure way to tempt a run-in with local police. At least it had been when she'd been a patrol officer.

"Max, check if there are any security cameras in the area," Vince said. "If you need help accessing, buzz Jason and get him on it."

"Working on it now," Max said.

She couldn't just keep standing around outside the

café. Not without looking suspicious. "I'm headed inside," Lana murmured and stepped into Jumped Up.

"Remember, get in, get your coffee, get out and go to the park. You would have seen it. It's the one across the street," Eamon said. "Stay in the open. Our target just rounded the block again."

"He's turned into the alley behind the café," Vince said.

"We're parking at the end of the alley, Lana."

"Mmm-hmm." It was the only response she could give without sounding as if she were talking to herself. She took a deep breath and allowed the warm, toasty aromas of hot butter mingling with pungent ground beans to pull away at least some of her stress.

Any other time she'd have loved to revel in the dark-wooded, Pacific Northwest feel of the café. With the dim lights and small guest tables, it reminded her of one of her favorite spots up in Seattle.

Most of the tables were occupied. A young mother broke off a chunk of banana to hand to her stroller-trapped toddler. A pair of college students seated at the window counter on bar stools tapped away on laptops while sipping out of frothy eco-friendly cups. Two older men were halfway through a game of chess that, to Lana's eye, looked like it would soon end in a checkmate, while a group of senior citizens compared prescriptions and tried to outbrag one another in the chronic conditions department. She might have smiled if her heart wasn't pounding in her ears. Just your ordinary neighborhood coffee stop.

The handwritten chalk menu overhead boasted everything from a blackberry dark roast to a word salad offering that had just as many syllables as the coffee beans it probably took to brew.

Lana got in line, bided her time and resisted the impulse to look behind her anytime the door opened.

Instead she focused on the glass pastry cabinet containing dozens of in-house baked goods while one of the employees was busy filling the sandwich trays for what Lana was sure was the upcoming lunch rush. Her stomach growled in anticipation of something she didn't dare ingest.

She'd have to come back another time. When her heart wasn't lodged solidly in her throat.

Lana took a step to the side, her eyes refocusing on the glass of the display cabinet in time to clash with the gaze of a man standing two people behind her. She slid her eyes away, then back again, only to see him shift behind the person in front of him.

Was she being paranoid? The back of her neck continued to prickle.

She could hear Vince and Eamon talking, though, discussing the plethora of delivery vans and trucks making their way in and out of the alley. Sunday morning deliveries setting up the eateries in the area for the upcoming week.

Lana wasn't in a position to talk to them or respond. What she could do was memorize everything about the man who continued to shift in and out of her sight. Tall, slender to the point of being almost skeletal, with close-set dark eyes and a locked jaw that she suspected might be made of steel. The dark suit he wore cost more than her first car, and his long jacket looked too heavy for the early summer weather currently assaulting the Valley.

Her pulse jumped, but she remained calm, pretended to continue to peruse the pastry offerings before she ordered her coffee.

"Thanks," she said a while later when she accepted the large cup. "Do you have a public bathroom?"

"Right back there." The server pointed to the narrow hallway on the other side of the counter.

"Thanks." Lana flashed a smile and circled around, noticing her tail had stepped out of line and taken a seat by the door.

She made her way to the one bathroom, hesitated with her hand on the door, glanced back to confirm her tail was still there. He was. And he'd shifted his chair out in order to keep her in his line of sight. Her gaze shifted down to the gun secured at his side.

"Lana?" Eamon asked as she ducked inside and locked the door. Her hands were shaking again. Her pulse raced, as if her system didn't know what to do with the adrenaline anymore. "You went awfully quiet. What's going on?"

"Not sure." Self-doubt battled against reason. It would make sense for them to have someone else on foot; someone she and Eamon hadn't anticipated, but this was why she'd reminded herself to stay fluid. Expect everything and have contingencies in place for whatever might come to pass.

It was, she recalled, one of her early lessons from her two years as an undercover narcotics detective. One thing she did know. She didn't want Eamon blowing his cover by having to come in and pull her out. Or worse, rescue her. The very thought was bitter on her tongue.

"You sound stressed. Talk to me, Lana." Eamon's urging didn't do anything to calm her down.

She looked down, fisted her hands to make them stop shaking. "Someone followed me inside. And yes, before you ask, I'm sure. He's waiting by the front door and he's armed. Eamon, if I've put these people in danger—"

"No one's going to try anything in publi—"

"They shot up a motel in the middle of the night," she reminded him and heard the panic in her voice. "I don't think a coffee shop is going to offer a deterrent."

Now wasn't the time to lose it. She braced her hands on the edges of the sink, ducked her head and tried to shove the images of Cynthia Randolph out of her mind. The thoughts of the family the woman had left behind— her parents and a brother, if Lana recalled correctly. The ripple effects were devastating and she was done causing them.

"Okay, it's okay." Eamon's voice in her ear again. "Just stick with the plan and make your way to the park. We'll be there in a couple of minutes. Max? We could probably use some backup—"

"No!" Lana cut him off. "No, Max, you stay at the bar. I mean it, Eamon. I don't want anyone else in the line of fire because of me. Just… I just need a minute." Her mind quickly sifted through her options. She couldn't erase the image of that mother and her baby, or the chess-playing pair. Going out the front door could very well get them hurt. That only left one option.

"Lana. You want out, you say the word," Eamon said. "We'll find another way."

"We both know there is no other way," she said. "They've already killed two people that we know of." She didn't want any more blood on her hands.

"Lana—"

"I'm going out the back." She picked up her coffee and carefully opened the door.

"Lana, no. I repeat, no on the back exit. The SUV—"

The occupants of that SUV were going to find a way to get what they wanted one way or the other. At least with her tracker, Eamon, Vince and Max would be able to see where the bad guys took her and maybe even lead her to Felice and the answers they sought. "I've got at least one guy with a gun on one side and the possibility of escape on the other," she told Eamon. "I'm going with option number two."

She didn't stop to look toward the front but focused on the neon Exit sign over the back door. She hadn't bothered with a purse, had her cell in the back pocket of her jeans, her ID, a credit card and some cash in the other. All she had in her hand was her coffee, which she could throw in someone's face as a last resort.

"Lana—" Eamon's anger came through loud and clear, but it was hopefully something she'd deal with later. "They're right outside. Don't you dare… Vince—"

She heard swearing and the blaring of horns as she pushed on the bar and opened the door into the alley.

Lana couldn't decide who was more surprised. The driver of the SUV or his copilot in the passenger seat. She turned slightly, saw the man from the café run-

"One Minute" Survey

You get up to **FOUR books** <u>and</u> a Mystery Gift...

ABSOLUTELY FREE!

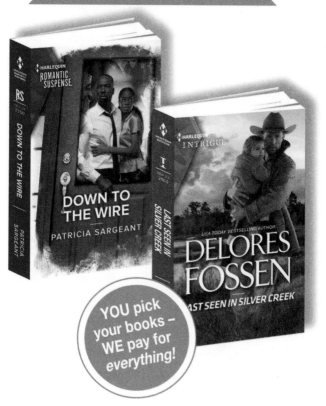

YOU pick your books – WE pay for everything!

See inside for details.

Dear Reader,

Your opinions are important to us. So if you'll participate in our fast and free "One Minute" Survey, YOU can pick up to four wonderful books that WE pay for when you try the Harlequin Reader Service!

As a leading publisher of women's fiction, we'd love to hear from you. That's why we promise to reward you for completing our survey.

IMPORTANT: Please complete the survey and return it. We'll send your Free Books and a Free Mystery Gift right away. And we pay for shipping and handling too! ← *We pay for EVERYTHING!*

Try **Harlequin® Romantic Suspense** and get 2 books featuring heart-racing page-turners with unexpected plot twists and irresistible chemistry that will keep you guessing to the very end.

Try **Harlequin Intrigue® Larger-Print** and get 2 books featuring action-packed stories that will keep you on the edge of your seat. Solve the crime and deliver justice at all costs.

Or TRY BOTH!

Thank you again for participating in our "One Minute" Survey. It really takes just a minute (or less) to complete the survey... and your free books and gift will be well worth it!

If you continue with your subscription, you can look forward to curated monthly shipments of brand-new books from your selected series, always at a discount off the cover price! Plus you can cancel any time. So don't miss out, return your One Minute Survey today to get your Free books.

Pam Powers

"One Minute" Survey

GET YOUR FREE BOOKS AND A FREE GIFT!

✓ Complete this Survey ✓ Return this survey

▼ DETACH AND MAIL CARD TODAY! ▼

1 Do you try to find time to read every day?

☐ YES ☐ NO

2 Do you prefer stories with suspensful storylines?

☐ YES ☐ NO

3 Do you enjoy having books delivered to your home?

☐ YES ☐ NO

4 Do you share your favorite books with friends?

☐ YES ☐ NO

YES! I have completed the above "One Minute" Survey. Please send me my Free Books and a Free Mystery Gift (worth over $20 retail). I understand that I am under no obligation to buy anything, as explained on the back of this card.

☐ **Harlequin®
Romantic
Suspense**
240/340 CTI G2AD

☐ **Harlequin
Intrigue®
Larger-Print**
199/399 CTI G2AD

☐ **BOTH**
240/340 & 199/399
CTI G2AE

FIRST NAME

LAST NAME

ADDRESS

APT.#

CITY

STATE/PROV.

ZIP/POSTAL CODE

EMAIL ☐ Please check this box if you would like to receive newsletters and promotional emails from Harlequin Enterprises ULC and its affiliates. You can unsubscribe anytime.

HI/HRS-1123-OM

ning down the hall toward her, his hand already on the
butt of his gun.

"You guys looking for me?"

The passenger looked out, confusion marring his
thick brow. The man had a neck thicker than her thigh,
and it wasn't helped by the black turtleneck he wore,
or the black knit cap obscuring most of his forehead.

"You going to open the door or what?" she demanded
as she popped the plastic lid off her large, steaming
coffee.

He looked back at his partner. The other man's shrug
confirmed her earlier suspicion that they were not dealing with rocket scientists. She felt some of the tension
and fear melt away. Abducting her hadn't been their ob-
jective. Otherwise they wouldn't be balking now. She'd
taken them by surprise, which gave her the advantage.

"Lana, I swear, if you get into that car…" Eamon's
voice trailed off, probably, she thought, because he didn't
want to voice what she knew he was thinking.

The back door of the coffeehouse burst open. Lana
pivoted and tossed the contents of her cup right in the
man's face. He jumped back. The door slammed closed
just as the passenger in the SUV jumped out and yanked
open the back door for her.

"Lana, don't you do it," Eamon shouted. It took her
a second to realize she hadn't heard him through her
earpiece, but from down the alley, where he was racing
straight for her.

She couldn't afford to keep watching him. They needed
answers. She needed to get this case closed once and for

all. And right now the only path she had to do that was in that SUV.

She climbed into the car. The door barely closed before the passenger was back inside shouting, "Go!"

Lana was thrown back in her seat as the car took off down the alley and made a sharp, tire-screeching turn onto the street. She turned around, eyes pinned on the alley as Vince's van made an equally sharp turn to pursue.

"What are we supposed to do now?" the driver demanded of his partner.

"Don't know." His hands were shaking as he pulled out his cell phone.

Lana frowned. She'd never encountered such uncertain criminals before. "Who do you work for?" she shouted over the roar of the engine.

"Shut up!" the driver yelled. "Do we go to the rendezvous?"

"The rail yards? Yeah." Cell phone guy nodded and dialed. "They said if we got into trouble to head there."

Curious, Lana carefully slipped her finger into the door handle and pulled, but they'd engaged the child locks. Her window didn't work either. "Eamon." She kept her voice low as they continued to argue. "We're headed to the rail yards." The area was in the early stages of redevelopment. She couldn't imagine anyone was there on a Sunday. At least, she hoped not. "Eamon?" She pressed a finger against her ear, looked behind her as they sped away and put distance between them and Vince's van.

"Eamon?" She tried one more time, only to realize that the voices in her ear had gone silent.

Chapter 10

"I can't hear her," Eamon yelled into the dash screen as he rebuckled his belt, now that he was back in the van. "Max? Why can't I hear her?"

"Signal's jammed," Vince answered in his marine-calm voice that scraped along the edge of Eamon's nerves. "Probably why we couldn't get a signal off them back at the bar. She's okay, Eamon. She's alive."

"She was alive when she got in the SUV," Eamon corrected, wondering if his heart was ever going to beat again. He pinned his gaze on the roof of the SUV that was gradually gaining distance on them. "We don't know what she is now. What was she thinking, getting into that car?"

"She was probably thinking she doesn't want anyone else getting hurt on account of her." Vince's matter-of-fact statement made sense, but it didn't sit well with Eamon. "I'd be more concerned about who the guy in the café was. Max? You get anywhere on surveillance in the area?"

"Yeah, hang on." Max's voice and activities were muffled before a second voice echoed on the other end. "Jason just got here. He's setting up and will hack into the feeds I was able to pick up on."

"If Jason gets busted for this, I'm going to expect a federal bailout," Vince warned Eamon. "Lana went with her gut." He switched lanes, stayed a good three car lengths behind the SUV. "We weren't there and we weren't in her head. Give her the benefit of the doubt."

"I should have been with her," Eamon said. "And her gut is what got her suspended from the force in the first place."

"Beating yourself up about this isn't going to do any good. Max? You've got us on your map, right? Where are we headed?"

"Three choices. Old Sac, I-5 or…"

"The rail yards." Vince and Eamon spoke at the same time.

"Max, you stay on her tracker and let us know the second it comes back on line."

"Way ahead of you. Jace, let's…"

Eamon blocked out the chatter. "She was jumpy. I should have seen it. Telling her about Cynthia Randolph probably pushed her over the edge." He should have gone with her. They should have revamped their plan so she wouldn't have been alone.

"Stop woulda coulda shoulda-ing," Vince ordered.

"And stop thinking with your…heart," he said with a wince. "You're a good FBI agent, Eamon. Start acting like it. You can begin by remembering she's a cop with a decade's worth of experience behind her. You know her. Better than the rest of us do. What was she thinking when she got into that car?"

It took some doing, filtering through the last few minutes to dig out what Vince was asking for. "Collateral damage. She'd do whatever she could to stop the fallout from affecting too many people."

"All right. Good. Max? You got anything on those cameras yet?"

"Not yet. Jason's having some issues getting into the… What?"

"Someone's in the system already." Jason's voice snapped through over Max's. "I'm trying to get in around them, but it's going to take some time so they don't know we're piggybacking in on their hack."

"Do whatever you can," Vince ordered. "Whoever that guy was in the coffee shop scared her more than the two guys in the SUV. And keep in mind, they drove off with her. They didn't shoot her then and there."

"Ah, the bright side," Eamon muttered. His hands fisted against his thighs. How had he not seen what was going on behind those eyes of hers? "When we do find her, I'm never going to speak to her again."

Vince surprised him by grinning. "Must be love." He glanced over at Eamon, his smile widening. "You never did hear the whole story about me and Simone getting back together, did you?"

"I heard enough," Eamon said. "Enough to know you've been where I am now."

"We'll get Lana back," Vince promised. "None of us are going to let her get away from you. I promise."

"Don't go making promises you can't keep," Eamon warned. "There! We were right. They're taking the turn-off for the rail yards."

"Okay. Okay, I'm going to back off. Give them some space and time to think." Vince eased his foot off the gas. "We don't want them feeling cornered. She didn't get into that SUV without an idea, Eamon. I know it's hard right now, but you need to ease up, okay? I'm going to call Jack and Cole in. Chances are we'll need local law enforcement's support."

"Okay, we're in!" Jason shouted over the line. "Max and I are going through the security footage from the parking lot across the street from the café. Give us a second…"

"There! Screenshot him, right there," Max said.

Eamon's pulse kicked up.

"Putting it through my facial rec program now…" Jason murmured.

"What facial rec program?" Eamon asked. "Did you hack into the FBI again?"

"Of course not," Jason said with a fair amount of offense.

"He's been developing one himself," Vince explained. "When he's not working at the teen center or studying for his degree."

"Gotta do something to put food on the table," Jason

said. "And I've already got interest from a private security company, thanks to a mutual friend."

"Slade," Eamon said, then shook his head. "I forgot, we're supposed to meet him—" He pulled out his cell and dialed. "Hey, Slade. Sorry, but I think Lana and I are going to be a little late for our meeting."

"Let me guess," Slade said in an overly calm tone so similar to Vince's that Eamon had to glance over to make sure Vince was still in the car with him. "Does this have anything to do with a visit to Jumped Up and an in-progress pursuit through downtown Sac?"

Eamon frowned. "I don't really know how to respond to that." He clicked onto speaker and held out his phone. "You've got me and Vince. And yes, we're currently tailing an SUV with Lana inside."

"Ah, guys?" Jason's suddenly uncertain voice filled the car. "I've got an ID on the guy following Lana into the café. His name's Boris Klineman. He's a former spook."

"CIA," Vince muttered. "Awesome. Just what we needed."

"What on earth does the CIA want with Lana?" Eamon asked.

"Nothing," Slade said. "Boris doesn't work for the CIA any longer." He paused. "He works with me."

"Okay, guys, this has been fun, but I've changed my mind. You really need to drop me off." Lana's sudden bravado had little to do with the panic coursing through her system and more to do with the fact that the men in the front seat looked more freaked out than she did. The rumbling and bumping their way through the rail yards was giving her a headache and sending the box on the seat beside her into some kind of frenetic fit. "Whoever you're working for, I'm betting they didn't see adding kidnapping to your résumés."

"You just…" The passenger swung around and pointed his cell phone at her. "Just shut up. We need to think."

"No." Now wasn't the time to be quiet. Causing more confusion was going to get her out of this car faster than anything else. Except maybe them shooting her and throwing her out the door. "What you need to do is to stop this car and let me go. Whoever that was back at the café—"

"You mean your boyfriend?" the driver spit.

"Actually, I was talking about the tall guy with the gun. But yes, the agent, too." She wasn't entirely sure how to feel about referring to Eamon as her boyfriend. It seemed so…juvenile. "Who I can guarantee by now knows exactly where you're headed. You aren't getting away. Not while I'm in the car with you. Give it a few minutes." She pointed behind her. "You'll see him again."

"FBI?" The passenger lost most of the color in his face. "Um…they didn't say anything about the feds being involved."

"Shocker. Someone lied to you." And she had a pretty good idea who.

Lana scooted forward in her seat as they pulled off the road and onto the endless gravel expanse. They bumped and jostled their way over the mishmash of old train tracks, avoiding various piles of rebar, steel beams and piping for upcoming projects. "Stop the car and let me out. I'll make sure everyone knows I got in willingly. No kidnapping charges." She crossed a finger over her heart before holding up three fingers when the passenger looked back at her. "Promise. Girl Scout's honor." Total bluff. She'd never been anything close to a scout.

"Gonz, maybe we should do what she says." The driver's hands tensed on the wheel as they slowed. "They've already paid us. We can just..."

Gonz? What, had she been abducted by a pair of Muppet wannabes?

"We finish the job," Gonz said, his thick brows vee-ing over equally dark eyes. All of a sudden the two men didn't look much like men, but rather overgrown kids who were in way over their heads. "As soon as we ditch the fed, we take our cash and make a run for the border to Mexico."

"You aren't going to ditch the fed." They were giving her a migraine.

"Yes, we are. We already have..." Gonz twisted around in his seat again, looked out the back window. "I don't believe it. She's right. He's still back there. Hack, I thought you said we lost them."

"He's giving you space," Lana said quietly. "To give me time to show you the error of your ways. From what I can see, the job was simply to watch and report. Right? Look—" Lana began as they hit another rail and she bounced high enough to hit her head on the roof. "Ow." She pressed a hand against the top of her head and grabbed the box before it slid to the floor. "Okay, that hurt. You two aren't in anything you can't get out of right now. Trust me. I know. I'm a cop."

"Disgraced cop, from what we heard," the driver said.

"Nice." Lana smirked. "What's your name, Hatch?"

"Hack." He glanced over his shoulder. "Short for Hacksaw."

"You wish," Gonz snort-laughed as they hit another bump that sent both Lana and the box beside her into the air once more.

"Leave that alone," Gonz snapped as Lana pushed the box back against the passenger seat. "That's ours."

"Let me guess," Lana said. "Your payment? How much is my life and privacy worth?" Hand-delivered this morning right out in the open where anyone could have seen. Her heart skipped a beat. Where anyone could and did see. She ran her finger over the cellophane tape holding the lid closed. "Were you supposed to be paid in cash?"

"Didn't think so," Hack said, glancing back before he had to take a hard right to avoid another stacked set of rails. "Thought it was going to all be online. We set up a new account and everything."

"Would you shut up!" Gonz ordered.

"Sure." She pried up a corner of the tape and pulled it back. "I bet you did." Resting the box on her legs, she removed the rest of the tape. The two sides popped open. Without taking the lid off fully, she could see the red light of a digital timer counting down. She closed her eyes, forced herself to take a deep breath. "Stop the car."

"We've been through this already—" Gonz began,

only to stop midprotest when she opened her eyes and looked into his. "What? What is it?"

"Stop the car. Right now. Hack, stop!" Her palms went clammy as she swallowed hard.

"Stop, Hack. Stop!" Gonz yelled.

Hack slammed on the brakes. It took all Lana's effort not to scream, but she kept the box steady.

As the timer continued to tick down.

One minute fifteen seconds. Fourteen seconds... thirteen...

She looked behind them, saw Eamon and Vince barreling across the rails toward them. "We need to get out of the car." She slid the box onto the seat and sucked in a breath when the contents shifted. "Unlock the doors, Hack. For all of us."

The two men were staring blankly at the bomb packed neatly into their payment box.

"Just in case you needed more information," she said in such a tight voice she feared her throat would close, "there's enough C-4 in this box to blast you and a good portion of this rail yard into the afterlife. So by all means, please. Take your time and think about it."

Fifty-nine seconds. Fifty-eight. Fifty-seven...

"Right." Hack nodded and clicked open the locks. "Prison's better than dead." He hopped out of the car at the same time Gonz did.

She grasped the handle and opened her door. With her eyes glued to the bomb, she gently released her hold as she lifted one foot out of the car.

She heard the sound of tires over gravel ramping up behind her. "Eamon!" she yelled, hoping, praying he could hear her. "Eamon, for the love of… Stay back." She twisted and her foot caught. She landed face-first in the dirt and gravel.

In her head, she could see the clock ticking down. Forty seconds, thirty-nine…

She wrenched her foot free of the car, shoved herself up, stumbled again as she tried to catch her balance.

"Stay back!" she yelled at Eamon as he leaped out of the car and raced toward her, Vince right on his heels. "There's a bomb!"

Twenty…nineteen…eighteen.

Her feet couldn't get any traction and she slipped and shoved herself forward, fearing, knowing she wasn't going to make it clear.

She nearly tripped again, only to find herself caught by two pairs of hands that kept her upright. "Eamon."

But it wasn't Eamon. Eamon was being dragged back by Vince, who was pulling them behind the van for protection.

"Run!" Gonz yelled as he and Hack all but lifted her off the ground and put as much distance between them and the SUV as they could.

"Five…four…three…" She couldn't help but continue the countdown.

"Get down!" Eamon's voice erupted over her the instant before the car blew up.

The shock wave took the three of them down, face-first, right in a pile of jagged debris. Heat blasted over them. She couldn't hear anything but the sound of her own heart hammering so hard in her chest she felt her ribs might crack.

She had no idea how long she lay there, how long she breathed in dust and dirt, smelled the acrid stench of burning fuel, metal and plastic. Lana cried out when rough hands grabbed her shoulders and rolled her over.

"Lana!" Eamon's voice broke through her foggy thoughts faster than his face appeared in front of her. "Lana, you okay? Can you hear me?"

She shook her head, coughed as he sat her up, moved behind her and wrapped an arm securely around her.

She blinked, tears streaming from her eyes as she watched the black plumes of smoke erupting from the bank of flames.

She could hear shouting then. And sirens. And... everything. Everything in the world seemed to be lodged firmly in her ears. She plucked an ear pod free and the odd noise vanished instantly.

"I've got it." Eamon popped the other one out, pulled her back so she was sitting up straighter. "You okay?" he demanded and carefully ran his hands up and down her arms and legs as if checking for any injuries. "What about you two?" She felt him shift and reach back first for Hack, then Gonz.

"I'm okay," she choked out as an odd energy zinged through her. "That was...seriously close."

"Too close," Eamon muttered. "Here come the reinforcements," he said as a fleet of emergency vehicles and other cars headed their way. She saw Vince turn and wave his arms, motioning for them to detour to his right, before he headed toward her.

"Hey." Lana attempted to grin up at him, but had to blink a few times to put him into focus. "You found me."

"Never lost you." Vince crouched, reached out and touched a finger to her cheek, and it was then she noticed the combination of relief and concern on his usually unreadable face. "Told you we had your back." He turned his head toward Gonz and Hack as they stumbled to their feet. "Fastest turnaround from criminal to hero I've ever seen." He stood, helped haul them up as two groups of paramedics jogged over, medical kits in hand. Behind them, two squad cars, lights spinning, emptied out, followed by Cole and Jack emerging from their SUVs.

"We need to get them to the hospital," Eamon ordered.

Lana heard something in his voice, something she couldn't quite identify. Or maybe she didn't want to.

"That bomb was meant for them," she whispered, in part due to her raw throat. "It was the package we saw delivered from the van." She pulled her legs in under her, but didn't get the chance to even try to stand. Eamon scooped her up into his arms. "Ah, jeez, Eamon. Don't do this. I can walk."

"I'm not talking to you right now."

"Yes, you are." Her attempt at humor was greeted by a steely-eyed glare. Because he seemed to need it, because she needed it, she lifted her arms around his neck and buried her face against him. "Don't be angry with me, Eamon. It's not even ten a.m."

"The way I'm feeling right now, I'll probably be angry until the end of time." He began to walk, bypassed the EMTs and took her straight to the back of one of the ambulances. "You got into that car. After I specifically told you not to."

"Funny how I have my own mind." She clung to him even after he set her on the edge of the back of the open ambulance. "I couldn't take the chance the guy with the gun wouldn't hurt anyone."

"But you had no problem risking yourself."

"It's the job," she shot back and was rewarded by a hacking, lung-searing coughing fit. One of the EMTs, a young blonde woman with a pixie cut, placed an oxygen mask over her mouth. Lana took a few deep breaths before she shoved it aside. "I'd never have forgiven myself if something happened to any of those people, Eamon."

He stood beside her, rested a hand on the back of her head and drew her against his chest. "I know. You were more than willing to die for all of them."

She nodded, reveled in the feel of the fabric of his shirt against her cheek.

"I do have one question for you. Before they take you off to the ER."

She shook her head, pushed back. "I don't want—"

"I don't care what you want at this moment." He bent over, his face so close to hers she could feel his breath, as hot as the fire that continued to burn in the distance. "You're so willing to die for strangers. I want to know, I need to know, if you are just as willing to live." He cupped her face in the palm of his hand. "For me."

She had no doubt, not in that moment at least, that he could see into her very soul. "I—"

"Don't answer now." He pressed his mouth to hers.

She tasted her own tears when he pulled away. "Think about it first. Because if the answer is yes, I plan to hold you to it."

Chapter 11

"Yes, sir, I'm certain Agent Barbosa will lead the team just as well, if not better, than I could at the moment." Eamon paced his way around the perimeter of the ambulance bay of the emergency room of Mercy General. Besides the chaos around him, the cell reception inside was horrific. Although chaos suited his state of mind at the moment. "I'm happy to assist where I can from a distance."

"Assist with what?"

He glanced over his shoulder, keeping a rein on the irritation that surged through his system. Eamon cupped his phone against his chest and glared at Lana. "Aren't you supposed to be on a gurney?"

Her eyes narrowed, but before she responded, the muffled sound of his boss's voice had Eamon lifting the phone again. "Yes, sir. I appreciate the update. I'll check in soon." He pocketed his cell. "It's not enough you semi-assaulted a former CIA operative a few hours ago in a coffee shop. Now you've broken out of the hospital."

"I didn't break—I walked. And why does it take longer to discharge you from the emergency room than it does to be examined?" She straightened the sweatshirt that one of the patrol officers had passed along to her at the scene. "I'm fine. And I know the doctor already told you."

Oh, the doctor had told him all right. Apparently countless scrapes, bruises, heat burns and a minor sprained ankle weren't cause for hospital admission, despite Eamon's plea to the contrary. What he wouldn't give to have her put under lock and key, preferably with a guard on her door.

"Vince is on his way to pick us up."

Lana had refused to let him ride in the ambulance with her. After he and Vince gave their statements and handed Gonz and Hack off to the sheriff's department, he'd had a quick conversation with Lieutenant Santos, who was not thrilled to be called to yet another fire-related incident connected to Lana. Vince dropped him off at the hospital before he headed home to check in and switch vehicles. Since then, he'd spent his time pacing, catching up on emails and getting thoroughly acquainted with Mercy General's spotty reception.

"Do we need to make a break for it before an orderly comes after you?"

"I'm fine." Her limp was barely noticeable as she moved toward him. "They've got their hands full with actual sick people. What's going on? They call you back on a case?"

"They wanted to." He spotted a small park bench across the lot by the exit. "Let's get you off that ankle."

"If I have to say I'm fine one more time I'm going to slug you in your badge." She touched a hand to his arm. "New case? Ongoing?"

"Doesn't matter. It's being taken care of."

"You're still angry."

"Now, why would I be angry?" Even now the terror he hadn't felt in more than twenty years pressed in on him. Until today, he hadn't thought anything could rival the uncertainty and fear Chloe's murder had triggered. But that was before Lana had nearly gotten herself blown to smithereens. "You did what you thought needed doing."

"Yes, I did." The steadiness in her voice only irritated him further. "The same thing you would have done in my position."

"Don't be so sure."

"But I am sure. I know what you're going to say, Eamon." Her breathy voice, the rush of words—he could tell she'd been rehearsing what to tell him. "I could feel you radiating tension all the way back in my partition. And thanks, but I'm not going to sit down, because once I do, I won't want to get up anytime soon."

"Lana—"

"Don't." She turned on him, rested her hands on his chest. "Don't keep dwelling on the what-ifs. Believe me, it's only going to make things worse."

He looked at her, unable to see anything other than

the red splotches from the heat burns and the scrapes on her face and neck. The barely-there evidence of something worse that could have happened.

"There's no need for an I-told-you-so, or a lecture on not following orders. For the record, I... Oh."

He dipped his head and kissed her. A kiss devoid of the anger and fear that had been building up over the past few hours. A kiss he'd never anticipated giving, especially not so publicly and impulsively. It was a kiss that, he hoped, would silence and comfort him and, maybe, if he was lucky, begin to restore his equilibrium.

"Okay." She curled her fingers into the fabric of his shirt when he lifted his head. "Have to admit, I didn't see that coming."

"Me either." He rested his forehead against hers, closed his eyes and, for a moment, reveled in the knowledge that she was alive, that she was safe and that she was in the one place he wanted her: his arms.

"I thought for sure I was going to have to wear you down in order to get you to do that."

He smiled in spite of his still-unsteady emotions. "I'm about to say something that will probably tick you off, but I need to get it out."

"Okay." Her voice was slightly muffled by his shirt, as she'd pressed her face against him.

"Don't ever do anything like that again."

"Eamon." He felt her entire body tense, from the top of her spine all the way down to her toes. But when she leaned her head back and gazed at him, there was nothing but understanding in those amazing depths. Along with the barest hint of humor. "I can't promise that."

"You could try."

"It's not just that I can't." She shook her head. "I don't want to. I haven't felt this alive, this useful, this *capable*, since before Marcus died. It's like I spent the past two years in this unbreakable fog, but when I was in that hallway near the bathroom, when I had to make that split-second decision, it all came back. That adrenaline rush, that going on instinct. An instinct that, for the first time in a long time, I felt as if I could actually trust." She reached up, flattened her palms on either side of his face and tugged his mouth down to hers for another kiss. "You gave me that. A chance at redemption. All the rest of it—the mistakes you think I may have made—"

"The mistakes you *did* make."

"No. There were no mistakes." The certainty, the confidence he'd been looking for ever since he'd first seen her sitting in the Brass Eagle waiting for him at that table, it was all back and seemingly, amazingly, firmly in place. He didn't know whether to be relieved...or worried. He was on the precipice of getting everything he'd ever wanted: her. Was he about to lose her because she'd found her true self again?

"I really am trying not to dwell on what-ifs myself," she said. "But what if I hadn't gotten into that SUV when I did, Eamon? What if I'd gone out the front door instead and that car remained parked there? Because that was the plan. They were told to follow me and stay put. In that alley behind the café."

"Lana—"

"There were dozens of people inside. Families. Babies."

Her brow creased, as if she could envision the horror of a different result. "They could have all been killed when that bomb went off. I'm not going to regret preventing that from happening."

"I know you're right." It hurt to admit, but he owed it to her. He didn't want her to think, for one second, that he wasn't proud of her, even if she had scared a good ten years off his life. "As an FBI agent, I don't have an argument to make. But as the man who…" He stopped himself from saying the words, but not fast enough he didn't see the shock in her eyes. "I guess I'm just going to have to get used to you being a badass again."

"I guess you are." She kissed him for a second time, smiled against his mouth when a horn honked. "I think that's Vince."

"Yeah." He tightened his arms around her before he released her. "Slade texted a little while ago. Since we missed our appointment with them at the hotel, he and his boss are waiting for us at the Brass Eagle. I think we're about to get read in on the story behind A&O Solutions."

"It's about time." She slid her hand down his arm, slipped her fingers through his and held on. "We okay?"

He nodded and squeezed her hand. "We're okay."

He might not have said the words, but she'd heard them. At least, Lana wanted to think she had, but the truth was, she was afraid she was reading too much into the moment between them. Between the adrenaline rush and subsequent crash, she suspected she could sleep for a week. It wasn't every day a woman saw her entire life—past, present and potential future—flash before her eyes.

Her stomach growled so loud once they entered the kitchen of the Brass Eagle that she made Vince laugh and take pity on her. He detoured to have his kitchen staff get them some food while she and Eamon made their way to where Slade was sliding out of a booth by the window.

She'd only met Slade Palmer once at dinner the previous night. If she hadn't, she might not have recognized him. Gone were the casual jeans and T-shirt that put most of his tattoos on display. Instead, this man was in full professional mode, right down to the sharply pressed dark slacks and crisp button-down shirt. The laptop he had open on the table was housed in a briefcase and reminded her of the kind of thing she saw in spy movies.

"You two sure know how to start the day with a bang," Slade said.

"How long did it take you to come up with that one?" Eamon said as they shook hands.

"Longer than I'd like to admit. Heard you had a close call." Slade brushed a hand over her shoulder. "Glad you're okay."

"Thanks."

"This is my boss, Aiden McKenna. He owns Minotaur Security."

The man seated across from him got to his feet, turned and offered his hand. He rivaled Eamon in height and build, but where Eamon was red-haired and fair, this man's hair was so dark it had shimmers of blue, and those green eyes of his were as sharp as broken bottle glass. There was a punch of attractiveness about him that Lana suspected had left many swooning in his wake. "Pleasure to meet the woman who knocked one of my best men down a few pegs. I'm going to have to add coffee defense training to my employees' schedule."

"My apologies to... Boris, was it?" Lana said.

"I will pass them along." Aiden straightened. "I'll also add my sentiments to Slade's. Happy to see you're both all right."

"McKenna." Lana frowned, trying to place the name. She glanced back at Eamon. "Any relation to the Boston police commissioner?"

"Only slightly." Aiden's lips curved. "She's my mother."

Lana's mind raced. The man was still looking at her with nothing less than approval and acceptance. Maybe Commissioner McKenna hadn't shared anything about their previous experience.

"Well, that explains that," Eamon said as he accepted the greeting. "We heard through the grapevine Commissioner McKenna was sending her best man to talk with us."

"Is that what she said?" Aiden straightened his shoulders. "I'll have to be sure to mention that when I see her for dinner next month. And time it for when my siblings are in earshot."

"Great. Now you probably started a family feud," Lana teased Eamon and did her best to bury her nerves. "Are you guys hungry?" She gestured back to the kitchen, where she and Eamon had ordered what was becoming their standard burger fare.

"We grabbed something on the way over, actually," Slade said and, after a nod from Aiden, held out his hand. "Lana, would you mind giving me your cell phone?"

"My phone? Why?" Even as she asked, she pulled her cell out of the back pocket of her jeans.

As soon as he had it, Slade plugged it into his laptop, typed something in, scanned the screen. "Yes, it's like you thought."

"What thought?" Lana asked. "What's going on? What did you find on my phone?"

"We'll get to that," Aiden told her before he produced what looked like a cell phone charger. He set it on the window ledge, flipped a small switch on the side.

"What is that? A signal jammer?" Eamon asked. "I haven't seen one that small before."

"Perks of the trade," Aiden said.

"You're saying my cell is bugged?" Lana asked. "It hasn't been out of my sight in months."

"There are multiple ways to track someone these days," Slade reminded her. "Or to hack into their devices."

"You being tracked would explain an awful lot, Lana," Eamon suggested.

"Awesome. For the record, this conversation is already ranking at the bottom of my desired activities list for the day. And I almost got myself blown up this morning." Lana tugged off her sweatshirt and hung it on the hook on the back of the booth while Eamon dipped behind the bar and came back with a water for her and a filled mug of coffee for himself. She glared at him as she waved him into the booth and slid in next to him.

"You really want liquid caffeine right now?" he asked.

She didn't answer but took a large gulp of her water. Before she sat down, she'd felt as if she hadn't had anything to eat in months. She'd been famished. Now? Eamon's thigh pressed against hers, sending her thoughts into a completely different arena. There was nothing like almost dying to remind you to live.

"Vince filled us in," Slade said as Vince appeared with a plate of onion rings and a trio of dipping sauces. Rather than returning to the kitchen, the private investigator grabbed a chair and planted himself at the end of the table.

"On what he could, at least," Aiden added.

"Sac police took the two men into custody," Eamon told them after giving them a quick rundown. "From what I hear, they're not holding anything back on the details."

"Let me guess," Aiden said. "Local guys. More brawn than brains. Questionable history with the law. Contacted online, supposed payout, also online, from a company that dead-ends about two shell companies in?"

Aiden made it sound as if what had happened this morning was an everyday occurrence. "They were smart enough to stop the car when they saw the bomb." Lana reached for a still-hot ring and submerged half of it into the house-made ranch before biting in. "But yeah, from what I gathered, they were in it for a quick buck. I wouldn't call them harmless exactly, but—"

"They came through in the end." Eamon reached his hand under the table and took a hold of hers. "I don't think it would require much to convince them to testify against A&O Solutions."

Slade and Aiden exchanged looks.

"What?" Lana asked.

"There are about a half dozen shell companies in between these two and A&O. It's something, but it's not anything we can build a solid case on. A&O has their business locked down so tight not even oxygen gets out. I bet right now they're already severing any ties with the shell that hired these two. Or at least that's the way it used to be." Aiden reached into a soft-sided briefcase Lana had missed before. He pulled out a stack of file folders, set them in front of him, along with a tablet computer that was already on. "There's a reason I came out here instead of passing this information to Slade over the phone." Aiden rested a hand on the top file. "What I'm about to share with you needs to be kept strictly confidential. For the foreseeable future, at least."

Vince glanced up at one of his servers who was re-filling coffees. The young woman's eyes went wide at Aiden's comment.

"Hold off on the food for a little while, Maya, please?" Vince said even as Lana's stomach growled. "I'll give you a heads-up when we're ready."

"Sure thing, boss." She hurried back into the kitchen, no doubt to share what she'd overheard.

"You want to take this upstairs, where it's more private?" Eamon offered.

"No," Aiden said. "This'll be fine." His eyes flickered to the cell phone he'd set near Eamon's shoulder at the window. The screen displayed the area behind him, giving him a wide field of vision outside.

Lana kept her expression passive as her mind raced. Until this moment, she hadn't considered there might be a replacement crew keeping an eye on her. Unless... unless she wasn't the only one Aiden was worried about.

"For the record, I was a little freaked out before," she admitted. "Now you're starting to scare me."

"Told you she was paying attention," Slade said to Aiden, who nodded in what Lana interpreted as approval. "You're on, Aiden."

Lana dropped her gaze to her cell lying dormant on the table, hooked up to what she assumed at this point was some kind of technological life support. Under the table, she squeezed Eamon's hand. Why did she feel as if she was about to take a massive dip down one huge drop of a roller coaster?

"I'm a rip-the-bandage-off-the-skin kinda guy, so I'm just going to jump in," Aiden said. "A little over three years ago, based on a reliable tip, the Department of Justice opened an investigation into A&O Solutions for a variety of crimes including, but not necessarily limited to, money laundering, corporate espionage, blackmail, conspiracy..." Aiden hesitated. "Murder."

"You can't be serious." Lana had guessed right—that coaster drop robbed her of breath. "You're suggesting A&O Solutions is what? Some kind of front for organized crime?"

"It's not a suggestion, Lana," Aiden said. "It's a fact. They've been operating in this vein almost since the company was established back in the eighties. They have their hands in everything. And not just in this country. All over the world."

"That human trafficking ring I was investigating last year? The one my cousin got caught up in?" Slade said to Eamon. "Aiden's seen evidence that suggests A&O had a hand in the initial financing of their operation."

"I can't believe this." Lana could only stare as a buzzing roared in her ears. "There has to be some mistake." Even as the protest escaped, she knew it wouldn't go anywhere. Information like this wouldn't be shared, however limited, if there wasn't irrefutable evidence of its validity. "Forget the fact Marcus never would have been involved in anything illegal. I've been to Christmas parties with these people," she said. "Office events, baby showers! Heck, a whole group of us went to Bermuda... What you're accusing them of makes it sound as if they're operating like something out of a bad spy movie."

"Lana, let him present his case," Eamon urged before he turned his attention back to Aiden. "I'm sor—"

"Don't apologize for me," Lana snapped and attempted to tug her hand free, but he hung on. "It's not the last four years of your life they're calling into question."

"That's not what they're doing." Eamon's jaw tensed. "Is it?"

Lana's stomach sank when neither Aiden nor Slade answered. "You'll let me know if I need a lawyer, yeah?" Between this revelation and her cell phone, she was beginning to wonder.

"I think we need to hear what they have to say," Vince said in a clear attempt to play peacemaker. "I've started picking up some government contract work, and while I'm sure my contacts and connections aren't nearly as good as yours," he said to Aiden, "I haven't come across anything about an investigation like this. Or about A&O itself."

"Good." Aiden nodded. "That means the wall of silence is holding. This entire thing is as high up as it can go. But that doesn't mean A&O isn't aware of it. They've got their own connections, their own operatives, everywhere. It's one of the reasons they've survived as long as they have. Secrecy isn't just a job requirement at A&O Solutions. It's a creed."

"Sounds like some weird secret society to me," Lana muttered. "One with a major profit margin."

"Clearly A&O isn't the only one with connections," Eamon said. "You found out about it, Aiden."

"It took calling in just about every favor I was owed." Aiden didn't blink. "I've got ten years with the Secret Service behind me and I left on relatively good terms." A hint of regret flashed in his eyes. A quick flash, but it was there. "That's always afforded me some significant goodwill. In the three years it's taken me to build Minotaur into what it is, I've been lucky and rarely missed a step. But when I started asking questions about A&O Solutions? I got major pushback. Pushback I've never experienced in all of my professional life. I'm not downplaying it when I say my reputation meant absolutely nothing where A&O was concerned. After seeing what little evidence my contacts were willing to share, I understand now why they literally suspect everyone of possibly being connected to them in one way or another. Even me."

"Just to expound on that," Slade said. "He's not joking about his standing in the business. His reputation was good enough to lure me into the private sector after how I parted ways with the FBI. Don't think I would have done that for anyone else. No offense," he added to Vince, who shrugged it off.

Lana glanced at Eamon, silently asking him what Slade's story was. "I'll tell you later," he answered.

"All this is to say that the information Aiden has is credible, Lana," Slade said. "He wouldn't be here if he didn't believe in it. And he wouldn't be taking a chance telling you if he didn't think the two of you could be trusted. Listen, please. It's important you let him tell you what he knows."

"Fine. Yeah, okay." Now it was Lana who shrugged, and as she did, she had the sickening feeling her life had just taken a significant turn.

"Eamon requested Cynthia Randolph's accident report and autopsy results."

"You did?" Lana asked.

"I did." Eamon accepted the file Aiden handed over. Lana leaned closer and scanned the information along with him.

"Her car is still being processed by Boston authorities," Aiden said. "But the DOJ has assigned a special forensics team to the lab. Last I heard, they hadn't found any evidence of tampering, but they're taking their time. If something's there, they'll find it."

"'Cause of death—blunt force trauma,'" Eamon read.

"Poor girl." Lana's stomach twisted around the onion rings she suddenly regretted eating. "She was really sweet. Innocent, you know? Smart, talented, dedicated. Marcus adored her. Whatever the report ends up saying, it can't be a coincidence she died after I spoke with her." She hesitated. "After she gave me Marcus's client list." Her heart skipped a beat. A list that, if what Aiden and Slade said was true, could very well be an investigative Holy Grail. But one that might set off cataclysmic alarms and fallout. "Eden." She grabbed Eamon's arm. "Eamon, Eden has that list. We have to get it back, make sure no one knows—"

"Way ahead of you, Lana," Aiden said.

"Eden reached out to me the other day," Slade said. "Looking for help with some information she'd found on the list. That's why I called Aiden. Something didn't seem right, and as soon as I mentioned Marcus and A&O Solutions—"

"Suffice it to say, Eden is fine," Aiden said, cutting him off. "I've already assigned one of my protection teams to Detective Delaney's family, and another two teams are watching the building and its other occupants."

Lana, thinking of the very pregnant Greta Renault, breathed a little easier. "Okay. That's good to know."

"No one's going to get anywhere near anyone in that building," Aiden assured her. "We aren't taking any chances with the lot of you. Especially after this morning. My guess? A&O has had someone watching you for months."

"Longer." Suddenly all those unexpected visits and

inquisitive calls from Felice made sense. "I should have been more careful. Certainly more cautious. If I had been, maybe Cynthia—"

"I told you not to blame yourself," Eamon said.

"Don't—"

"Eamon's right. Don't blame yourself." Aiden's tone had a bit of a military clip to it. "Cynthia worked for A&O Solutions, Lana. She was on borrowed time and her expiration clock started ticking as soon as Marcus was killed. Speaking of Marcus, I need to ask you questions about him and his work."

"Ask whatever you want," Lana said with a shrug. "But like I told Eamon, we didn't talk about his work very much." If all they were telling her was true, she finally began to understand why. Even as she started to question everything she knew about the man she'd married.

"What do you know?" Slade asked.

"He was recruited out of college, thanks to Felice Covington. She'd sponsored him through school, helped him get financing, housing, stuff like that. Then he went to law school and straight to work for A&O. He was already head of their legal department when we met four, almost five years ago."

"You met in Seattle?"

"Yeah. He was there scouting spaces for a possible satellite office that never opened. I stopped for a drink with my partner at the time and Marcus chatted me up at the bar. We went out to dinner the next night, and it took off from there." The sentimentality of those memories was quickly becoming tarnished under the weight of reality. "He was the first guy I'd met who wasn't intimidated that I was a cop." He'd told her countless times it was one of the things he loved most about her— her independence and down-to-earth mentality. Doubt circled like a bloodthirsty shark and she braced herself, holding her breath in anticipation of Aiden telling her that her meeting—and marrying—Marcus had been some kind of setup.

"But you didn't talk about his business that much?"

"Hardly ever. When something was bothering him, I guess, but he never let things get to him very much." She was beginning to second-guess everything. Everything about Marcus. Everything about their life together.

"How about a man named Felix Sorento?" Slade asked. "Did Marcus ever mention him?"

"Sure." She breathed a bit easier and glanced at Eamon. "He was the A&O board member who died while on vacation with his family in Japan. It was a heart attack, I think?" That pool of dread was expanding inside her. "Why? What does Felix Sorento have to do—"

"Felix Sorento was the man who tipped off the DOJ about A&O Solutions. He was going to be their main witness in the case," Aiden said.

"Sorento was a whistleblower?" She balked. "You're kidding. No, of course you aren't kidding," she said quickly. "Sorry. Stupid question. I don't know why I keep doing that." She winced as she wished she'd just let whatever truth they were on the verge of uncovering be buried with Marcus. "What made him turn on A&O?"

"There was a young woman, Julia Conti…" Aiden paused when Lana nodded. "You knew her?"

"Yes, actually. Marcus hired her. She worked at A&O for a few years. There was a gas leak in her apartment building and she...died." Lana swallowed hard. "It wasn't an accident, was it?"

"DOJ reinvestigated. No," Slade said. "It wasn't an accident."

"Sorento and Conti had been having an affair for months. A few weeks after her death, Sorento made the approach to DOJ, said he was convinced Conti had been killed because of something she'd seen or heard at the company headquarters."

"Marcus was devastated by her death," Lana whispered. "I'd never seen him so shaken before. It was the one time he refused an assignment. He let someone else make the arrangements for her funeral."

"Sorento agreed to give testimony about the company's business practices and their suspected criminal dealings in exchange for immunity and relocating him and his family. It took years to work out the details, and during that time he continued collecting information on A&O and passing it off to his contact at DOJ. He was due to testify the week after his trip to Japan."

"The rabbit hole just gets deeper. This whole thing..." Lana broke off, took a deep breath. "Okay, I'm just going to ask. What does any of this have to do with Marcus specifically?"

Slade exchanged a look with Aiden, a look she herself had used multiple times when questioning witnesses. Or suspects.

Was that where this was going? But hadn't they already said they didn't suspect her of being involved with

A&O? She pulled her hand free of Eamon's and wiped her suddenly damp palms hard against her thighs. "If you want to hook me up to a lie detector, do it," she said. "I have nothing to lose and nothing to hide. Ask whatever it is you want to ask." At this point she was ready for anything.

"All right," Aiden said slowly. "When did you first hear about Felix Sorento?"

"Not until Marcus got the call that he'd died." She cast desperate eyes to Slade, then to Eamon. "It was at two, maybe three in the morning? We joked about me usually being the one who got the midnight calls. He got on a flight later that day."

"I don't suppose you remember the exact date he left?" Slade asked.

"I do, actually." An odd sensation began swirling inside her. Something cold. Chilling. Ominous. She lifted her hand to grip the key and wedding bands hanging around her neck. "It was right before our anniversary, which is on March eighteenth. I'd just caught this armed robbery–homicide case that was going to take serious overtime. I didn't think I could take even a night off to celebrate, so I was actually relieved when Marcus had to leave town a few days before then. Yeah. He flew out on the fifteenth. And before you ask, I remember because he made a joke about the Ides of March."

"And what did he say he was going for?" Aiden asked.

"To help the family. Sorento's wife and two sons were with him. Marcus was supposed to take care of all the travel arrangements, deal with the local officials. Make certain the family didn't have to worry or think about anything other than each other. Marcus even planned the funeral himself. It's what he did. He took care of people."

"Lana," Eamon said in that overly patient tone of his.

"Don't Lana me," she snapped. "It's obvious they're leading up to something that I'm either not going to like or they think I had something to do with." Whatever was coming was going to hurt.

"We do not think you're involved," Slade said. "If we did, Aiden would have suggested we hold this conversation in a more official federal setting."

"Oh, well, then happy happy joy joy." She swallowed a rush of angry tears. "That leaves option number one on the table. Just spit it out already, Aiden. What is it you think—"

"Felix Sorento didn't die on the fifteenth of March, Lana." Aiden pulled a solitary sheet of paper out of one of his folders and set it in front of her. "This is an official copy of the death certificate. As you can see, he died on the eighteenth."

She tasted bile in the back of her throat and stared at the document. It blurred for a moment before her vision cleared. "No." She touched tentative fingers to the paper. "No, that can't be right. Marcus only left Seattle on the fifteenth. I know he did."

"I don't think they're disputing Marcus's travel dates, Lana." Eamon's tone could only be interpreted as cautious. "Are you, Aiden?"

Lana ignored his hand that reached for hers. Instead, she shoved both of hers under her thighs and dug her nails into the vinyl. She couldn't explain the overwhelming urge to run that sped through her, but suddenly she felt trapped by information she couldn't seem to process. But the longer she looked at the death certificate, the deeper she felt she was falling.

"There's a logical explanation," she whispered. "There has to be. I mean, how could he have known Felix Sorento was dead before he…died?" And yet he'd told her it was a heart attack that had killed Felix Sorento. Three days before he actually did.

She looked at Eamon, but for the first time since she'd met with him in this same booth a few nights ago, she saw doubt on his face. "Eamon?" She glanced at Vince, then Slade, and finally she focused on Aiden McKenna. "What is it you're saying?"

Aiden hesitated.

"Show her," Slade said. "She has a right to know, Aiden."

Another file folder, this one in blue, was placed in front of her. Aiden flipped it open. "These photos are stills from the security feed at Tokyo's central garden. Notice the date."

She followed his finger to the bottom corner. "March eighteenth." She leaned closer. "That's Marcus." She pointed to Marcus wearing the beige trench coat she'd bought him for Christmas. He was standing off to the side with another man whose back was to the camera. Tall, lanky, with shiny dark hair. Marcus was clearly handing him something.

Slade flipped to the next picture. Same date. Same Marcus in the same coat in the same place, only the man he'd been speaking with had moved off, heading toward a small group on a guided tour of the garden. A man, woman and two young boys.

"Is that Felix Sorento?" She spoke as if from outside her body. Her ears were roaring so loudly she almost couldn't hear Aiden's response.

"Yes." He flipped to the next picture showing Marcus's companion walking past, directly behind Sorento, his right hand raised.

The next photo showed Sorento pitched over, clutching his left arm. The final image was of Sorento on the ground, his family and garden employees hovering. She shifted through the rest, the images coming together like a kind of macabre flip-book. Marcus's companion circled back, before the two walked off in the opposite direction and out of sight.

"The cause of death was correct. Sorento did die of a heart attack," Aiden said. "He'd had a heart condition for years that he took digitalis for, but it was under control and had been for a while."

"At the request of the DOJ, a subsequent tox panel was performed," Slade said. "It confirmed what the DOJ suspected. Felix Sorento was poisoned. An overdose of oleander caused the heart attack."

"Oleander." Lana felt the blood drain from her face. "You're certain it was oleander?"

Aiden nodded. "One hundred percent."

"What?" Eamon asked.

"I don't know. It could be nothing." But that wasn't the way her luck was running, was it? She cleared her throat, attempted to put her thoughts in order even as panic threatened to cut off her air. "Neither Marcus nor

I had a lot of time for hobbies," she choked out. "But Marcus, one of the reasons he loved the house we bought was because of the greenhouse in the backyard. He liked to garden." She raised terrified eyes to Aiden and Slade. "He had an affinity for medicinal plants, even dangerous ones. Foxglove. Pennyroyal. Dogbane. He had a bunch of books on their historical uses, how they were cultivated. I've been trying to…keep them all alive since he died. They were the only things he really paid much attention to other than me. I'm terrible with them, but I couldn't just let them… There must be seven or eight oleander plants."

She shoved the photos away, rested her head in her hands.

"I know this is difficult to hear," Aiden started.

"That the man I was married to for three years was actually moonlighting as a floral hit man for a crime syndicate?" She dropped her arms on the table and looked at him. "What makes you think that would be hard to hear?"

"He might have planned it…" Eamon rested a hand on her back and she hated that her initial reaction was to shake him off. "But he didn't do the killing himself."

"Really?" She could feel the tears burning behind her eyes, but she was determined not to let a solitary one fall. "Semantics? You really think that was candy he was handing off to that guy? Looked like a hypodermic needle to me."

"That was the official assessment, actually," Aiden said. "But Eamon makes a fair point, and it was one Slade and I considered before we came here to speak with you. We don't think Marcus was a hit man necessarily."

"Oh, good." She patted a hand against her chest. "What a relief."

"You know what a fixer is, right?"

"They specialize in taking care of certain types of problems for the people who can afford them," Eamon said. "They're like corporate caretakers who are sent out to solve potential issues, prevent scandals. Cover up wrongdoings."

"Stop witnesses from talking to the Department of Justice," Vince added. "Fixers make sure the rich and powerful aren't held responsible for their actions."

"The best ones tend to know their way around the justice system. Being a lawyer would definitely be a bonus," Aiden said.

"So Marcus wasn't a killer—he was just someone who provided the weapons and opportunity." She didn't have any energy left with which to fight. "The distinction, while negligible, is noted." Lana turned her head, lowered her voice before it broke. "Can I have the key to your apartment, please, Eamon?"

"Sure." He pulled it out of his pocket. "I can come with—"

"No." She shoved out of the booth, knocking her knees against Vince's chair. "No, I'd rather be sick in private, thanks. I'll…" She'd what? She honestly didn't know what she was going to do other than put one foot in front of the other, which she managed to do.

The nausea intensified in that all-too familiar post-drunk way, only instead of cloudy, vague regrets, she had the abject terror of realization swirling through her system. She was a cop. A decorated one who had been admired. It was all she'd ever wanted to be.

Justice. Law and order. Right and wrong. It had all been crystal clear to her since before she'd first stepped foot into the academy, and yet...

And yet she'd married a man who had apparently been an integral cog in the organized crime wheel that turned not only within the confines of the United States, but all over the world.

What was worse than that?

She had no trouble believing it was true. And that was the truly sickening part.

He wasn't the man she thought he was. How could he be and be responsible for what she'd seen in those photos? And she had seen it. In his eyes. Even from a distance, she'd seen the detached determination, the flash of, what—approval?—when the deed was done.

Lana dived up the stairs, taking them two at a time to the third floor; her hands shook as she shoved the key into the lock. She stumbled into the apartment and hit the bathroom floor on all fours, just in time to empty her stomach of its meager contents into the toilet.

She heaved and choked and cried until her ribs and throat ached. When she sat back and swiped her cheeks she did so with an anger and ferocity that left her skin raw.

The rage coursing through her, the anger at the fact that every single thing Aiden McKenna had told and shown her fit the puzzle she'd been trying so hard to put together. She couldn't argue with any of it. Not one little bit. Everything Marcus had ever been about had been a lie.

A lie she'd bought into, hook, line and sinker.

Fury shoved her to her feet. Determination had her cleaning up and throwing cold water on her face, brushing her teeth and pushing herself out of the bathroom and into the open space of Eamon's apartment.

She stood there, chest heaving as she tried to grab hold of some thread of decency about the man she'd been married to. The man she should have seen through.

"What a fool I was. How could I have been so naive?" She'd never once questioned. Never once believed he was anything other than who he portrayed himself to be. And none of it, not one word he'd spoken to her, had been true. "Why me?" She stared at the window. "Why did he have to pick me?" Was it the challenge of her being a cop? Or was it some kind of assignment from his employer, a way to keep an ear on the rumblings within law enforcement so they could be ready when and if the government came calling?

The very idea had her doubling over, crouching into a ball, until she braced her hands on the floor, head bent over her knees. When she opened her eyes, the necklace hung free, and the key pendant and wedding bands she'd kept safe these last months dangled and shimmered in the afternoon sun streaming through the blinds.

She gripped the chain in one hand, ripped it over her head and, as she stood back up, tossed it onto the kitchen table before striding over to the cabinets. This time she knew where to find it and she did. The bottle of Scotch felt cool and comforting in her hand.

The empty glass she dragged down clattered onto the counter that she rested her hands on before she bent over, her forehead brushing the polished marble edge.

The temptation and promise of absolute oblivion, of erasing the pain slicing through her, throbbed so painfully she nearly sobbed. Without looking, she grabbed hold of the bottle, focused on the feel of it against her palm as she found herself silently begging for the strength to stop.

"Lana."

She squeezed her eyes so tight stars exploded behind them.

"He lied to me." The loathing in her voice shocked her. "Every single day, simply by existing, he lied to me. He was a killer. A manipulator. A user. And I didn't see it." She turned her head, looked at Eamon standing there, so tall and handsome and strong, in the doorway of his makeshift home. Looking at her with so much understanding, the shame ripped through her like a tidal wave. "I didn't see anything except what he wanted me to see. No wonder I broke as a cop. He broke me."

"Not possible." Eamon barely made a noise as he walked across the room to stand beside her. He didn't touch her. Didn't move the glass. Or the bottle. Nor did he pull her hand free of the death grip that numbed her fingers.

He simply rested a hand on her forearm, his gentle fingers offering a moment of comfort she couldn't help but think she didn't deserve.

"I can't tell you not to take that drink."

"Sure you can," she whispered and choked on a laugh.

"All right, then. I won't." He moved closer, until the

warmth of his body began to ease the chill of hers. "You're the only one who can make that decision, Lana. But you and I both know that nothing you're holding on to right now is going to make any of this better."

The tears she'd fought against so hard emerged once more. She struggled to keep them from falling, but instead she saw the tears splash onto the floor. "I don't want to drink." But the desire, the bone-deep yearning that felt like another entity surging inside her, slapped back, a challenge she either had to surrender to or triumph over.

She stood up, knowing she could step back and Eamon would put the bottle in the cabinet, along with the glass. But it wasn't up to him to do this. It was up to her.

Eamon released his hold as she picked up the bottle and took a step around him to the sink, where she emptied the Scotch straight into the drain. "I'll reimburse you," she said in a futile attempt at humor. When the final glug of alcohol spilled out, she let the bottle clatter in the sink as he turned her into his arms. She rose up on her toes, locked her arms around his neck as he held on, his arms the only thing that felt real. Lana buried her face in his neck, inhaled the male scent of his aftershave, lost herself in the feel of his skin against hers.

"You were right. Holding that bottle wasn't going to make it better," she whispered. "But holding on to you does."

"I think that's the nicest thing you've ever said to me." He turned his head, pressed his mouth against the side of her neck. "I know this is the last thing you want to hear right now, and it's probably the absolute worst time to tell you, but I'm going to say it." He pulled back, just enough to look into her eyes, to lift a hand to her face and stroke her cheek. "I love you. Trust might be in short supply for you right now, but I think I'm pretty good in that department where you're concerned. If you can't believe anything else right now, believe me. I love you."

She felt the doubt circling once more, attempting to grab hold, to convince her she had no right believing anything anyone ever said to her again, and yet...

She couldn't imagine going through these last days without him. These last hours. The last few minutes. There wasn't anything else in this world that could keep her on her feet, that could keep her moving forward, like Eamon Quinn.

"Yeah," she said and smiled back at him as her eyes filled yet again. "Yeah, you're quite reliable with the truth." It should have come as a surprise that she had won this man's heart, and she wished, with all of hers, that she trusted herself enough to tell him she felt the same. But she couldn't. She could barely trust what she could see with her own eyes at the moment, let alone what her heart might be screaming at her.

Not yet, anyway. Not until she was finally free of the past that only now did she realize had no basis in reality. Reality...

She frowned, her mind finally skipping over the stones of betrayal as she hit on something Aiden and Slade hadn't addressed. "There's more. There has to be more." She pulled free of Eamon, stepped back, cast a cursory look to the necklace she'd thrown on the table.

"Eamon, there's a question we haven't even asked, not them, not ourselves."

"What's that?"

"Marcus." She steeled herself to step into the arena for the final battle for answers. "If he was such a vital employee, if what he did was so important for A&O Solutions, then why is he dead? Eamon, why did they kill him?"

Eamon blinked, his expression shifting from affectionate back to serious again. "That's a really good question."

"Yes, it is. And I think I know where we can find the explanation. The one place Felice couldn't get to." She stalked over to her bag, dug inside and pulled out her set of keys that included, among other things, the key to Marcus's apartment. "We need to get to Boston."

Chapter 12

Since the age of fourteen, Eamon had made it one of his primary goals to get to the end of his life without regrets. It was that mindset, and almost thirty years of focusing on that goal, that had him admitting out loud the one thing that, if said at the wrong time, could blow a hole in any hope he might have for a future with Lana Tate.

He'd known her, loved her, for more than three years, but until that moment when he walked into the apartment and found her hunched over that bottle of Scotch, he hadn't realized how desperately he'd needed to confess his feelings. Not to stop her from taking a drink. He'd been right about that—there was nothing he could do to prevent her from drinking if that was what she decided to do.

Eamon had needed to tell her because in those seconds, he truly feared he was going to lose her. Maybe for good this time.

Perhaps his timing could have been better. Admitting to being in love with her so quickly after she'd discovered the truth about her late husband's double life probably wasn't the best idea he'd ever had. She was on shaky ground where everything was concerned, let alone an awful thing so potentially wrought with complications. And no, she hadn't responded with professions of her undying affection for him. But she hadn't rejected his admission either. She hadn't run and hid or thrown it back in his face. She'd held on to him, clung to him. Accepted him.

And that, he told himself as the fog of possible regret faded away, was more than enough. For now.

The cockpit door of the private Bombardier Challenger popped open and Lana stepped out, looking surprisingly calm despite her longtime aversion to small aircrafts. She stopped at the built-in drink station, grabbed a bottle of water out of the mini-fridge, offered him one.

"Thanks." He watched, amused, as she made her way past the sofa-like seat and plopped down in front of where he was seated in one of the four leather-upholstered swivel seats. Behind them, both Slade and Vince had slept their way across the country, each stretched out in one of the other chairs, while Aiden McKenna had been plugged into his laptop and on a call with various members of his staff, checking in on current jobs and potential assignments.

"Well?" Eamon asked Lana. "Feel better about this thing now that you've spent some time in the copilot seat?"

"Let's just say I've felt worse." She slammed a death grip on the arm of the sofa when the plane did another slight shimmy. "I can't stop thinking about a friend telling me the smaller the plane, the rougher the ride."

"Trust me, this baby is as smooth as ice compared to others I've flown in." Aiden popped his earphones out and closed his computer. "I had to hand out Dramamine to my people whenever we boarded my first jet."

"Yay, progress," Lana said with a hint of a smile before her gaze drifted to the window and she looked out into the night sky. "I'll be very glad to get on the ground. The captain said we should be landing in Boston in about twenty minutes or so."

Eamon glanced at his watch. "Puts us into Boston International at around midnight local time."

"Hear that, Slade? Vince?" Aiden reached back and gave Slade's black work boots a nudge. "Little over an hour and you'll get an actual bed."

"Hallelujah." Slade stayed exactly as he had been for the past six and a half hours, legs stretched out, arms crossed over his chest.

Vince sat up, instantly wide-awake, thanks to his military training with the Marines. "Coffee." He scrubbed both hands down his face. "Need coffee."

"Help yourself." Aiden motioned to the fully decked-out espresso and coffee machine above the refrigerator.

"Make that two, please." Slade sighed and folded himself back into a seated position.

"I thought you didn't like to travel too far from home," Lana said.

"Ashley and I make exceptions for family." Slade's smile was quick but genuine enough. Gratitude surged inside Eamon. "To be honest, I think we could have filled up the plane with all the people who want to help. Apparently Eden and Cole had quite the discussion about her ability to be backup from a stationary position."

"She probably just wanted to ride in the plane," Eamon said.

"Good to know that's a temptation," Aiden said as the plane began its ear-popping descent. "She's really good on the research side of things. The work she's done on that client list you turned over is going to save DOJ a ton of time. I know she typically focuses on cold cases, but do you know if she's ever considered contract work?"

Lana's gaze jumped to Eamon's. She was thinking what he was. That Eden was looking for other employment options now that she was expecting her second baby. "I would feel safe in saying it's worth an approach," Eamon said. "Especially if there's schedule flexibility in the offering."

"Agreed." Lana stared down at her cell phone, which had been lying on the table beside Eamon's for most of the flight.

"Having second thoughts about us keeping that malware active that Felice sent to your cell with those pictures of Marcus?" Aiden asked.

"Only because I feel like the darned thing is possessed." She sighed. "I want it gone, but if we remove the program, A&O or at the very least Felice is going to know we're on to them. All the more reason to leave it turned off. Speaking of Felice, she texted me at least three times before we left California. I mentioned the apartment. Let her know it was on my mind."

"Planting the seed." Aiden nodded. "That's good."

"One thing I don't get," Eamon said. "If your assumption is right, Lana, and Marcus has something in his apartment that A&O wants, why not just go in and get it? They know the address."

"Biometrics," Lana said. "Growing up, Marcus's favorite TV show was *The Jetsons*. He was always reading up on the newest gadgets, systems. Programs. This particular apartment building is one of the first to use the Xenon Two Thousand."

"Quadruple-layered security," Aiden said at Eamon's blank look. "Key, fingerprint, personal access code, full biometric scan. And as close to a hack-proof server as I've ever encountered. Try to bump a lock in that building or use a passkey without other verification? Instant lockdown and the cops are called. It's all four or no joy. And don't get me started on the steel-plated elevators."

"Please no one tell my brother about this," Vince said. "Jason would sell his soul for a chance to hack the thing."

"I thought you said you'd never been there," Eamon said to Lana. "How will you—"

"Xenon sent out a special programming team for my print and scan. Kind of like what they do to make 3D models. I am literally the only person who can walk into that apartment."

"Makes it a darned good hiding place," Aiden agreed. "Smart."

"Also explains why you're still alive, Lana," Slade said. "They need you to get in."

Aiden smirked. "All their resources and A&O couldn't get into a simple two-bedroom apartment. Gotta love the irony."

"They lured me here," Lana said. "They wanted me to come to this place. Seems only fair I should return the favor and lure them in, too."

Eamon gnashed his back teeth together. He understood the advantage of being able to use Lana as bait for this case, but that didn't mean he had to like it. Besides, there was no faster way to tick off Lana Tate than to go all protective bodyguard on her.

"Stick close to the truth," Eamon said instead. "Just say you decided to follow her advice and came out to check the apartment before you sell. She'll take the bait."

"But wait until we've got our surveillance lined up before you respond to her text," Aiden said. "We want to make sure we've got all the angles covered."

"We've run a background check on the dozen or so other tenants in the building," Slade said. "We didn't find anyone else with any employment history with or connections to A&O Solutions. And we dug pretty deep."

"I'll take that as good news. I won't feel like I'm walking into some kind of den of thieves." Lana's repeated attempt at humor did not work on Eamon.

"We also sent a team to the building earlier this afternoon as a maintenance crew," Slade added. "We found a way to hook into the internal and external security feeds. We'll have you in sight until you get into the apartment at least."

"But not after?" Eamon asked.

"Oddly enough, there aren't any security cameras in the apartments," Aiden said. "She'll be fine, Eamon. We'll be right outside the entire time."

"So when are we going to do this?" Lana asked. "Tonight?"

"Negative," Aiden said. "Even if you hadn't had a close call this morning, it's been a long day for the rest of us. I want us coming at this with a clear and well-rested mindset. We'll assume, since your phone's been off, she won't know you're here. In the meantime, we'll get everyone checked into a hotel for the night. Don't worry," Aiden said to Eamon when he frowned. "My mother recommended it. It's a place that's been used for stashing witnesses and those in protective custody. It's also a favorite of politicians and celebrities, so the security's better than most. Trust me. It's safe. Even from A&O."

"All right," Eamon said as the lights of the airport appeared in the distance. Out of the corner of his eye, when Vince asked anyone else if they wanted coffee, Eamon noticed Lana pulling out her sobriety chip that she clasped between her hands, almost as if it were a talisman.

Uncertainty wove through him, and he opened his mouth to say something. Vince cleared his throat and, when Eamon glanced up at him, shook his head. Instead, when Vince made his way to the back of the plane, he inclined his head in a way that had Eamon getting up to follow.

"Now isn't the time," Vince murmured as Eamon joined him near one of the compartments that housed a selection of nonperishable snacks. "If she wants your help, she'll ask for it."

"You know?"

"That she's an alcoholic? She came into the bar three nights in a row, didn't drink anything other than club soda and had that chip in her hand most of the time. Plus I haven't seen her drink anything stronger than a soda. Yeah," Vince said. "I know. How long does she have?"

"Four months and change." He didn't particularly like the idea of talking about her behind her back this way, but if anyone was going to understand… "That's all I know."

"You know she's struggling," Vince said. "That's enough."

"Maybe." Eamon wasn't so sure. "It's not easy."

"Being in love with an alcoholic, even a recovering one, never is." Vince plucked out a couple of packages of trail mix and handed him one. "Just ask my wife."

"Still? But you've been sober for years." Eamon shook his head, not wanting to believe. "I've never seen you—"

"And hopefully you won't, but I'll never say never. There are periods I have to take it a day at a time. And others when it's an hour at a time. I can go months without a meeting and then something crops up that sends me right back for a refresher and reset."

"It's such a difficult road to walk," Eamon said. "And yours is even harder, owning and running a bar."

"I'm a glutton for punishment." Vince's lips twitched. "Strangely enough, it's not as hard as you'd think. It's easier when you've got some stability and people to lean on." He hesitated, as if debating to continue.

"What?" Eamon urged. If Vince's impulse was to say something, it was worth hearing. Whether Eamon wanted to or not.

"Simone started going to Al-Anon meetings when we got back together. She said she needed to understand more, and to be aware of pitfalls and triggers. I'm sure she'd be willing to sponsor you or give you information about where you can go."

Eamon looked over at Lana, who had settled back in her seat and looked a bit less stressed. "I don't want to get ahead of myself. Lana and I aren't exactly official or anything."

"Then you're the only one who doesn't see it." Vince ducked his chin. "Together or not, your feelings for her aren't going anywhere. Tackle the challenges head-on, Eamon, but don't make it the focal point of your relationship. She's far more than her disease and dependency."

Eamon let out a long breath. "Is it me, or does this feel like a really bad time to be sending her into the lion's den of A&O Solutions?"

"Maybe. Or it could be the perfect time. She's had a lot thrown at her in the last couple of years, the last few

days, but she's still standing. Still fighting. She hasn't
had a genuine safety net in a really long time, but you've
given her that. She's been alone and that can feed an ad-
diction more powerfully than any treatment can combat. If she can stay sober during the rough patches, it'll
make the good times ahead even better. All you can do
is love and support her, so long as you understand the
difference between support and enabling."

"And how do I do that?"

"By leaning on your friends." He rested a hand on
Eamon's shoulder. "I'll text Simone once we land, let
her know you'll be in touch when you get home. Take it
a step at a time, Eamon. Just one step at a time."

Lana flipped the switch on the bathroom fan and
swiped a towel across the steamed-up mirror. After
a long day and an even longer flight, she'd hoped the
state-of-the-art shower would ease the ache in her mus-
cles and siphon the stress of the day straight down the
drain.

Instead, she found herself keyed up as the promise
of what awaited her in just a few hours loomed large.
The only thing worse than the anticipation was how
antsy she'd gotten without being able to use her cell
phone. She pulled the towel off her head and tossed it
over the shower door.

"Lana?" Eamon knocked on the bathroom door.
"Aiden had room service send up something to eat. It's
ready when you are."

It was on the tip of her tongue to tell him she wasn't
hungry, but she was. She'd been too nervous to eat on

the plane. Too nervous about a lot of things. She stood in the middle of the spacious white-and-gold bathroom and wished everything could stop. Just for a little while. Long enough to catch her breath, to get her bearings and her thoughts in order.

"I'll be out in a sec." She gave herself credit for sounding utterly fine. She'd never felt this way before, as if some kind of pressure-sealed door had opened and she'd taken a step into the inevitable. The last two years, maybe the last six, had been leading her right to where she was now. Standing between what was and what could be.

What could be. She turned, pressed her fingertips against the steam-slick door. It had been a long time, too long a time, since she'd had a clear plan of action in her mind about anything.

The desire to find out the truth about Marcus's death had been planted long before it fully bloomed. But it had been there, lurking beneath her grief and loss and her self-destructive way of coping with losing him. It wasn't until she'd followed the impulse to find Eamon that she'd made progress.

It wasn't until she was with Eamon that she'd finally been able to see the reality of her life with Marcus. Lies.

It had all been lies. Who he was. What he was. Nothing Marcus had ever said to her had been the truth. How could it have been, when the biggest part of him had been something utterly abhorrent to her?

There was anger now. More anger than she knew what to do with. Some at herself for being duped for so long, but mostly anger at Marcus for not being the man she'd believed him to be.

There was no way to fix this. No way to get out from under the truth. She'd been married to a criminal who was responsible for…for offenses and horrors possibly too numerous to count.

She rubbed a hand just over the towel knotted between her breasts. How could she be standing here, thinking what she was thinking, feeling what she was feeling, given everything that had happened? How could she possibly trust herself again when it came to a man?

"Because he's Eamon." Honorable, devoted, steady Eamon. A man who had never let her down, never disappointed her. A man who had shown, long before he'd said the words, that he loved her.

She took a deep breath, abandoning the futile fight. From the start, they'd shared a connection. A connection she hadn't let herself feel or contemplate at the time for various reasons; not the least of which was that she was married. Marcus had had his suspicions, but now she had to wonder what his nonchalant, amused reaction had actually meant.

"Stop. Just…stop." Marcus didn't matter anymore. Not the way he used to. How could she mourn someone who had never existed? Instead, she made him the means to an end. An end that if they weren't careful would rob them all not only of their professional futures, but quite possibly their lives.

Lana ducked down, dug out the box of condoms Eden had packed as a "just in case" inclusion. Leaving her bag on the floor of the bathroom, Lana pulled open the door and stepped out.

The cool air from the hotel AC chilled her damp skin. She shivered, but not from cold. From the sight of Eamon Quinn standing in front of her. Alone. In their room.

"I was beginning to think maybe you'd drowned in there." Eamon had his back to her, was busy fiddling with the room service cart and the large silver domes. "When Aiden said we'd be staying in a hotel, I'd have bet most of my savings it would be a hole-in-the-wall hovel. Instead, we've got…this." He took a step back, waved his arm at the large suite they'd been given, decorated in similar gold tones to those in the bathroom. "Makes me sorry we can't enjoy…" His voice trailed off when he faced her.

The fog that crossed over his face, the quick dilation of his pupils, the slow, dazed smile that stretched his lips sent a new wave of energy zinging through her system.

"Confession time," he said.

"Oh?" She arched a brow.

"Yeah." He blew out a breath. "Of all the outfits Eden gave you, I think this one's my favorite."

"I was thinking of you when I put it on."

He didn't move. She thought it a bit strange, that a self-assured man like Eamon Quinn should be frozen in place as if she was Medusa weaving her spell.

"You know what else Eden gave me?" She held up the box.

"I don't think I've ever loved that woman more. Remind me to send her a basket of muffins or…" He stopped when Lana took a step toward him, grabbed hold of the towel knot and twisted it free. "Roses. Yeah, she's definitely earned a basket of roses. Or maybe diamonds."

Lana's lips twitched as she turned and threw the box into the bedroom behind them. "You're overdressed, Special Agent." She could feel the heat of him radiating against her as she moved closer.

"So it would seem." He glanced over his shoulder to the closed curtains at the windows overlooking Boston Harbor. "Hang on. Just…" He held up a finger, darted down the short hallway to the door and flipped the security latch. "Aiden has a key. I'm not taking any chances. Not after waiting this long." He was back at her side and hauling her into his arms in the next moment. "Tell me you're sure." His breath was hot against the side of her neck, sending chills down her spine for an entirely new reason. "Tell me this isn't me asleep on the plane having a dream."

She couldn't help it. She laughed. "Only you would think of something like that."

"Just kind of seems to be the way my luck runs where you're concerned." He straightened, caught her face between his hands and stared so deeply into her eyes she could see the reflection of his soul. "I've wanted you for so long, Lana. So long." He brushed his mouth against hers. "But it's been a really, really rough day. For both of us. If you have any doubt—"

Anger blazed afresh and she embraced it, embraced him. Locking her arms around his neck, she kissed him with every ounce of courage she held and pressed her naked, damp body against him.

Every cell in her body surged to life. Even through the fabric of his clothes the charge between them was enough to set her on fire.

"I should have showered first," he murmured against her lips.

"Later," she promised. "Together." She grinned, pulled back enough to trail a finger down to his lips and tease them apart. She felt him go instantly hard against her. "If you're a good boy."

"Challenge accepted." He bent down as he slid his hands along her bare back, over the curve of her butt. He cupped her, hauled her up, and as he began to walk to the bedroom, she locked her legs around his waist. The pressure and friction of the fabric against her core had her whimpering against his throat. It wouldn't take much, just lowering that zipper of his and…

"Hold on," he urged. "Just hold…on."

They made it as far as the door before he pressed her up against a wall, kissed her and set her entire being on fire.

It was like being caught in the beginning embers of a firestorm. Instant, intense and painfully pleasurable. The heat wove its way through her extremities, stoking in her center as she opened her mouth for him, her tongue dancing with his. She tightened her arms around him to ensure he'd not turn to ash.

She couldn't recall ever being kissed like this, as if his very life depended on his touching her, tasting her. Devouring her.

"Eamon." His name was a drug on her lips, promising ecstasy and escape even as he loosened his hold and let her legs drop to the floor. He backed away, leaving her feeling utterly abandoned and unfulfilled. "What are you—"

"Don't!" He held up a hand, walked over to the bed and pulled the sheets and comforter off the king-size mattress. On his way back to her, he stopped, picked up the box of condoms and had a foil packet out before the smile on her lips could fully form. "You didn't honestly think I was walking away."

She hadn't wanted to. But the doubt was there. Doubt she quickly shoved into the deepest corners of her singed soul. Her body tingled, desperate for his touch, and she pushed away from the wall, joining him at the bed, their bare feet tangling in the sheets that lay forgotten on the floor.

He reached down, grabbed the hem of his T-shirt, but she shook her head and slipped her hands down his arms to do it herself. She had to rise up on her toes to get the T-shirt over his head, but the instant he was free of the fabric, her hands were on his bare chest, reveling in the slight dusting of red hair covering his torso.

Lana pressed her lips against his heart, smiled at the staccato beating she took pride in being responsible for. A wave of sadness threatened to douse the flames of desire. All this time... All this time he'd wanted her and she'd committed herself to a man who had only ever lied to her.

"Lana." Eamon's voice broke through the pain. "Lana, stop thinking. Be with me. Now." He kissed her. Then again, longer, deeper. "Be with me here in this moment. Nowhere else."

She nodded, hating the tears that burned and blurred her vision. Vision she wanted filled only with him. "Yes." She reached up, slipped her hand through his hair as he turned her so her knees hit the back of the mattress. "I'm here with you, Eamon." She gazed up at him, longing for, anticipating the moment when he'd slip inside her body and claim her, heart and soul.

When she'd claim him.

"Only you."

When he let her go this time, it was only long enough to divest himself of his pants, to unwrap the foil package and cover himself. She glanced down and frowned.

"A word of advice?" Eamon said, an unfamiliar waver in his voice. "Don't ever look down at a man in this condition and frown."

She laughed, lifted her head and leaned into him. "I was only thinking how I'd wanted to do that."

"Temptress." His mouth caught hers, drew the kiss out long enough to have her moaning in anticipation and frustration. "Next time," he breathed and slid his hand down between their bodies and cupped her.

She dropped her head back, her mind spinning at the pleasure building inside her. "Not this way," she managed. "I want you inside of me." She held on to his shoulders and in one fluid move toppled both of them onto the mattress.

Before she caught her breath, he rolled onto his back and drew her over him so she straddled his hips.

His back arched as his hands came up, searching

for hers. As he filled her, she slid her fingers through his, pressing their hands together while she moved over him. The power she felt, riding this man, pushing him into the same throes of passion she now realized she'd only dreamed about, acted as a quickening, renewing her entire being to one of strength and triumph.

The buildup was slow, but more intense than she could have imagined. She stared down at him, her breathing ragged as he tightened his hold on her and tucked his chin in to meet her gaze.

"Go over," he ordered. "I want to watch you when it happens."

She tried to hold off, to extend the exquisite pleasure between her legs, inside her, but his command was one she couldn't refuse. She rocked herself hard against him, pressing down as she drew him in as deeply as she could as the climax crashed over her and she dragged him with her.

She released his hands and collapsed over him, sobbing. His arms held her tight and she relished how strong and safe she felt. "Eamon." It was all she could think to say. "Eamon, I—"

"Not now." His lips brushed against her temple.

"But I—"

"Tell me later," he whispered. "Tell me later." He turned her face to his, brushed his lips over hers once more. "After."

"After what?" Even as she asked, she felt him stir inside her. "You're kidding me." Her laughter felt as if it had been bottled up for years, only to flow free and unheeded now.

"Never about this." He slowly skimmed his fingers over her skin. Slick with sweat, it prickled beneath his touch. "Never about you."

He kissed her and started again.

Chapter 13

"Why don't you want me to tell you?"

Lana's quiet question drew Eamon out of a light sleep. For a long moment he reveled in the idea that she was, finally, in his arms. In his bed. It wasn't just a dream his subconscious had cooked up in an effort to quell his seemingly impossible desires.

He could, he thought, draw out her question to the point of teasing. He could distract her—far too easily, he knew. Or…

"Because I want you to be one hundred percent clear-headed when you tell me you love me." He reached down to pull the sheets and blanket more securely around them as he shifted her more fully against him.

Bundled up in bed with her, behind her, being able to bury his face in her hair with a mere turn of his head, knowing she was content being exactly where she was, he couldn't recall a more perfect moment in his entire life.

"What makes you think I'm not clearheaded?" Rather than anger or irritation tingeing her voice, he heard dismay, confusion and perhaps a tad bit of defiance.

"Because I wouldn't be if I was in your position."

She reached back, slid a hand down his hip. "And what position is that?"

He nuzzled her neck, hid his smile in her hair. "You had a lot thrown at you the last few days. I'm betting you can't help thinking that the years you spent with Marcus feel somewhat tainted now. I don't want your feelings for me tangled up in whatever you might be feeling about him."

She sighed. "When you say astute things, I have to wonder if you're altogether real." She drew his arms more tightly around her body, snuggled back against him. "A statement like that really should tick me off. But somehow it manages not to."

"It's a gift." His cell phone buzzed from its spot on the nightstand.

"Aren't you going to answer it? It might be work."

"It could only be work." His main reason for not answering. The night was beginning to fade, turning into what he hoped would be a good day for answers. A good day to take a good chunk out of A&O Solutions' stability and hold them accountable for everything they'd done. What he didn't particularly care to deal with at the moment was what was waiting for him at the Bureau once his leave was over. "I'll call them back. What?"

"What what?"

"I can hear you thinking." He pressed his lips to the back of her head. "What is it?"

"I was considering how hard your job must be. How dark you have to go into the human psyche working the cases that you do. Don't you ever worry about losing yourself? Losing your soul? It has to—"

"It does. But it's tempered by other…interests." His hands began to wander, but they didn't get far before she turned over, lifted a hand to his face. Stroked her fingers down his stubble-covered cheek. It was, he thought, a beautiful way to start any day.

"How does it not consume you? How do you keep the anger, the rage, at bay?"

"Sometimes I don't. Other times I allow myself to get distracted by someone else's demons and ghosts." He kissed the tip of her nose. "Sometimes a damsel in distress allows me to be her defender and slay her dragons instead."

She snort-laughed, smacked him lightly on the shoulder as her smile brightened up the darkness. "You're in quite a vulnerable position to be calling me that."

"I'm a risk-taker, too. You know, if we don't get some sleep—"

Someone knocked on the hotel room door.

They frowned at one another, as if confirming they'd each heard it.

The knock came again.

"What the—" He threw back the covers and climbed out of bed, jumped into his jeans before he grabbed his sidearm and, keeping it low next to him, headed to the door. "Lana, stay—" But it was too late. She was already out of bed and tugging on his T-shirt.

He unhooked the safety latch and opened the door. "Aiden. What's wrong?" He pulled the door open farther and stepped back as Lana switched on the lights.

"What's going on?"

"Did you turn your cell back on?" Aiden asked.

"What? No." Lana picked it up from the coffee table in front of the gray upholstered sofa. "It's still off. See?" She handed it to him. "I haven't turned it on since before we left the bar back in Sacramento."

Aiden barely gave it a glance. "The unit I've had watching Marcus's apartment building just called. They've spotted three surveillance teams staking out the apartment building."

"They know she's on her way?" Eamon asked.

Aiden shook his head. "I don't think so."

"He's right," Lana said. "They checked your phone, Eamon. It's clean. They don't know I'm coming. But they are anticipating my arrival."

"They have a plan," Eamon said.

"Me not answering Felice's messages probably put them on alert," Lana said. "They're tired of waiting." She reached back and slid her fingers through his. "And so am I."

"What?" Lana mumbled around a mouth full of French toast and looked across the table at Eamon. It was barely after seven, only a few hours since Aiden had knocked on their hotel room door, and after grabbing a few fitful hours of sleep, she found herself not only energized, but absolutely famished. They'd since moved everything over to Aiden's business suite, which included a delivery of room service breakfast fit for a film crew. "Sue me. I'm hungry and it's mostly your fault."

"If I'd known that's all it would take to get you to eat, we should have slept together days ago." The strained patience in his voice was a reminder Eamon was not, in any way, happy with her and Aiden's plan.

"Have to work off the nervous energy somehow. Since other avenues aren't available to me at the moment." It was as if she had an entire beehive buzzing inside her.

Eamon rolled his eyes.

"You don't get it, do you?" She chewed and swallowed, wiped her mouth and reached for her coffee.

"Pretend I don't."

"I have something they want," Lana explained. Again. "Something they need. And they're desperate to get it." Seriously. What was up with that? "That's all good news, Eamon. It means we have the upper hand."

"Doesn't seem that way from where I'm sitting."

"Then I suggest you switch seats." She hadn't felt this clearheaded, this positive, in ages. Maybe it was the prospect of finally putting the last eighteen months behind her. Or maybe this was the aftereffect of having spent a good portion of the early morning hours exorcising what she hoped were the last of her marriage-related ghosts. It could even be that she was being proactive and productive rather than allowing life to steamroll over her. More than likely, it was a combination of the three.

Whatever the reason, she planned to run full tilt at

the situation, even if she ended up smacking headfirst into Felice and A&O Solutions.

"I don't like the idea of using you as bait."

"You forgot the *again*." She arched a brow at him. "You mean you don't like the idea of using me as bait *again*. Funny how it wasn't a problem yesterday when it was your idea."

He blinked, frowned into his coffee. "All right." He paused. "I'll admit you are not altogether incorrect."

She dropped her fork. "You just admitted you were wrong. You really are the perfect man, aren't you?" She considered the smile he offered her a small triumph. "I hear you, Eamon. I do. And I understand where you're coming from, but I know you see this from my perspective, too. This is something I not only have to do, I also need to do it." She had to close the book on the last couple of years, on her marriage, on Marcus's sham of a life, before she had a hope of moving forward with her own. A future she hoped would include Eamon Quinn. "Look at it this way," she added when he didn't appear convinced. "I'm trusting you to make sure I make it through today in one piece. You and your friends. This time last week I'd have considered that an impossibility."

"We're your friends, too." Vince and Slade entered Aiden's suite in time to counter her statement. "We're ready to be brought up to speed."

"And eat," Slade added as he grabbed a plate and piled it high with eggs and bacon. "Definitely ready to eat."

"All right, we're all set with the Boston PD," Aiden

said as he clicked off his cell phone. "They'll set up a surveillance perimeter around the public garden near the apartment building. Plenty of cover so they won't be seen as you draw them in. Keep it simple and straightforward from the moment you pick up the car, which is when you turn your phone back on. You'll pick up a tail along the way. Just be ready for that and don't lose them."

"You've got eyes on Felice's teams, right?" Eamon asked.

Aiden nodded. "I brought in three more cars. The watchers are being watched. We'll have eyes and ears on you the entire time, Lana."

"See?" Lana plastered a smile on her face and aimed it directly at Eamon. "Easy peasy." Lana took her last bite as Aiden sat at the head of the table, his own food having gone cold ages ago. She got up to refill her coffee, barely noticing the nervous trembling in her hands. "In case I don't—in case I forget," she quickly amended as she faced the four men seated around the table. "I just want to thank all of you. Not only for stepping up to help with this nightmare of a scenario, but for trusting me with my part in things." She offered them each a shaky smile. "It means a lot."

"You've earned your wings with us, Lana," Slade said. "The only thing we ask is that you trust us. None of this works out without trust."

"Right. Trust will get us through." As she spoke, guilt grabbed hold of her stomach and squeezed. She had every intention of sticking to their plan.

But that didn't mean she didn't have one of her own.

One she wouldn't hesitate to put into play if she thought, even for one minute, Eamon and their friends were in trouble.

She'd ask for forgiveness later. If she was still alive.

"You're a guy who listens to his gut, right, Aiden?" Eamon couldn't decipher where the unease was coming from as he sat like a stone in the passenger seat of one of Aiden's black SUVs. But it was definitely there. They were parked far enough away to stay clear of any potential countersurveillance, yet close enough they had the building—and Marcus's second-floor apartment in particular—in sight. Aiden's surveillance van was parked where it had been for the past day, directly across the street from the entrance, its plain black color boring enough that it drew no one's attention. Six cars behind sat a more conspicuous cable repair van that rocked enough to betray three or four people were inside. *Amateurs*, Eamon thought. The arrogance of power, thinking they were too good to be caught. "You get the feeling something's not right? With Lana?"

"Yep." Aiden didn't flinch. He rested his head in one hand, his index finger against his mouth, stared at the building as if he could somehow manifest an end to the situation with his mind. "I do indeed."

"How do you…?"

"Being able to read people has kept me alive for most of my life," Aiden said. "That and trusting my instincts." He angled his gaze at Eamon. "Listening to my gut."

"When did you know?"

"As soon as I finished running down the plan," Aiden

said. "She thinks my way of approaching Felice is wrong. She didn't say it, she played along, but she disagrees."

"Why didn't you call her on it?"

"Because no amount of research we might have done can come close to what she knows about someone she knows personally," Aiden said. "Add to that she respected me enough not to question me in front of my people." He glanced at Eamon. "She's been conned by the woman for years. In some ways, she has far more at stake than we do. I'm okay giving Lana some leeway if it means she can throw some dirt back in Felice's face. Especially if it helps us get what we want."

"All I want is Lana out of there, safe and sound."

"That's definitely at the top of the list." Aiden pressed a finger against the device in his ear. "Slade? You have eyes on our sparrow?"

"She's headed into the nest now," Slade responded into both their ears. "Just turned the corner into the lot."

"Don't let her hear you call her *sparrow*." Vince's voice echoed next. "She'll fry you both over an open fire."

"Sparrows are hardy creatures," Aiden said. "They can fly through any storm and come out relatively unscathed, sometimes even stronger than before. Mobile one, report in."

Eamon looked out his window into a lush yard in front of a small cottage-style house. It was a quiet neighborhood, far enough outside the main hub of the city to give off suburb vibes. The rotating reports, mobile one, mobile two, mobile three… They all left him feeling slightly disconnected. He didn't like this feeling, sitting out here while she stepped into whatever waited for her inside. "She shouldn't be going in there alone."

"You go in there with her, you risk scaring everyone who's watching." Eamon's phone chimed with Aiden's texted reminder to rotate the broadcasting frequencies to the team. "You want this over, Eamon? Trust her to get the job done. And trust me and my people to make sure she does."

"Right. Yeah." Eamon took a deep breath. "I know. Sorry."

"Stop apologizing for worrying about the woman you love."

"And with that," Slade said, "Vince owes me fifty bucks. I told him this would turn into a therapy session."

"Heads up." Aiden sat up straighter as Lana's rented blue Prius zoomed its way into the parking lot. "Here we go. I know I say this every time, but I need every one of you to hear me. Be ready for anything. And I mean anything. Lana's got the lead on this. Let her have it."

Eamon couldn't help but think Aiden was speaking directly to him.

"She's got this, Eamon," Aiden said.

Eamon nodded. "I know." But that didn't mean he wasn't terrified their first night together may very well have been their last.

Lana parked in one of the two reserved spots for her and Marcus's apartment. The other slot was empty; it had been since the day after Marcus had died. He'd driven a company car, one Felice had been eager to retrieve.

She climbed out, grabbed her duffel bag out of the trunk, her purse out of the back seat, and made her way around to the front entrance, adjusting the oversize button-down dark blue shirt so the button cam Aiden's team had added could have an unobstructed view. She resisted the temptation to adjust the pod in her ear.

"We've got you, Lana." Aiden's voice was loud and clear. "Doing great. We've identified three vehicles in the area, each with at least a two-man team inside. Up to now, no one other than tenants have approached the building, but I'm going to assume that won't last. First hurdle ahead. Let's see if the security system is everything it's touted to be."

It was starting to feel like a dream, being here after all this time, given the obstacles she'd overcome, some of her own making.

The steel-and-glass construction gave the apartment building a cold, almost industrial look. There were no soft angles here, no gentle touches. Everything about the building screamed *stay away*. Even the landscaping came across as a deterrent, with its blackthorn and common holly bushes planted along the perimeter.

It was almost funny, how she could see both sides of Marcus's life reflected in the structure he'd chosen to live in. She should have come here sooner, if only to put those remaining pieces of the puzzle into place. So much made sense given what she knew now. His reticence when it came to talking about his work, his odd fascination with security systems and home protection. The number of books he owned on the topic of toxic plants and substances. The place looked impenetrable, which, given the secrets he'd had, made it the perfect place for him.

She rounded the corner and stopped at the thick glass panel door with a massive brass bar handle. The fingerprint scanner pad was tucked into a discreet alcove, beside a bank of brass mailboxes. She'd thought Marcus was teasing when he'd told her about the various levels of protection. Even the visit from the security system people hadn't convinced her. Obviously he had not been exaggerating. Getting into the lobby was going to be work. She glanced up at the cameras—one on either side of the enormous door. "Okay, boys. Here's where we find out how welcome I really was."

She inserted her key into the slot, twisted it, then held her thumb on the pad, waited for the neon green light to move up and down. When she was prompted, she keyed in her unique eight-digit personal code before removing the key.

"Welcome, Detective Lana Tate." The sultry female voice sounded. "Please, enter and have a nice day."

The lobby door clicked.

"What was that?" Eamon asked in a way that had Lana fighting a laugh.

"The inventor had a thing for new tech," Aiden said. "Can't blame him really. Okay, Lana, remember, once you're upstairs—"

"Disable any signal jammers that might cut us off and prevent the apartment from being monitored. Yes, Aiden, I know." She pulled open the lobby door and stepped inside. When it closed behind her, there was a gentle *woomph* as if the room had been repressurized.

Her shoes squeaked on the polished tiled floor as she bypassed the elevator for the staircase.

"Mobile one, report," Aiden said.

"Got her in sight," the unfamiliar voice said. "Stairway cameras operational. Elevator cameras check. Button cam clear. Good to go."

Lana took the stairs to the second floor, her hand gripping the rail with more pressure than necessary. The adrenaline surge had gotten her to this point, but now the nerves were setting in. Nerves she needed to get under control if this plan of hers was going to work.

Another keypad awaited her on the second-floor landing. She entered her code again, scanned her thumb again, turned her key again. When she pulled open the door on the second-floor landing, she spotted a middle-aged couple emerging from the door across the hall from Marcus's apartment. They were both tall, slender, and wore enough designer clothes to open their own store. Lana silently swore. Marcus had told her about them, but for the life of her, she couldn't recall their names.

"You're Lana, aren't you?" The surprise on the woman's face was at least friendly as she made her approach, arms open. "Lana Tate? Marcus's wife. I recognize you from Marcus's pictures. How are you? You know, after…"

The dramatic tone, along with the perfectly manicured nails, razor-straight black hair and Botoxed face, triggered the memory. "Veronica. It's nice to meet you. Marcus spoke very highly of both of you." She readjusted the bag on her shoulder to avoid the unwanted hug and air-kiss greeting. "I'm doing okay, I think. Good days and bad. How are you and…?"

"Gordon," Aiden supplied from the van. "He's in finance and she's into spending his money. They also have a Tibetan mastiff named Chanel."

"Of course they do," Eamon muttered.

"Gordon," Lana said, finishing her thought with a glance toward the husband. "And Chanel, of course. Marcus told me all about your beautiful dog."

"Oh, aren't you the sweetest." Veronica rested a hand against her heart and gave her the "I'm sorry your husband is dead" head tilt. "With everything you've been through, you remember our baby. Gordon, isn't she the sweetest?"

Gordon looked as if he couldn't be bothered. "Nice to meet you." He held his thumb on the keypad beside their door to engage the lock before he strode toward them to claim his wife. "We're going to be late."

"Oh, yes, of course." She smiled at Lana as her husband escorted her to the elevator that was waiting for them. "Bye, Lana. Maybe we can get drinks before you…" The rest of her offer faded into the elevator as the doors closed.

Lana gave an absent wave before making her way down the hall to the last apartment on the right. Yet another keypad, only this one had a full hand scanner. She lifted her right hand, flexed her fingers. "This is getting ridiculous. NORAD doesn't have this many levels of protection." She took a deep breath and rested her hand on the plate.

The laser moved up and down, once, twice, three

times before she heard the top lock click. The second lock didn't release until she keyed in her code again. The nerves were back, making her hand shake as she twisted the knob and opened the door.

"Well, this is…disappointing." She stepped far enough inside to let the door close behind her. "I was at least expecting—" She yelped and jumped back as a scanner embedded in the ceiling focused on her. She looked up at the bright red light, winced as it moved up and down her body.

"Lana?" Eamon's voice came through loud and clear. Too loud. "What's wrong?"

"I'm being probed." She eyed the comm unit on the wall, saw a video feed of the front lobby on the screen beside an intercom.

"Detective Lana Tate. Primary resident. Entry approved. Welcome home, Detective Lana Tate. My name is Angie. If I can be of assistance, please don't hesitate to ask."

"Uh, thanks, Angie." She dropped her bag on the gray-tinted hardwood floor even as she wondered what on earth she'd ask of a security system. The air smelled slightly floral, and more than a little stale. It made sense. As far as she knew, the only person who had been in this apartment since Marcus's death was the property manager, who'd emptied out the fridge and disposed of any perishable items. As for the rent, that was being paid out of the only account of Marcus's she'd left open. "Guys, can you all hear me?"

"Five by five," Aiden responded. "Ready to make your call to Felice?"

"In a minute." She hadn't anticipated needing to get her bearings. After all, it was just an apartment. She might own it, but it wasn't like it was home. Not her home, at least. No, while her name might be on the deed, this wasn't her space.

The small entry table displayed an old abalone shell with some loose change and a few solitary keys, along with a framed photo of herself: a candid shot Marcus had taken with his cell phone shortly after they'd started dating. She waited for the grief to descend. The sorrow. The regret. Even anger. But none of that came. Instead, all she felt was an unexpected sadness over someone she'd clearly never known.

The short hallway opened up almost immediately into a nicely furnished great room with an angled fireplace. Her sneakered feet were silent on the hardwood floor as she moved around. There was no balcony, only a bank of curtained windows overlooking the wooded area behind the property. There was nothing special about the apartment. It could have easily been a display model with which to tempt potential owners.

The only personal touches she saw, other than the practical furniture choices, were photos. Enough that the number surprised her. She lifted the largest framed one off the mantel, the one that displayed her personal favorite from their very private wedding.

Instead of seeing a happy bride with the beach at her back, her new husband's arms holding her close, Lana only saw a naive woman who'd been fooled into complacency. Who'd been lied to. A woman who just a few short years after this was taken would realize what she'd had then didn't come close to what she had now.

She set the frame facedown on the hearth as an image of Eamon floated through her mind. Despite the anger she felt twisting to life inside her, an unexpected wave of calm washed over her. Eamon had a way of doing that. Bringing her peace, even as he drove the rest of her to distraction.

She made her way toward the kitchen, looked to her left and down the hallway she assumed led to the solitary bedroom. Across the room, on the other side of the kitchen, a half bath, the door slightly ajar, and another secured door beside it.

"Lana?" Aiden asked. "You still with us?"

"I just need...a minute."

She keyed in her code, waited for the click. This time she didn't jump when the laser hit the top of her head and ran far more quickly than the previous scan. After a slight pause, the door opened.

"Granting access, Detective Lana Tate. Welcome, Detective..."

"Oh, shut up." Lana poked her head inside. Once again, nothing special. A simple mahogany desk, matching built-in bookshelves and cabinets. A ridiculously expensive leather chair that looked as if it belonged on a space shuttle. She glanced at her watch, noted the time. She was almost out of it. Lana performed a quick inventory of the cabinets and drawers. The books on the shelves were collectible leather editions that had never had their spines cracked. The file cabinet in the corner? Empty. The only thing she found of interest was a thin laptop in a bottom desk drawer. "Good enough." She snatched it out, held it against her chest as she left the office, pulling out her cell phone. She turned it on and set the laptop on the circular glass coffee table between the sofa and fireplace.

She started to dial when a quick flash caught her attention. Lana looked up, glanced around the room. She must be seeing things. She ducked her head. There it was again. This time, she raised her chin in time to see a thin beam of light flash across the room and hit the back wall of the kitchen.

"What the—"

"Lana? What's going on? You find something?"

"I don't know. Maybe? Hang on." Even with the light gone now, she followed the movement to the fireplace and ran her fingers over a small notch in the wall behind where the picture frame had been. "That's…weird." She stepped back, walked around on one side, then to the other. "The walls are uneven. One side cuts off but not the…other." She returned to the hearth, planted both hands on the mantel and shoved.

Nothing.

The light flashed again. This time when it hit, she saw the odd shape it took. Part circle, part rectangle. Almost like a…

Her stomach dropped.

Almost like a key.

She reached for her necklace, nearly panicked when she found it wasn't there, then remembered she'd taken it off back in Eamon's apartment.

"Lana—"

"I need a few more minutes," she snapped. "Please, Aiden."

"We've got movement out here, Lana. At least two of the cars are pulling in closer to the building and we have four men headed to the building."

"Well, they can't come in unless I let them in. Give me some time."

She ignored Eamon's sigh of frustration. She didn't know what she expected them to do. She certainly didn't want them getting into some kind of shoot-out simply because she'd been distracted by a beam of light.

Except it wasn't just a beam of light. She hurried over to her bag, dug around and into the side pockets until she felt the chain. She yanked it free, dangled it to grab the key and went back to the fireplace.

"Suddenly I know why *National Treasure* was his favorite movie." Lana hesitated only a moment before she slid the key into the recess of the wall. She turned it.

She heard a click and the revving of a motor before the entire panel housing the fireplace slid out and to the side. Behind it sat a safe room door made of solid steel, much like a bank vault door.

"What the…?"

"She really needs to stop saying things like that," Aiden complained. "Especially if she's not going to explain herself."

Another keypad, but she didn't hesitate and inputted her numbers. Zero eight one six eighty-seven. The lock disengaged and she pulled down on the handle and opened the door.

The voices in her ear faded into white noise when she

stepped inside, but she barely noticed. Overhead lights blinked on, illuminating the cramped room filled with multiple computers, a personal server and two industrial metal shelves filled with file boxes organized by year. The bulletin board over the desk was covered in pristinely arranged sticky notes with names, dates and various methods of death with question marks beside some of them.

"Recognizing Detective Lana Tate." Angie's voice drifted out of the speakers. "Welcome, Lana Tate. Initiating program Marcus Is Dead."

Lana spun around as the desktop computer blinked to life. She gasped as Marcus stared back at her from the screen.

"Hey, hon." His smile was drawn, tight, his dark eyes shadowed. She could see it now. The weight of what he'd done, in his eyes. His face.

She moved closer, stretched out her hand as if expecting to be able to touch him.

"If you're seeing this, then my plan didn't work and I'm dead. It also means you're in some serious trouble, so I'm going to do what I can to help. Too little, too late, I know. But…" He sighed, and whatever amusement had been in his eyes faded. "I should probably start by saying I'm sorry, but I'm going to assume by now that's the last thing you want to hear from me."

Tears scalded her eyes. "You—"

"I know you're angry," Marcus went on as her knees went weak and she sank into the only chair in the room. "And if I'm honest with myself, I'm glad I'm not there to see it. But before you slam the door and walk away, I need you to do one thing for me. Just listen. Please listen to me for just a few more minutes, Lana. Because I have a story to tell you."

Chapter 14

"We've got no way to get inside," Eamon said as Aiden alternated between teams, telling them to stand down for now while at least one of his people worked on hacking into the apartment's security system through Lana's cell phone. "What is she doing in there?"

"Confronting her past?" Aiden answered without missing a beat. "She's not going to lose the plot, Eamon. She's just gone off course for a bit. She's safe in there, remember. But we might not be."

"Maybe they'll assume we're with them?" Eamon suggested as a pair of dark coverall-clad men wearing even darker knit caps made their way around the perimeter of the apartment building. "How insulated are they from one another? With the way A&O hires local heavies, it's possible none of them have ever met each other before."

"Good point. One that could work in our favor," Aiden said. "Ditch the jacket. Toss it in the back. And the tie." Eamon did as he was told, rolled up his shirt-sleeves and unbuttoned the top button on his collar, but when Aiden looked at him, he shook his head. "Doesn't matter what you wear, you still look like a fed. Slade? Keep trying to get through to Lana."

"Just getting static. It's like she's moved into a dead zone."

For the first time since Eamon met Aiden McKenna, the other man flinched. "Okay. Okay, we're going to give it ten minutes. If she isn't back by then, I'm call-ing in the local PD. We breach that building without them on-site, I'll never hear the end of it." He glanced at Eamon. "Especially from my mother."

"Understood," Slade confirmed, before the rest of the teams did the same.

"Ten minutes." Eamon set his watch, returned his at-tention to the men patrolling the building. "Let's hope she's back with us by then."

Through the waves of anguish and betrayal, beneath the roar of logic and acceptance, against unmitigated resistance and reluctance, Lana listened. Processed.

Accepted.

She reached over and hit the escape key on the key-board of the desktop computer, freezing Marcus's hand-some face on the screen. His smile came across as part apology, part regret, and all charm. It was the man she remembered, a man she'd never really known.

She stood, surprised her legs actually held her up,

and waited until the light on the front of the computer stopped blinking green.

"Download complete," the computer told her. "Please remove flash drive."

Before she pulled the drive free, she opened Marcus's email program, logged out so she could log in to her own, then forwarded the entirety of downloaded information to not one, not two, but three different allies.

Only then did she pull the drive free and, after another glance around the room, stashed it on the top of the highest shelf behind yet another framed photograph of the two of them together.

When it was put away, she zombie-walked back to the door. The instant she stepped out of the room, voices exploded in her ear.

"Three minutes."

"Three minutes to what?" Lana asked as she turned and pushed the door closed, keyed in her code to lock it. Pulling the key free of the notch had the panel sliding back into place. The room settled back into normalcy as if she hadn't just stepped into a portal of clarity.

"Lana. There you are. We thought we'd lost you completely."

"Not completely," she whispered.

"What happened? Are you okay?"

Not yet. But she would be. "I'm sorry I dropped out of range. I...I found something. I'll explain later. I'm calling her now." She retrieved her cell phone, but before she could dial, it rang. Felice's name appeared onscreen. "Felice. Hello. I'm sorry I haven't returned your messages. I was on a plane."

"I'm just glad to hear your voice," Felice said with what Lana could only interpret as false concern. "Where are you?"

Lana caught movement on the security monitor by the door. She walked over, stood in front of it, eyes narrowed as she watched three different teams of men approach the panel in an attempt to find a way in. "You know where I am." She'd never felt quite so calm in her life. And the idea of that terrified her. "You've always known where I am, haven't you? From the very beginning. You've always known."

She heard Eamon swear, but she couldn't think about him now.

"Lana." Felice's voice tightened. "I don't know what—"

"You can drop the act, Felice. Honestly?" She sighed and dropped her head to her chest. "I'm exhausted and I'm too tired to deal with it. I have what you want. The files. The records. All the information about Project Orbana."

Lana winced at Eamon's and Aiden's protests before she ripped the pods out of her ears and tossed them onto the counter behind her.

"You have no idea what you're playing at." Felice's voice was devoid of the affection Lana had always heard until now.

"You slipped, didn't you, Felice? You made the horrific error of caring for one of your vulnerable orphans. The ones you trained to be killers. You cared for Marcus, didn't you? You were blind to him and didn't notice everything he was doing behind your back. All the information he was collecting. You didn't see it until it was too late. That's why he had to die, wasn't it? Because he was going to turn on you and your bosses at A&O."

"You're signing your own death decree," Felice spit. "Stupid woman."

"You were already going to kill me." Lana reached behind her, pulled the gun out from the waistband of her jeans. "The only thing I can do now is make it more difficult for you. Come and get it, Felice. Come and get all the files he kept." She released the safety on the weapon. "I'll be waiting."

Lana hung up and tossed the phone into her bag.

An odd serenity washed over her as she walked over to the window. Feet planted, shoulders straightened, she stared out into the trees and waited.

"She's gone completely off the rails." Eamon dropped his head into his hands. "I was afraid something like this was going to happen." Even as he accepted it, he couldn't find any way to blame her. A switch had been flipped inside her. One that might never be flipped back.

"She does seem to have set her own course. Man, sometimes I really hate being right." Aiden blew out a breath. "Team roundup, prepare to implement contingency plan Lana One, over."

"Confirmed." The responses came as Eamon stared, somewhat dumbfounded.

"You have a plan in place for this?"

"I told you," Aiden said. "I read people. I know them. And I always, *always* have a backup plan. This is when I tell you that if you step foot out of this vehicle you will follow my orders to the letter. Do you understand me, Agent? To. The. Letter." Aiden, cell in one hand, his earpiece still in place, shoved out of the car as Eamon hurried to catch up.

"This probably isn't the right time," Aiden said as they crossed the street and ducked into the foliage cover near the apartment building. "I've been putting together a plan for a dedicated unit specializing in child crimes both here and overseas. I need someone to take the lead. Someone who knows how the law works in this country and elsewhere. Someone who might want a little extra leeway in how a case gets handled but still understands how these kinds of criminals operate. Know anyone who might be interested?"

"Uh—" Eamon blinked. Aiden was either the king of bad timing or a genius. Leaving the Bureau to work for Minotaur could be the best of both worlds. The resources he'd have at his fingertips to do the job he did better than just about anyone else? "I think maybe I do."

"Maybe's good enough for now," Aiden said over his shoulder. "Mobile one in position? Over?"

"Confirmed, over."

Aiden crouched, and Eamon followed suit as a pair of the countersurveillance men headed in their direction. Aiden shifted so Eamon could read his hand signals. Aiden was going after the lead guy, Eamon had the second. Eamon nodded.

They waited until the men were nearly past them before leaping out, locking arms around their necks and dragging them back into the bushes. Eamon's target fought back, kicking and slamming his hands down on Eamon's forearm, but he tightened his hold, twisted ever so slightly until the man passed out. He dumped him and was about to roll him over to secure his hands with a zip tie, but Aiden stopped him.

"Strip him down first. We need those coveralls. And the hats," Aiden added as he pulled his shirt over his head. "Time to make a switch before Felice gets here."

It surprised Lana that it was taking Felice so long to arrive. Considering the woman had known for a good half hour before speaking to Lana where Lana actually was, the delay just seemed… What was the word? Rude.

"Angie?" Lana turned from the window, pulse hammering as the adrenaline began to build once more. Something Marcus had said, something Felice confirmed, had opened up a whole floodgate of ideas. Ideas Lana had finally filtered down to one.

"Yes, Detective Lana Tate?"

Lana rolled her eyes. When this was over, she was going to rip Angie's wiring out by the roots. "Can you show me the schematics to the building?"

"Of course, Detective Lana Tate. Where would you like me to display them?"

She eyed the laptop on the sofa. "Do you have access to electrical devices in this apartment?"

"Yes, Detective…"

"Display on biggest screen, please."

The TV hanging on the wall blinked to life.

"What am I looking at?" Lana asked as she scanned the blueprints of the seven-story structure.

"The schematics you requested, Detective Lana—"

"Show me the staircase and elevator system, please?" Lana stepped closer as the image changed. "Angie, do cell phones work in the elevators?"

"Yes, Detective Lana Tate."

"How?" The steel plating was bound to block the signals.

"Multiple signal boosters have been installed throughout the building, Detective Lana Tate. Including one in each elevator."

"Perfect." She recalled Aiden mentioning the security cameras in the elevators as well. "Angie, do you have access to the operations system of the elevator?"

"I have limited access, Detective Lana Tate. In order to facilitate emergency situations."

Lana inclined her head. "Can I talk to you in the elevator?"

"Yes, Detective Lana Tate. I have vocal interfaces in every part of the building, including the gym, meeting room—"

"Are you able to implement an emergency elevator stop?"

"Yes, Detective Lana Tate. Although it is not recommended."

"What other emergency protocols do you have access to, Angie?"

"I am programmed to assist all residents in various emergency situations. Fire evacuation, flood protection, assault lockdown…"

Bingo! "Do you know how many residents are currently in the building?"

"Yes, Detective Lana Tate. There are currently six

apartments occupied. Thirteen other apartments have vacated for the day. Apartment 1C is expected back…"

"Angie, stand by to implement emergency lockdown for all apartments currently occupied. No one in or out until reversed by me or a man named Eamon Quinn. Understand?"

"Yes, Detective Lana Tate. Standing by."

"Thanks."

"Of course, Detective Lana—"

"Just Lana, please." She didn't think she'd ever hear the word *detective* in the same way again. The buzzer by the door sounded. "Stand by, Angie."

"Standing by, Lana."

Even on a screen the size of a tablet computer, Felice Covington made an impression. She wore a tailored suit of the deepest blood red, her jet-dark hair pulled into a knot at the back of her neck. She smoothed a hand down her torso, turned her head toward the men Lana knew were lurking just out of camera range.

Lana hit the intercom button. "Second floor. Use the elevator."

Lana grinned at the flash of irritation on Felice's face. Then she bent down and grabbed her bag to stash in the kitchen. She quickly replaced one of her ear pods, twisted it on to reactivate it. "Aiden? Eamon?"

"Lana?" Eamon whispered. "What the—"

"No time. Aiden, I've got an idea. Is your team still wired into the surveillance system in the elevator? Can you make a recording?"

"Stand by," Aiden said. "Mobile two, please confirm."

"Mobile two confirming. That's a go on the elevators. Recording in progress."

"Okay." Lana felt more confident already. "Okay, good. This is gonna work. We're going to pull this off."

"Pull what off?" Eamon asked.

"I don't want to jinx it." She'd had enough bad luck the last year and a half. She was focused on turning it around, on shutting A&O down once and for all and, hopefully, getting all of them out of this alive.

She heard shouting, voices she didn't recognize coming over her feed. "Where are you?"

"Not something we can explain at the moment," Eamon murmured.

"You and I are due for a discussion at the conclusion of this operation, Detective Tate," Aiden said. "A long one."

"Seconded," Eamon chimed in. Both of their voices had dropped significantly from when she'd first entered the apartment.

"Copy that." Now wasn't the time for second guesses or regrets. On the bright side, she couldn't be fired from a job she'd never had. "Angie, unlock the door, please. Allow my approaching visitor to enter."

"This is not recommended, Lana, as it is against security protocols."

"Understood. Override protocols and unlock the front door."

"Unlocking door." Lana swore she could hear the AI gnash her cyberteeth together.

The click echoed in the empty space. Her heart hammered in her chest as the front door pushed open. The clack of Felice's heels sounded like gunshots as she walked down the hall, turned and stepped inside.

She approached in the same way Lana stood, with her hands behind her back, a disapproving expression on her schoolmarm face. She stopped a few feet away from Lana. "You disappoint me, Lana. I truly believed you were smarter than this."

"No, you didn't." Lana forced herself to relax even as her hand tightened around the butt of her gun. "You tolerated me because I was married to your favorite orphan. The terrified little boy you programmed and trained to do your bidding. Yours and that of A&O Solutions."

"Where are the files?" Felice sounded bored.

"Safe. Where's your backup? You didn't come alone."

"They're in the hall." Felice glanced over her shoulder. "They're armed. All of them. In case you were curious. Even if you did get past me, they wouldn't let you take two steps before firing."

"Well, at least I'm prepared." Lana's smile was quick and cursory. A few weeks ago, even a few days ago, she might not have worried so much about dying, but now? She held strong to the image of Eamon, to what it felt like to be so completely loved. It was, quite simply, the best thing to live for. "I have a few questions for you. Before we conclude whatever this business is between us."

"Stalling before I end your life." Felice sighed. "How predictable."

"Do you plan to kill me yourself or will you be outsourcing this to one of your minions?" Felice's eyes narrowed in a way that bolstered Lana's confidence. "Project Orbana. You know it needs to end. You've ruined hundreds of lives. And that's just the children you manipulated. I told you," Lana said at the flash of disbelief across Felice's face. "I know everything."

"You're the only one who will." Felice reached into her pocket and withdrew a small hypodermic needle. "Just to build the anticipation. It'll be a lot more tidy than a bullet wound. Blood makes such a mess."

"Always planning ahead." Lana's gaze caught the shift of shadows out in the hall. The men who had been circling in and around the lobby cameras. She checked the monitor. No one there. They must all be inside.

"I plan and I watch," Felice confirmed. "For instance, your little stunt at the coffee shop. You confirmed what I always believed to be your weakness. You care too much. Collateral damage, it's unspeakable for you." Her lips flickered. "It's why I've ordered my men to go door-to-door and fire on every single person inside should you refuse to come with me."

"Come with you?" Lana frowned and her heart skipped a beat. "Why would—"

"As fitting as it might be to have you die of an overdose in your late husband's home, I can't take the chance of leaving something behind for the authorities to find. My sweeper team is on the way. This is what I meant about disappointing, Lana. You see, they can only be let in by someone on the inside. You've removed a significant obstacle. Now…" She stepped closer. "Where are the files?"

Lana swallowed hard, let her arm drop to her side, weapon tight against her thigh.

Felice scoffed. "You aren't going to use that."

"Why not?" Lana aimed it at Felice's chest. "The apartment is soundproofed. No one will hear."

"You kill me, you'll never make it out of this apartment, let alone this building, and neither will anyone else. The files, Lana. I tire of asking."

Lana hesitated, did her best not to look to the sofa, where the laptop sat.

"Ah. You are off your game." Felice spotted the computer and brushed past Lana to claim it. "Now come." She stepped forward, held out her hand. "Give me your weapon and we'll leave together. Peacefully. Let everyone else be safe."

Lana's hand trembled. It made a grotesque kind of sense that she'd walked right into a trap after being so careful about creating her own. She knew without a doubt that if she did what Felice wanted, if she left this building with her, she'd never make it back to Eamon alive.

But there were others to worry about besides herself. Others she had sworn to protect. She wouldn't allow any more innocents to die.

"All right." She raised her hand, let the gun slip free and spin in her hold, the muzzle rotating until it pointed at the ceiling. "All right. I'm putting it down." She walked over to the small dining table and left it there. "You lead, I'll follow."

"I don't think so." Felice, needle still in hand, stepped aside. Every muscle in Lana's body tensed as she moved on. She counted her steps, keeping an eye on the shadows that shifted into solid forms as she reached the door. On the bright side, there were only two men in the hall.

On the other hand, they were two men armed with semiautomatic pistols.

She could feel Felice behind her, drawing closer with every step. Just let her get a little bit...

Lana spun, grabbed Felice's hand and yanked her forward before she quickly let go. As Felice plowed into one of her men, Lana dived for the door handle and before she pulled it closed yelled, "Angie, lockdown mode, now!"

She heard every lock on the second floor slide into place as the door to Marcus's apartment clicked shut.

A masculine hand caught her shoulder and jerked her back. She ducked and turned in one quick motion, pivoted and drove her foot directly into the nearest man's solar plexus. He slammed against the wall.

She didn't stop to think. She ran. Full out. Eyes locked on those sliding metal doors. "Angie," she yelled. "Open elevator A."

She didn't have time to contemplate the fear that had plagued her most of her life as the elevator doors slid open and she dived inside. She hit the floor, immediately pushing herself over and into the corner as heavy-booted footfalls echoed toward her.

"Angie, close doors!"

A hand slammed into the door opening, shoved the nearly closed doors open once more as one of Felice's guards stepped in, gun in hand, and aimed the muzzle directly at her head. Lana blinked, unable to see anything beyond that black, dark barrel.

"Enough!" Felice's voice snapped and she clipped along the hall toward them. She shoved her foot soldier inside before joining them, her injured hand clutched against her chest, the hypodermic needle still in her grip.

Lana's breaths came in short gasps as she pushed farther into the corner, shoving the terror aside as she stared up at the woman responsible for turning her husband into a monster. For robbing him of whomever he'd been meant to be.

The doors slid closed. Lana's vision cleared as she looked at the now lowered gun. "Angie, sixth floor." The elevator took off, its whine a symphony of gears and ingenuity as Lana grabbed hold of the railing above her head. "Angie, emergency stop!"

The car stopped abruptly. Felice shrieked, stumbled against the wall, only to be righted by the man in black. Lana raised determined eyes first to Felice, then to the man who had retrained his gun on Lana.

A man with beautiful, familiar hazel eyes. And the faintest hint of red hair escaping the hem of his cap.

Love so powerful she almost whimpered draped over her as her confidence surged. "He trusted you. He was a child, a lost little boy, and you made him believe you cared about him."

"He was useful," Felice said. "Until he wasn't. My only regret is that I wasn't the one driving the car that ended him." Felice crouched, wobbling on her bladelike heels as she stared into Lana's eyes. "But I heard you scream for him." She touched a finger to Lana's face. "And that brought me more pleasure than anything has in a very, very long time."

"You betrayed him," Lana whispered, her voice breaking. "He trusted you more than he ever trusted anyone. He loved you and you betrayed him. You killed him."

"He betrayed me first. Betrayed all of us. After everything we'd done for him, everything we made him, everything we gave him, he was going to walk away. For you. For you and whatever brat offspring you hoped to give him." She seemed to catch herself, as if she'd admitted too much. "We simply couldn't allow it. He was ours. He was never yours."

"You didn't have to kill him. He was trying to do the right thing."

"Oh, don't be so melodramatic. Marcus Tate wasn't a victim," Felice spit. "And he certainly wasn't a hero. He wasn't going to turn that information over to the authorities. He was holding it over our heads. He wanted money. Enough for the two of you to start over. To disappear. Did you know that Marcus Tate wasn't even his real name? He was made up. I made him up. I created him. He knew the price for betraying the syndicate and he did it anyway. The second he did that, he forfeited both your lives."

"You turned him into a killer." Lana stared. "How many people did he kill for you?" she asked on a whisper. "How many deaths is he, are you, are they, responsible for? Murders. Bombings. Shootings. Poisonings."

"More than you'll ever know," Felice boasted as she stood. "And they're all up here." She tapped a finger against her temple. "I am the human record of our success. And now that I have the only other record—"

"Do you think that's enough?" Lana glanced up at Eamon as he pulled the black knit cap off his head and holstered his weapon.

"Should do it." He glanced up at the camera. "Aiden? Did it come through?"

"Loud and clear and in full Technicolor."

Felice blinked, her confusion obvious. "I don't—"

"That's okay." Lana pulled herself up and brushed herself off. "After you take some time to replay this all in your head, you will."

Felice's eyes darkened and sharpened as she turned on Lana. Her hand came up, the needle poised to plunge. "Angie, first floor. Express!"

The elevator plummeted. Felice lost her balance but stumbled toward Lana, who grabbed her hand and whipped it behind her. The needle clattered to the floor as Lana pressed Felice up against the wall of the elevator as it came to a sudden stop on the first floor.

"Lana." Eamon moved in behind her, rested a hand on her shoulder. "Aiden, cut the feed."

"Here's what's going to happen, Felice." Lana released the woman, although she didn't turn around. "You have a choice to make. You can testify against A&O Solutions and help put them out of business once and for all, or you can take full responsibility for every single crime your orphans committed. Not that you'd live long enough in prison for that to happen. I'm sure there's another Marcus out there who would like to take you out. You know, because it's his or her job."

"I think she gets the point," Eamon said.

"Speaking of points."

Lana turned at the sound of Aiden's voice. He stepped into the open elevator, bent down and picked up the hypodermic needle. "I'm betting this is oleander."

"I should have poisoned your Scotch when I had the chance," Felice said. She strode past Lana and into the custody of two of Aiden's men waiting just outside the elevator. "I certainly had plenty of chances, didn't I. You're a disgrace, Lana. A drunken, pathetic disgrace who never deserved Marcus."

"Only one of us is a disgrace," Lana said calmly. "And it isn't me. Aiden, I'd recommend keeping her in one of your vans until the feds can get here. There's sensitive information upstairs in the apartment we wouldn't want her to see." She looked at Eamon as Felice was led away. Sirens blared in the distance, a sound that brought her such comfort she felt as if she could breathe again. "You should call it in."

He shook his head. "Not my call to make." He looked to Aiden.

"I think it would make a pretty big last call," Aiden said. "Earn yourself some serious DOJ goodwill on your way out the door?"

Lana caught Eamon's arm. "Out the door? Where are you going?"

"We have some details to work out." Eamon glared at Aiden. "Suffice it to say, I've been made an offer I'm not entirely sure I can refuse."

"You Godfathered him?" Lana straightened as a cacophony of emotions battled for control. "Aiden Mc-

Kenna, you really are one smart cookie. Speaking of cookies, I'm starving."

"We can fix that," Aiden said. "Vince? Slade?"

"On our way," Vince said amid the rustle of food packages.

"Meet us upstairs at the apartment," Lana said as she stepped back into the elevator. "There's something I think you all might want to see. Coming?" She held out her hand to Eamon, who looked surprised.

"You hate elevators."

"I do." She nodded and sighed, tugged him in as Aiden followed. "But I'm just not up to tackling another flight of stairs right now."

Chapter 15

"I need to get to the airport." Eamon eased his arm out from around Lana's shoulders and sat up. But he wasn't without her for long as she shifted her legs under her and scooted up behind him, pressed her lips against his bare shoulder. "If I'm lucky, I'll get back just in time to get Jason to his tuxedo fitting. Sure you don't want to come back with me?" He reached back, found her hand and squeezed.

"Not yet." Lana sighed, a big smile on her face. Aiden had been gracious enough to extend their room reservation for a few days, and they'd made very good use of both the bed and room service. A bonus incentive, he'd told them, to sweeten his job offer.

"To be honest," Lana continued, "I'm really not in

any rush to get back on a private jet. I'm good with commercial for the foreseeable future."

It had been two days since Felice Covington's arrest by federal authorities. A little over thirty-six hours since the story broke on the truth about A&O Solutions. And twenty-four hours ago the first round of arrest warrants had been issued.

Aiden had been right. It was the perfect case for Eamon to end his FBI career on. Among other information found in the files Marcus Tate had left in the care of his wife had been countless evidence trails that would shut down multiple child trafficking and exploitation sites around the world.

"I can come up to Seattle this weekend, help you decide what you're going to do." He drew her arms around him, resisted the temptation to press her back into the mattress and lose himself in her.

"If you come up to Seattle, I won't be capable of thinking about anything other than you. No. I need to do some serious self-examination," she said. "I need to figure out where I go from here. Although I'm thinking there might be room for me with you in Sacramento? I heard through the grapevine those final two apartments in Greta's building are finally finished. Not entirely sure I can afford it—"

"I have an in with the landlord," Eamon said. "But it would be awfully greedy of us to take both of them." Eamon grinned. "Plenty of space for both of us in one."

"Yeah?" She shifted around and straddled him, wound her arms around his neck and kissed him. "You want me to move in with you?"

"Yes." He kissed her again. Her body stiffened, and for a moment, he thought he'd spoken too soon.

"Wow."

"Is that a wow as in yes or a wow as in I don't think—"

"Eamon." She clasped his face in her hands, stared into his eyes. "I'm not in the right frame of mind to answer that question right now. How about…three weeks. Give me three weeks."

"Three weeks as in Kyla and Jason's wedding?" His initial flood of disappointment vanished.

"Is it?" She mock-gasped. "Well, so it is. What a coincidence. Three weeks." She lowered her mouth to his. "How about we take a shower before you head off to the airport?"

"You heard about the water shortage in Boston, didn't you?" He shifted around, held on to her as he stood up. "We need to double up to conserve."

"Whatever you say, Special Agent Quinn." She buried her face in his neck. "Whatever you say."

It had been far too long since Lana had felt anything close to excitement about the future. But as she slid the "Offer pending" plaque on the top of the For Sale sign in front of her house, that was precisely what she felt. Excited. For whatever this new life of hers was going to bring. She was two days shy of the three weeks she'd promised Eamon. Her rented trailer was mostly packed, her resignation with the Seattle PD processed, and, thanks to a stellar real-estate agent, she was just a few days from entering escrow.

She turned to walk back into the house when a dark

SUV pulled into her driveway. Her heart leaped, as she assumed at first it was Eamon surprising her, but then she remembered he was neck-deep in wedding festivities, so she tempered her disappointment until she saw who it was.

"Aiden." She stopped, pushed her hands into the back pockets of her jeans and smiled as he approached. He was business casual today, dressed in dark slacks, blazer, no tie. With his black hair, he looked far more intimidating than she knew him to be. "This is a nice surprise. Everything okay?"

"I was in town for a meeting. Thought I'd stop by, give you an update on the Covington case."

"Oh. Sure." She shrugged. To be honest, she didn't want to give another thought to Felice Covington, A&O Solutions, or the crimes they were responsible for. "Come on in. I haven't packed the coffee machine yet. You want some?"

"That'd be great, thanks."

She had a pot brewing before he joined her in the kitchen. "Place is a mess, I know. I'm selling most everything with the house. The rest that I want to keep is already packed. It's a little sad, but it all fits in the smallest trailer they rent."

"You're smiling, so I think that means it's the right move."

She laughed, pulled two mugs out of the dish dryer. "You've spoken to Eamon."

"Didn't have to. The man is broadcasting on every platform available. I'm kidding," he added. "But I have been talking to him. It's going to be an adjustment for him, moving from the Bureau to the private sector."

"You couldn't have found a better man for the job. I know he'll still be working in the field some, but it's important that he knows he's making a difference."

"The Bureau's giving him a lot of credit for the A&O Solutions indictments. He's going out on a high. That's good for him."

"And for you." She took the filled pot and poured. "I've done some checking up on you, Aiden McKenna. You pride yourself on hiring the best of the best. That goodwill he's earned is going to rub off on your firm."

"You think?" He sipped, but not before she saw his grin. "Never crossed my mind. So. Felice."

She rolled her eyes. "Don't tell me. Someone shanked her in the prison yard."

"Hardly. She took the government's offer and is singing like the biggest canary in the coal mine."

Lana frowned. "I think you're mixing your metaphors."

He shrugged. "The deal she's getting only takes the death penalty off the table. She's in for life. Hard time, too."

She nodded. "Couldn't happen to a worse person."

"So, how are you doing?" His gaze drifted to the ninety-day chip she'd left on the counter. "Dealing with the fallout about Marcus."

"It is what it is. He was what he was. I loved him. Who he pretended to be." She searched her cabinet for the last package of sandwich cookies. "I've stopped blaming myself for that. The video he left, it helped me see that at least he hadn't married me because of my job. He loved me, too. Enough to try to break away from Felice and A&O. That means something."

"I think it does," Aiden agreed. "And work?"

"That is the big question. I put a call in to Lieutenant Santos in Sacramento. Asked if he had any openings for a detective." She hesitated. "I haven't heard back yet."

"Might be a reason for that."

"Ya think?" She couldn't blame the lieutenant. She hadn't gone out in a blaze of glory like Eamon had. She'd done serious damage to her career. It was going to take a lot to earn the trust of people she hadn't yet worked with. Even though she had. Kind of. "So, what was this meeting you had out here?"

"Funny you should ask. It was with Captain Davis."

"My Captain Davis? Or rather my former—"

"One and the same. I had some questions about you, thought maybe she'd be a good one to ask."

"And yet here you are." Butterflies the size of bats took flight in her stomach.

"Taking all things into consideration, she confirmed what I already know. You're a good detective with excellent instincts and a talent for thinking out of the box. You knew my plan for Felice Covington wasn't right. The only thing you did wrong was keep it to yourself and left us to play catch-up."

"Sorry about that." She shoved a cookie in her mouth. "At the time," she said after she swallowed, "I was thinking if I was wrong, at least the only person that would get hurt would be me. Hindsight's a…well, it's something."

"Things could have gone very wrong, but they didn't.

You saw all the angles. And now that you know me better, I'm guessing you wouldn't have any issues telling me I'm wrong."

She narrowed her eyes. "Where is this going?"

"I'm on my way down to Sacramento before I head back to DC. I'm going to suggest a partnership with Vince Sutton, make Sutton Investigations a part of Minotaur. Expand our reach to the West Coast. He's got good people around him, a lot of excellent resources. And it'll allow Eamon and maybe his future wife to stay put. Close to their family."

"I think that's great." But she still didn't see what it had to do with her.

"Vince isn't manager material. I want someone heading up the office I can talk to honestly, be told what works and what doesn't. Someone who knows how local law enforcement works and to liaise when needed. Starting salary would be double what you were making with Seattle PD. And there would be benefits, of course."

"Of course." She blinked, swallowed hard. "I, uh, don't really know what to say. Would I still…? I really like being a cop." The idea of abandoning a career she'd worked so hard to build on didn't completely sit right with her.

"You're always going to be a cop, Lana. It's in your blood. It's who you are. I'm just asking you to think about expanding your horizons a bit. You'll get to travel. Flexible schedule. And best of all, you'll get to shoot me down on occasion."

"Well, when you put it like that." She felt that zing of excitement shoot through her system. The same zing that struck whenever she heard Eamon's voice, felt the touch of his hand. Imagined his face. "When do you want me to start?"

"We can talk details on the plane." He folded his arms over his chest. "I am on a roll. We're wheels up in an hour. You can hitch a ride to Sacramento with me."

"An hour?" She shook her head. "I've still got packing to do—"

"Make a list of what needs doing and I'll get it taken care of. You didn't want to make that drive down by yourself, did you? I've got friends in the moving business. Consider it done."

She hesitated. She didn't want to disappoint him right out of the gate, but this was one of those times when she had to put herself first. "I'm sorry, Aiden. I've got something in about a half hour that I can't reschedule or miss."

"You're acting as if you think that's a deal breaker." He pulled out his phone and texted someone, got almost an immediate answer. "My pilot's looking into a later window. In the meantime, I'll call my moving contact. Will after seven tonight work?"

"Sure." She smiled, imagining Eamon's face when she showed up two days early. "After seven is perfect."

"Okay, then. I'll be back to pick you up later." He finished his coffee and headed out.

Lana glanced at her watch, gathering her jacket and purse before she locked up the house. Aiden was driving down the street as she pulled out of the driveway and headed in the opposite direction.

Twenty minutes later she parked in the lot of the

nearby community center, made her way inside and through the double swinging doors into the meeting room. She forwent the coffee for a change, ignored the doughnuts and surrendered to the pull of the homemade brownies that frequently made an appearance.

"Evening, Lana."

Lana looked up and smiled at the young woman taking a seat next to her. The folding metal chair was hard against her back, but she draped her coat over her knees and settled in as the other attendees joined them.

"Hello, everyone." Marsha, the leader of their group, welcomed the two dozen people sitting in a circle. "It's good to see everyone here. Let's just jump into it, shall we? Who would like to start?"

Lana fisted her hands in her jacket before unclenching one of them and raising it. "I'll go."

"Okay," Marsha said with an encouraging nod. "The floor is yours."

Lana took a deep breath. "Hi. My name is Lana. And I'm an alcoholic."

Ever since he was a little kid, Eamon Quinn had detested surprises. He was a nightmare at Christmas, and the kid who secretly searched the house for his gifts weeks before the big day. Birthdays? Forget about it. He'd been given one surprise party and it had traumatized him for years.

So hearing from his new boss that he'd be making an unexpected stop in Sacramento and bringing Eamon a surprise did not make his evening of frivolities more enjoyable.

Instead, as he mingled with his friends on the private patio of the Brass Eagle, he found himself constantly looking toward the door, hoping he'd soon be put out of his misery. He looked at his watch. It was already after ten. If Aiden didn't get here soon, the party was going to be over.

"You do know this is a celebration, right?" Jason Sutton, the groom-to-be, slung an arm over Eamon's shoulders and futilely attempted to put him in a headlock.

"Don't mess with the fed," Vince warned him.

"Ex-fed," Eamon corrected him. "Or I will be in another forty-eight hours." He'd put in for his pension a little over two weeks ago, about twenty-four hours before Aiden sent him a list of possible contenders for his child crime task force. Needless to say, he'd pretty much been working two jobs ever since. Add to that moving into the empty two-bedroom apartment in Greta's building and counting the hours until Lana arrived, hopefully with an answer to his proposal, and he'd kept busy.

The music was constant, the drinks flowing and the food grilling as the bride and groom and their close family and friends dived into the pre-wedding celebration full bore. Eden and Greta were holding court in the back corner of the patio, away from the smoke of the grill, and toasting one another with various nonalcoholic concoctions. Allie and her husband, Max, along with Riordan and Darcy Malloy, were having some kind of comical dance competition that could have made them a small fortune on social media.

Simone waved Vince over so she could hand off baby Caleb in order to go grab a plate of food while Kyla and

Jason drifted toward one another in a dreamy waltz that made even Eamon a bit misty-eyed.

"Up!"

Eamon glanced down at little Chloe Ann, dressed in an adorable white-and-red polka-dot dress, her arms stretched toward him. "Up, Amu." Her tiny fingers wiggled as she did a little shimmy.

He set his beer aside, bent down and lifted her, settling her into the crook of his arm as she grabbed hold of his neck. "You do like your parties, don't you, Chloe Ann."

"Party!" She lifted both arms up and squealed, grabbed hold of him again and planted a wet kiss on his cheek. "Love Amu."

His throat tightened and he touched a finger to her cheek. "I love you, too, Chloe."

"Hey! Look who's here." Jason abandoned his bride-to-be and made his way toward Aiden McKenna. "Welcome to the party."

"I don't want to intrude," Aiden insisted as he looked pointedly at Eamon. "Eamon didn't tell me there was a party when I said I wanted to stop by."

"Well, it's too late to leave now," Jason insisted. "Kyla, this is—"

"Aiden McKenna." Kyla, her tropical-flowered dress flowing around her lithe figure, approached with her hand out. "I've heard a lot about you. Welcome. Please. Join us."

"Happy to, thanks."

"I'll get you a drink. Beer?" Kyla offered.

"Ah, sure."

Eamon grinned at his new boss's discomfort. "It's your own fault," Eamon told him once he was within earshot. "You're in the circle now."

"Not that I need to earn any more goodwill, but I've got that surprise for you around here somewhere. Hello, there." He inclined his head at Chloe Ann. "And who might you be?"

"This is Chloe Ann. Chloe Ann, this is Aiden."

"Den!" Never leery of strangers, she pitched herself forward. "Hi, Den!" She grabbed hold as he lifted her free.

"Look at that. Got me an instant friend at the party. Now, let's see who your mom and dad might be."

As he held Chloe Ann securely in his arms, Eamon turned, his heart swelling. "Lana."

"Hey." She moved toward him and didn't stop until they embraced. "Surprise."

He folded her into him, his hands sliding down her back as he felt every nerve in his body settle. "I'm so glad you're here."

"Me, too." She stepped back, looked down at her simple black dress. "I hope this is okay. I packed most of my clothes in the trailer already."

"You look beautiful." He bent his head and kissed her.

"Sorry we're late. I had a meeting." She snuggled against his side, rested her head on his shoulder. "Have I got news for you."

"Yeah?"

"Oh, yeah." She beamed up at him. "But I think I'll start with saying I love you, Eamon Quinn. I am so, so grateful you didn't give up on me. That you were waiting, however far in the wings. I love you for now and always."

He didn't have any doubt. But hearing the words, seeing the absolute certainty on her face, he could feel those wounds on his heart finally begin to heal. Eamon slid his hand into the pocket of his jacket, pulled out the ring he'd been carrying around for the past two and a half weeks. It was a simple band, nothing fancy and flashy. Gold with a rounded diamond that caught the twinkling lights of the strands strung across the patio.

"Pretty!" Chloe Ann yelled as she reached up to try to catch the reflection in her fingers. "Amu and Lala pretty."

The crowd quieted, all eyes turning on them.

He didn't have to ask. He only had to look into her eyes as she smiled. And nodded.

"She said yes?" Eden yelled from across the patio.

Eamon nodded. "She said yes."

Lana chuckled as the cheering exploded and Vince hurried inside and returned with two bottles of sparkling cider. As he poured, the whole group moved closer, everyone encircling them.

"This is Kyla and Jason's night," Lana said as she wiped tears of happiness off her cheeks. "I don't want to—"

"You're part of the family now, Lana." Greta reached out and slipped an arm through hers. "I'm afraid you're stuck with all of us now. Congratulations."

"Thanks." Lana smiled up at Eamon, tears glistening in her eyes. "I love you."

"I love you, too." He drew her close and smiled.

Above the laughter, and the whoops and hollers and congratulations, there was the familiar memory of the sound of a little girl's laughter. He squeezed his eyes shut. "I miss you, little sister."

When he opened his eyes again and looked up, a star shot across the sky.

"She's here," Lana whispered. "She always will be. And so will I."

He kissed Lana, and he knew, without hesitation, that he was finally where he belonged.

He was home.

* * * * *

*For more great romances in this miniseries
from acclaimed author Anna J. Stewart and
Harlequin Romantic Suspense, visit
www.Harlequin.com today!*

#2263 COLTON THREAT UNLEASHED
The Coltons of Owl Creek • by Tara Taylor Quinn
Sebastian Cross's elite search and rescue dog-training business is being sabotaged. And his veterinarian, Ruby Colton, is being targeted for saving his dogs when they're hurt. But when the resurgence of Sebastian's PTSD collides with danger, romance and Ruby's ensuing pregnancy, their lives are changed forever.

#2264 CAVANAUGH JUSTICE: COLD CASE SQUAD
Cavanaugh Justice • by Marie Ferrarella
Detectives Cheyenne Cavanaugh and Jefferson McDougall are from two different worlds. When they team up to solve a cold case—and unearth a trail of serial killer murders—they're desperate to catch the culprit. But can they avoid their undeniable attraction?

#2265 TEXAS LAW: LETHAL ENCOUNTER
Texas Law • by Jennifer D. Bokal
Ex-con Ryan Steele and Undersheriff Kathryn Glass both want a new start. When the widowed single mom's neighbor is killed and the crime is posted on the internet, Ryan and Kathryn will have to join forces to stop the killer before his next gruesome crime: live streaming a murder.

#2266 THE BODYGUARD'S DEADLY MISSION
by Lisa Dodson
After a tragic loss, Alexa King creates a security firm to keep other women safe. Taking Andrew Riker's combat and tactical class will elevate her skills. But falling for the ex-marine makes her latest case not only personal...but deadly.

Get 3 FREE REWARDS!

We'll send you 2 FREE Books plus a FREE Mystery Gift.

FREE Value Over **$20**

Both the **Harlequin Intrigue®** and **Harlequin® Romantic Suspense** series feature compelling novels filled with heart-racing action-packed romance that will keep you on the edge of your seat.

HARLEQUIN
PLUS

Try the best multimedia
subscription service for romance
readers like you!

Read, Watch and Play.

Experience the easiest way to get
the romance content you crave.

Start your **FREE TRIAL** at
www.harlequinplus.com/freetrial.